SYDNEY COVE, BOOK 2

Longings
of the Heart

BONNIE LEON

Revell
a division of Baker Publishing Group
Grand Rapids, Michigan

© 2008 by Bonnie Leon

Published by Revell
a division of Baker Publishing Group
P.O. Box 6287, Grand Rapids, MI 49516-6287
www.revellbooks.com

Second printing, July 2009

Printed in the United States of America

Library of Congress Cataloging-in-Publication Data
Leon, Bonnie.
    Longings of the heart : a novel / Bonnie Leon.
        p.   cm. — (Sydney Cove ; 2)
    ISBN 978-0-8007-3177-9 (pbk.)
    1. British—Australia—Fiction. 2. Young women—Fiction. 3. Australia—
Fiction. I. Title.
PS3562.E533L66 2008
813′.54—dc22   2008026662

This book is a work of fiction. Names, characters, places, and incidents are the product of the author's imagination or are used fictitiously. Any resemblance to actual events, locales, or persons, living or dead, is coincidental.

1

Hands grabbed for her, strong arms pinned her down. She could smell the vile scent of sweet lozenges. She tried to wrench herself free, but the faceless man held her firmly. She tried to cry out, but terror paralyzed her.

Somehow she managed to scramble free, running toward escape, but darkness pervaded the room, and she couldn't find the door. And then the hands found her again and dragged her back to the bed, pinning her down. *Please don't hurt me. Please. Help! Please, someone help!* Her sobs brought no mercy from her assailant.

Suddenly Hannah was awake. She sat upright in bed. The room was dark. Where was she? Shivering with emotion, she wiped damp hair off her face and pulled her blanket up about her neck.

There was movement in the bed. Someone was with her! Panic bolted through Hannah, and she jumped out of bed and moved through the dark room like someone blind. The only light was that of dying embers in the hearth. She stumbled over something, and it clattered to the floor. Feeling her way, she sought escape. Where was the door?

"Who's there?" came a familiar voice out of the darkness.

More asleep than awake, Hannah kept trying to find the door. Instead, she bumped against a table and nearly toppled it.

"Hannah? Is that you?"

Still trapped within the nightmare, Hannah was confused. She recognized the voice. Did she dare answer?

"Hannah. What is it? Is something wrong?"

John! It's John. She let out a breath of relief. It wasn't Mr. Walker. It was her husband. "Thank you, Lord." Hannah couldn't hold back tears.

She heard him move from the bed, and then the room was illuminated as a candle was lit in the hearth. John held it aloft, and his eyes found her. "What is it? You're white as a ghost."

Hannah fumbled for an explanation. She'd hidden her past from her husband. How could she explain her nightmare? "It was just a dream. I'm sorry I awakened you."

John moved toward her. "Oh, luv." He pulled her tightly against him. "You're quaking. What were you dreaming about that frightened you so?"

"It was nothing. I . . . I'm fine now." In truth, she was far from it. He was still close—Judge Walker and his attack still too real. Hannah melded into John.

"Come back to bed, then." He draped an arm about her shoulders and walked her back to their bed. She climbed in, and he gently covered her with the light blanket and then moved around to his side, set the candle on the night table, and lay beside her.

Hannah closed her eyes. Why would she dream about Judge Walker on her wedding night?

Her thoughts returned to the previous evening. As they'd prepared for bed, she'd been anxious. But there'd been no need. John had been tender, very unlike Judge Walker who had forced himself upon her. And her new husband seemed to have no notion that she'd come to their marriage bed tarnished.

Remorse jabbed at her. Mrs. Atherton had beseeched her to tell John the truth, but she'd not done so. Had her mistress been right? Should she have confessed her sin?

Hannah had gone to John, but he'd shushed her. He hadn't wanted to know the truth.

Even while justifying her decision, she knew her choice had been deceitful. But if she had told him, she might have lost him. She glanced at John in the glow of the candle and her heart fluttered. He was exceedingly handsome and a fine man. How was it that she had been so blessed?

He has a right to know. He's my husband. Until I tell him he doesn't truly know who I am. She closed her eyes, and an image of his shock and revulsion erupted in her mind. Trepidation wrapped itself about her, and she pulled the blanket up more tightly under her chin. *I can never tell him. Never.*

John pulled Hannah close. "Are you better now?"

"I'm fine. Truly."

"Good." He kissed her. "I love you."

"And I love you."

John kissed her forehead and then pressed his lips to one cheek and then the other. He gazed at her in the flickering light. "How is it that I'm the lucky one who wedded you?"

"It is I who am fortunate," Hannah whispered, barely able to find her voice.

"Mmm, to wake up beside you every day for the rest of my life . . ." John let the sentence hang in the air. "God has shown me great favor, though I am undeserving."

"It is you who are a gift to me." Hannah cradled his face in her hands and kissed him and then held him as tightly as she could, and still it wasn't enough.

John's embrace became more powerful, and his lips sought hers.

Love drove away the nightmare. Passion flamed inside Hannah, and all she knew was her husband.

Reaching her arms over her head, Hannah stretched and then opened her eyes. John lay beside her, still sleeping. The previous day's events rushed at her—the wedding, dancing, and revelry. And then she remembered her first night as Mrs. John Bradshaw. Hannah could barely catch her breath. It was too wonderful to comprehend. She rested a hand on her chest, the joy nearly more than she could withstand.

Then she closed her eyes, and unexpectedly the nightmare rushed back at her. Taking a slow deep breath, she refused to allow its ugly tentacles to remain with her. That was the past; now she had a future with a wonderful man.

Rolling onto her side, she rested her cheek in the crook of her arm and studied John's muscled back. *Why have you blessed me so, Lord? I don't deserve him.*

John's breathing was quiet and steady. Hannah gently pressed her hand against his warm skin. He stirred slightly and then rolled onto his other side, facing her. His eyes remained closed.

She gazed at her husband. He was most certainly handsome. Dark hair cascaded onto his forehead and down a cheek, framing his strong, angled face. Although he still slept, Hannah could feel the love she saw in his vibrant hazel eyes whenever he looked at her.

She remembered their nuptial kiss. It had been gentle and respectful, and yet she'd felt his restrained passion. *Why me? Why does he love me?* She rested an index finger on his arm and gently caressed his skin. His breathing became less steady and his eyelids flickered open. His gaze settled on Hannah and he smiled.

"Good morning, wife." He draped his arm across her side and nuzzled her neck. "My love."

Hannah snuggled against him, resting a hand on his broad chest. She relished the security she felt at his strength and his familiarity.

"Mrs. John Bradshaw. The name has a lovely sound." Hannah smiled. "When I was a girl, my mum bought a bell for our door. We couldn't afford it, but I wanted one, and she did it because she loved me. Each time the door opened or closed, the bell would chime, and I thought there was nothing in the world more grand. It wasn't much, really, but I knew Mum had purchased it out of love." Hannah closed her eyes for a moment and then looked at John. "The sound of Mrs. John Bradshaw is even lovelier than the ringing of that bell."

John chuckled. "I never thought much about my name, but it sounds quite agreeable when spoken by my wife."

"Perhaps we can buy a bell and hang it from our door."

"It can be a reminder of your mother."

"And a reminder of love and devotion."

John kissed her and then fluffed his pillow and leaned against it. Cradling Hannah in one arm, he closed his eyes and breathed deeply.

"It was a grand wedding, don't you think?" Hannah nestled in close.

"Indeed it was." He looked at her. "When I saw you step into

9

the sanctuary, you took my breath away. I daresay you were stunning." He smoothed her brown hair. "I was stricken when I saw you, so much so that I could barely keep my legs under me."

"You're teasing."

"I'm not. I was absolutely beset by your beauty and with the knowledge that you were mine . . . for all time."

Hannah raised up on one arm. "Beset? Really?"

"Absolutely. I was." He grinned at her. "You don't believe me?"

"I do." Hannah settled back into the crook of his arm. "Mrs. Atherton provided the fabric for my dress. She's the most generous person I know."

"I must thank her. I was completely bewitched by you."

Suddenly, the stink of sweet lozenges and the feel of Judge Walker's hands engulfed Hannah. *Bewitched* was the word the judge had used when he'd assaulted her. He'd accused her of bewitching him, meaning that she'd caused his uncontrollable desires.

Her thoughts overwhelmed by Mr. Walker and his awful assault, Hannah pushed away from John and rested her back against the headboard beside him. Hoping to regain her composure, she folded her arms behind her head and made an effort to relax. *Think only of today. Forget about the past.* She tried to come up with something mundane to say. "I'm hungry. Are you?"

"Yes. But only for you," John said, a twinkle of devilment in his eyes.

Hannah turned a slab of pork that was roasting in an iron pot. Juices drizzled out. She pushed the pan closer to the fire and returned to the resting dough she'd left on the sideboard countertop. After shaping it into biscuits, she placed them in a skillet and set it in hot coals in the hearth. It felt good to be cooking for her husband. This would be the first meal she'd prepared for him as his wife, and she wanted it to be just right.

Wiping her hands on her apron, she straightened and walked to a cabinet, taking out a bowl of fresh eggs. She cracked them into a pan and whisked them with a fork.

John stepped through the doorway, his arms loaded with firewood. After setting the wood in a box beside the hearth, he crossed to Hannah and circled his arms about her waist, kissing the back of her neck. Hannah shivered with pleasure.

He pulled her closer.

"John, we must eat sometime. The morning is nearly gone and we've not breakfasted yet. If we don't eat and emerge soon, I'll be too embarrassed to step outdoors."

John didn't loosen his hold. "I daresay, I'd not want you discomfited," he teased.

"It's not funny." She wriggled out of his arms and set the eggs on a shelf over the fire. "Our breakfast is nearly ready." Hannah stirred the eggs, checked the meat and biscuits, and then straightened. She glanced at the tiny table sitting against the wall of the kitchen. "I've set places for us."

"Just one more kiss, eh?" John pulled her into his arms and kissed her.

Hannah smiled and met his ardent gaze. He made her feel as if life could be perfect.

"You're the most beautiful woman I've ever known, Hannah Bradshaw."

"No need for flattery. You've already turned my head."

"It's not flattery. You are beautiful. And it's more than your physical appearance I'm speaking of. You're even lovelier on the inside." He chuckled. "On the ship when I first laid eyes on you, you knocked the breath right out of me. I knew then that we belonged together."

"How could you? You didn't know me. And I was an absolute mess of a human being. We all were."

"You were dirty and your hair needed combing, but I could see you—lovely and proud and gracious."

Hannah felt a flush in her cheeks. "I must admit there was something I saw in your eyes that caught me right off. But your wild hair and beard covered up this handsome face." She rested a hand on his cheek, remembering how dreadful he'd looked.

Without warning the oppression and vileness of the convict ship and the agony of those days swept over her. "I want to forget all of that."

"I never will. And I don't want to. That's where I met you, and as ugly as it was, our days at sea made us strong. We'll need that."

"I suppose you're right." Hannah crouched in front of the hearth and stirred the eggs again. They were sticking. "I can be thankful for that. But the rest of it . . ." She looked at her biscuits. They were nearly brown. "I can never justify what happened to us." She straightened. "Now sit. Your breakfast is ready."

John moved to the table. "What would you like to do today? It's a fine morning. The heat's holding off, but we can expect it to warm up; it is November."

Hannah removed the food from the fire. She cut slices from the roasted pork and set them on John's plate, then ladled eggs alongside the meat and placed two biscuits on the dish. She set it on the table in front of him. "The eggs are a bit overdone."

"They look perfectly grand." John closed his eyes and

breathed in through his nose. "Smells good. Thank you, luv."
He crooked his finger at her, and she bent down so he could
kiss her cheek.

Wearing a smile, Hannah went to the hearth, and using a
towel to grasp the handle of the kettle, she lifted it from the
crossbar and filled the cups on the table with coffee.

John took a bite of egg. "Very good."

After returning the kettle to its place over the fire, Hannah
served herself a small portion of eggs and a biscuit and then sat
across the table from her husband. "It was kind of the Athertons
to give us this day together."

"Indeed. But tomorrow it will be back to work." John cradled
his cup between his hands and sipped. "More time together would
be outstanding, of course, but I'm grateful for what we have."

"I doubt we'll ever manage to find enough time together."
Hannah smiled and then took a bite of her biscuit. "Did you
notice the new physician, Mr. Gelson, at the wedding?"

"I did. We chatted for a bit. Seems a fine fellow and Parramatta is in need of a good surgeon. He plans to set up an office
and apothecary here in town."

"Lydia seemed quite taken with him, don't you think?"

Mischief lit John's eyes. "She did at that. And I'd say he wasn't
at all put off by her."

"It would be lovely if Lydia could find a noble gent to wed.
She so wants to be in love." She smiled at John. "Like us."

A frown creased John's brow. "I feel sorry for Perry, though.
He's smitten with her. He seemed a bit down at the party. I
found him outside on his own. When I asked if everything
was all right, he told me he was just getting a breath of air. It
was more than that, though. I doubt he could stand the sight
of the two of them."

"Perry's a fine man. I like him. And I wish Lydia felt something more for him than friendship, but she's told me she doesn't. She cares for him, but not the way a woman should feel for her husband."

"I know. I doubt he'd have given up though, at least not until last night." John rested his arms on the table.

"Lydia wants more than friendship. She wants passion." Hannah grasped John's calloused hand and held it between both of hers. "She's unwilling to settle for less."

"As I well understand. I refused to settle." John pressed Hannah's hands to his lips. "Perhaps David Gelson is a good match for her, eh?"

"Perhaps. And I was thinking Gwen might be right for Perry. She works here on the estate, and she's a fine person. When I first came here from the Female Factory, she was friendly right from the start. And she's from prison just as Perry is, as most of us are, and I'm sure wrongly convicted like us." Hannah set her fork on the plate and took a sip of coffee. "She can be a bit chatty, but she's delightful and a hard worker. From time to time I've seen her watching Perry. She may well be interested in him. Perhaps you could say something to him?"

"I'll do what I can." John didn't sound enthusiastic. "I'd hate for Gwen to get hurt. I doubt Perry will ever feel about any woman the way he does Lydia."

"That may be, but sometimes practicality must take precedence."

"I suppose so." John's lips turned up in a crooked smile. "I'm glad I wasn't practical."

Quiet settled over the couple. They were content just to be together.

It was Hannah who spoke first. "How shall we ever thank Mr. and Mrs. Atherton?"

John shook his head. "We owe them a great deal. Obtaining pardons for us was something I never expected and I'm sure cost them dearly."

"I want to do something to thank them."

"In all my life I've never met anyone in the aristocracy with such decency and compassion as the Athertons. And I've known many in the upper classes."

Hannah sometimes forgot about John's past. She'd not known him before his imprisonment. "So, you did quite a bit of business with those of nobility?"

"I did. And in some circles I was considered gentry myself."

"At our shop, Mum and I met many highborn women. She had a reputation as one of the finest seamstresses in London." Sorrow touched Hannah. "Mum had few possessions, but she was a fine lady. And she died too young." She felt the sting of tears. "Even with the snobbish types, she was pleasant, genuinely so. I doubt she had any callousness in her."

"I'm sorry about your mother. I know how much it hurts to lose one's parents. At least we have each other." John took another drink of coffee. "Have you considered what we ought to do now that we're free?"

"I thought we might stay on here for a while. The Athertons have been good to us. I'm not sure I feel right about leaving them."

John gazed out the window toward the main house. "I don't think they'd want us to remain in servitude. They gave us our freedom believing we'd do more. And we can."

"What is it you want, then?"

"I've been considering starting my own farm."

"You've always been a toolmaker."

"True, but I've long wanted to try my hand at something else." He rubbed his freshly shaven cheek. "In London, just before I was arrested, I dreamed of adventure and of putting my efforts into something new and interesting." He gazed at her. "This could well be my chance. There's free land for those who want to work it."

Hannah reached across the table and grasped John's hand. "All I need to be content is to be with you. I want whatever you want."

He gently squeezed her hand. "Together, we can do anything we put our minds to." The golden glints of color in his eyes blazed. "God has blessed me with a most excellent wife. I think of our future and am inspired." He smiled. "You'll make a fine mother. How many children shall we have?"

Hannah's breakfast suddenly felt heavy in her stomach. She couldn't meet his eyes.

"Are you all right? You've gone quite pale."

"I'm fine." Hannah wasn't fine. She was afraid. What if there were no children? After all, she'd done a heinous thing. She'd wished for the death of her own child. Such a sin could not go unpunished.

John leaned back in his chair. "I say we should have a half dozen at least." He grinned. "Three boys and three girls would be just right. They'll be handsome too. Like their mother."

Hannah poked at her eggs with her fork. "It's God's choice about children, when and how many. We'll have to wait and see what his plans are for us, eh?" She glanced at John. He'd trusted her and she'd not told him the truth. What if God withheld the blessing of children because of what she'd done? What would she tell him then?

2

A knock sounded at John and Hannah's door. "Who would come calling this morning?" John asked, his voice tinged with irritation. He didn't rise, but sipped his coffee instead.

Another timid knock trembled against the door.

John set down his mug and folded his arms over his chest. "I'll not answer, not on our first morning together."

"Perhaps we should. What if it's something important?"

John shook his head and remained seated.

Again, a knock rattled the door. This one was more resolute.

"I'm going to answer it." Hannah moved to the door. When she opened it, an anxious-looking Perry stood on the porch.

He tipped his head slightly. "Mornin' to ye. I trust ye had a good night." His face reddened. "I mean, I hope yer well."

"I am." Hannah smiled.

Hands clasped behind his back, Perry shifted from one foot to the other. He looked past her and into the house. "I know this isn't a good time, but I was wonderin' if I might have a word with John."

John stepped to the doorway, protectively circling Hannah's waist with his right arm and leaning the other against the doorframe. "What's so important that you come calling the morning after a man's wedding?"

"Sorry. But I needed to speak with ye." His eyes darted toward Hannah. "Alone." His voice was apologetic.

John glanced at Hannah. He didn't want to leave her, especially not to spend time with Perry. Friendship only went so far.

"You go ahead. I've dishes to do," Hannah said.

John tightened his hold around her waist and dropped a kiss on her forehead. "I won't be long." He shot Perry a reproachful look, grabbed his hat and settled it on his head, then stepped outside, closing the door behind him.

"I'm sorry to bother ye," Perry said. "But I've got to talk to someone and there's no one else."

"It better be important." John shoved his hands into his pockets and walked alongside Perry, who was moving at a quick pace up the drive and toward the river. "Good Lord, Perry, this isn't a race. What's got you so agitated?"

Perry slowed his steps. "It's Lydia," he blurted. "Did ye see the way she threw herself at that Gelson fellow?"

"I saw no throwing," John said wryly.

"Every time I looked at her she was talking to him and smiling in that way."

"What way is that?" John was losing patience. He'd planned to spend the day with Hannah, not with a fretful Perry. The day was heating up quickly. Soon it would be too miserably hot to enjoy much of anything.

"You know . . . ye can tell she's . . . interested. There are times when she smiles that it looks like she's lit from inside." He knit his brows. "And she danced with him more than once."

John stopped and folded his arms over his chest. Perry kept

walking. When he noticed John was no longer beside him, Perry stopped and looked back, then turned and faced his friend.

John studied him. "What do you think I can do about how Lydia feels? I've no influence over her."

"No. But ye might say something to Gelson. Tell him Lydia's partial to me."

"Is that the truth?"

"I don't know. We're fine friends. It could be."

"You know it's not true." John looked into the branches of a tree where a redheaded bird with a yellow chest fluffed its feathers while making a terrible racket. "You're beginning to sound like one of the blooming birds 'round here." He softened his tone. "You're no more than friends. And what would you have had Lydia do at the party? She's friendly. It's her way."

"You think that's all it was?"

John considered lying to Perry. He wanted to end the conversation and return to Hannah. Instead he posed another question. "Would it have suited you if she'd talked to no one? Just stood aside and watched everyone else have a good time?"

Perry dug a toe into the dirt. "No. Course not."

"Well then, I'd say you need to let Lydia be herself, and you need to stop worrying and meddling."

"But she was battin' her eyes, and then Gelson would say something and she'd laugh." Perry rubbed at his patchy beard. "She's partial to him. I can see it." He looked at John in a way that said, "Tell me I'm imagining things."

John clapped a hand on the smaller man's shoulder. "Don't trouble yourself so. It was just a party. And a good one, I might add—my wedding." He grinned. "Which reminds me . . . I have a bride waiting for me."

Perry shook his head and paced back and forth in front of

John as if he'd not heard John's reference to Hannah. "Ye know how I feel 'bout her. She's the only one for me."

"I know." John felt a touch of guilt at his own selfishness. His closest friend was hurting and all he could think about was that he was being put out. "Sometimes the people we love don't return the sentiment, at least not the way we want them to." John glanced up at the simmering morning sun. It was moving higher into the sky. He resumed walking. He knew Lydia was about to break Perry's heart, and he wished there were some way to lessen the hurt, but there truly was nothing he could do. "Lydia's kindly disposed toward you."

"That's not enough."

"You can't make her love you. I wish it was in my power to change her heart, but I can't." He grasped Perry's arm. "The two of you are quite good friends. Enjoy that. And be thankful for it."

"Thankful?" Perry sounded resentful. "I can't settle. I won't."

"You may have to."

Perry glared at John. "Now that ye've got Hannah, ye don't care what happens 'bout me and Lydia."

"That's not true." John's frustration intensified. "What am I to do? Or for that matter, what can either of us do?"

John stopped beneath an acacia tree and grabbed a low-hanging branch. He broke off a small limb. "Perhaps she'll fall in love with you, given time. For a long while Hannah would have nothing to do with me. And now . . ." He glanced back at his cottage. "Now, she's my wife." He was unable to keep the tenderness out of his voice. He cleared his throat and looked back at Perry. "When she told me there could be nothing between us, I nearly gave up." He tossed the branch and watched it drop into bushes along the drive. "'Course if she'd not changed her mind, I would have had to accept her decision."

"Right. But if Lydia never comes 'round, how do I do that?" Perry looked disheartened.

"I don't know. You just do."

"I can't lose her." Perry stared at Lydia's cottage where smoke drifted from the chimney. "I'll never love another."

"I don't believe there's only one woman for a man. Look around. There are other fine ladies in the district. Even here on this estate."

"That may be so, but even if I were to find someone else, I'm worried 'bout Lydia. I don't trust Gelson. He's most likely a philanderer and will likely take advantage of her."

"I doubt you've any worries there. She's a strong, sensible woman."

"Ye don't know her the way I do. She's vulnerable. And when it comes to love, all women are alike; they forget about being reasonable."

John kicked at a pebble. He wished he had answers for Perry. "I doubt you've any worries when it comes to David Gelson. Seems most the women 'round here are taken with him. With so many to choose from, he's not likely interested in Lydia."

"If only that were true." Perry didn't sound optimistic. "Do you think I ought to say something to her?"

"I don't think she'd take kindly to your interfering."

Perry gazed at her cottage. "She's a handsome woman—her green eyes and that wild auburn hair. And she's got spirit."

"Give things time." John rested a hand on his friend's back. "Try to be patient."

"I'm afraid if I give her too much time, David Gelson will steal her from me."

21

"Perry," John said gravely. "Dr. Gelson can't take something from you that you don't own."

Surprise and then truth touched Perry's eyes. "S'pose yer right, there."

"Gwen's a handsome woman," John said, his tone lightening. "Perhaps you ought to consider her. I have it on good authority that she likes you."

"Really?" Perry almost smiled. "She's a fine lady. And I do like her. But she's not Lydia."

"Perhaps there's more to her than you know." John gazed at distant wheat fields cooking beneath a hot sun, their hearty fragrance heavy in the air. "It's possible that when Lydia sees you've another interest, it might spark hers, eh?" Even while John was speaking, he knew it was unlikely, but he didn't have the heart to be completely forthright.

"It might at that." Perry looked thoughtful. "It's an idea. I might drop by and speak to Gwen this afternoon." He smiled, looking slightly more confident. "Sorry to have taken so much of yer time. I'd better get back to work." Perry tipped his hat and walked toward the shop.

The next morning, John stood inside the door and pulled Hannah close. "I wish I didn't have to go to work and could stay with you today." He kissed her. "I'll be thinking about you. And knowing you'll be here when I get home will make the day more tolerable."

Hannah wrapped her arms around John and snuggled close. "If only we had another day together, just the two of us." She smiled up at him. "But we'll be together tonight. And I'll see to it that I have a first-rate meal ready when you get home."

"It's not my stomach that will be hungry." John grinned down at her and lifted an eyebrow.

Hannah giggled. "That will be fine with me. How lovely to know that at the end of the day we'll have each other."

John hugged her more tightly. "All right, then. You'll be in my thoughts."

"Perhaps we could luncheon together?"

"I wish we could, but Mr. Atherton has business for me in Port Jackson. I mean Sydney Town. I forget myself. Not used to the change. It's a bother, changing the name of a town." He kissed her again and then looked over the property. "I want a place of our own. I want to work for us and the family we'll have one day."

"Family will come at the proper time."

"I'm going to speak to Mr. Atherton about it right away. I think we ought to apply for a land grant. The government will give a man thirty acres—and another twenty if he's married."

"I've heard of that, but us, so soon?"

"Why not? I've decided a sheep farm will be the thing." He grabbed his hat from a stand beside the door and pressed it onto his head. "You should tell Mrs. Atherton so she can be looking for a new housekeeper."

"All right. If you're sure we'll be moving soon. I'm not certain how or what I ought to say. The Athertons have been exceedingly good to us; I feel as if we'll be deserting them."

"They're the ones who gave us our freedom. It's what they want. I'm sure of it."

"I'll speak with her."

John kissed her once more and then opened the door and stepped outside.

Hannah watched as he strode toward the tool shop. When

he was out of sight, she closed the door. *I'd best hurry. Mrs. Atherton will be wondering where I am.* She walked to the bedroom, took a clean apron out of the bureau, and tied it on as she hurried toward the main house.

Stepping through the back door, she nearly collided with Elvine Goudy, who wore a starched white apron and a warm smile as she always did. "Good day," the cook said. "You look well."

"I am, thank you."

"Marriage agrees with you, then?"

"That it does." As Hannah walked into the kitchen, she knew she was smiling broadly but couldn't keep from it. She felt extraordinarily happy. "It smells wonderful in here."

"It's baking day."

Hannah glanced at the stone oven beside the hearth where she knew several loaves of bread were tucked inside baking. "Perhaps one day I'll have an oven."

"I'm sure you will."

Dalton, the houseman, walked by and offered a quick nod.

Hannah said "Hello," and moved toward the scullery and stopped at the door. Gwen was up to her elbows in soapy water. The young woman flashed her a smile. "Good day."

"Good day to you." Hannah glanced at a stack of baking pans and utensils. "Looks like you've a load of work to do."

"That I have. Baking day's always a busy one for me." Using the back of her hand, Gwen brushed blonde hair out of her eyes. "It was a lovely wedding. Thank ye for including me."

"It was lovely, wasn't it? And I'm glad you could join us."

Still smiling, Gwen returned to work.

Hannah moved toward the stairway. *I suppose I ought to begin with the beds*, she thought, climbing the steps.

Mrs. Atherton met her on her way down. She moved slowly. "Good morning, dear. How pretty you look today."

"Thank you. It seems everyone thinks I look especially fetching this morning. Is there something different about me?"

"Of course there is. There's a light in your eyes I've not seen before." Mrs. Atherton patted Hannah's cheek and then took another step down. "I'm on my way into Parramatta to see the new physician."

"Are you ailing?"

"No. But I'm hoping he might have something to ease the pain in my joints."

"I pray he has something to offer you."

"It would be a blessing." Mrs. Atherton eased past Hannah. "Good day, dear."

"Oh, Mrs. Atherton. Do you have a moment?" Hannah knew she must say something to her mistress about her and John applying for property and their possible move. Just the idea of it made her feel disloyal.

Mrs. Atherton stopped. "What is it, dear?"

"Well . . . John and I have been talking, and we plan to move onto our own place. He'd like to raise sheep. I don't know how long it will take to get a piece of land, but I thought you ought to know. That way you can be looking for someone to replace me."

Sadness touched Mrs. Atherton's eyes, but only for a moment, and then she smiled. "That would be spectacular, dear. I'd hoped you two would set out on your own." She took a gentle hold of Hannah's hand. "But I'll miss you terribly."

"I'm sure we won't move far. We like it in Parramatta."

"Good. At least that way we'll be able to see one another."

25

She let Hannah's hand drop. "Bless you, dear," she said and then continued down the steps.

The morning passed pleasantly enough. Hannah moved from bedroom to bedroom, her mind on John rather than her duties. What was he doing? Was he safe? When would he return? Time dragged. With the last of the bedrooms tidied and dusted, she made her way down the staircase and into the dining room.

Lydia stood at the heavy wooden table, silver laid out in front of her. She set a polished spoon in a row with several others. "Hannah, how grand to see you!" She hugged her friend. "How are ye?"

"I'm quite well. I love being Mrs. John Bradshaw."

Lydia placed her hands on her generous hips, mischief in her green eyes. "I've thought about ye and wondered how everything was between ye two."

"Splendid. I don't remember ever feeling so contented as when I'm sleeping in my husband's arms." Remembering the sweetness of their union, Hannah moved to the window, pushed aside delicate silk curtains, and looked out onto the shaded veranda.

Lydia picked up another spoon.

Hannah turned back to her friend and asked, "How have you been? I noticed you and the young surgeon spent quite a bit of time together at the wedding. You two seemed to be enjoying each other's company."

"He's quite handsome, isn't he? And he's kind." Lydia clasped her hands in front of her, trapping the spoon between them. "He asked if he could call on me."

"Really? Do you think he has serious intentions?"

"How can I know? I've only just met him." Lydia smiled.

"But I do hope so. He seems a fine gentleman." She gave Hannah an inquisitive look. "And how 'bout ye and John? Was it heaven?"

"Surely such things should remain private between a husband and wife."

"Yer not serious!" Lydia exclaimed. "Ye'd withhold that from me?"

Hannah giggled. "I suppose I can tell you. But you mustn't breathe a word to anyone."

"I'd never."

Hannah sat at the table and rested her chin on her hand. "It was wonderful. John was tender and kind. Mrs. Atherton had said that sometimes intimacy between a husband and wife can be bliss—it was." She closed her eyes for a moment and smiled, then looked at Lydia. "I love him so much."

"And he had no idea that you weren't . . ."

Hannah sat more upright, her spine stiff and her good mood fading. "No. He had no idea."

"Will you tell him now that yer married?"

"Why? There's no reason for him to know." Hannah's insides felt tight. She glanced about to make sure they were alone. She wasn't sure she could share this even with Lydia, but she felt too great a burden and needed to say something. "I didn't tell you everything . . . about the baby."

Lydia sat across from Hannah. "What do you mean?"

Hannah set her hands on the table in front of her, one on top of the other. "When I knew I was in the family way, I was distraught—you remember. And what can a woman do with a child in prison? It's even worse on board a convict ship. The child's life would have been ghastly." She met Lydia's intense gaze. "And my honor could never be reclaimed."

Once more Hannah glanced at the kitchen door to make sure she and Lydia were alone. "I prayed and asked . . . God to take the baby. I . . . I just couldn't have it."

Lydia gasped and clapped a hand over her mouth. Her eyes filled with tears. "How could ye wish for such a thing? Children are a gift from God."

"I know that now. Every time I think about it I want to scream. I committed a horrible sin. For a long time I thought it too much even for God to forgive. But he has forgiven me. Can you?"

Lydia didn't answer right away. "Of course. I'm not without sin." She shook her head slightly and then reached for Hannah's hand and grasped it. "But ye must tell John. He should know."

"I can't. I can't bear to see the loathing I know will be in his eyes." Tears spilled onto Hannah's cheeks. "Every time he looks at me, all I see is love. If I tell him, I'm certain I'll not see love but hate instead. I simply can't endure that." She wiped at her tears. "Please pray for us. Pray that I can live with what I've done and that John will never know the truth."

Lydia hesitated before answering. "I'll pray for yer happiness, but I'll also pray that one day ye'll be free of yer fear and that John will know the truth and yer love will be stronger for it." She looked Hannah straight in the eyes. "I hope ye'll find the courage to speak to him. This is too dreadful a secret to keep from yer husband."

Hannah understood that, but she also knew she couldn't tell John, not ever.

3

Mrs. Atherton stepped onto the front veranda and waved at Hannah and John. "Could you wait a moment? I have someone I'd like you to meet." She moved back indoors and a few moments later reappeared with a young woman in tow.

Moving slowly, Mrs. Atherton limped across the lawn toward John and Hannah. "I can barely get about today." She shook her head. "Even in this heat my rheumatism is a bother."

"Sorry it's troubling you so." John tipped his hat.

"I shall survive."

"Are the remedies Dr. Gelson prescribed of no benefit?" Hannah asked.

"I've not seen any improvement yet." Mrs. Atherton straightened slightly. "But I'm not here to talk about my maladies. I want you to meet the new housemaid."

Hannah's attention turned to the stunning stranger standing beside Mrs. Atherton. The woman smiled, but the gesture didn't touch her muted green eyes.

"I'd like you to meet Deidre O'Neil," Mrs. Atherton said. "She comes to us from Norfolk Island."

Deidre brushed white-blonde hair off one cheek. "I'm thankful to be rid of that place."

"Norfolk prison, you mean?" Hannah asked.

"Yes. I was there two years. It's a dreadful place."

"I've heard it's appalling."

"That it is." Harshness flashed across Deidre's face, but quickly vanished. She turned to Mrs. Atherton. "I'm thankful ye've allowed me to come to work for ye. Ye've rescued me from what I'm certain would have been a terrible end. I'll do a fine job for ye."

"I've no doubt of that. Grace Williams recommended you and I trust her judgment implicitly." Mrs. Atherton turned toward Hannah. "Deidre, this is Hannah Bradshaw. She was our housekeeper until she married this fine gentleman, John Bradshaw."

Deidre offered Hannah a cursory nod and then reached out to John and took his hand. "It's a pleasure." Her voice changed, reminding Hannah of bells in a soft breeze.

"John manages our machine shop and oversees quite a lot of the business for my husband."

"Welcome," John said. "I'm sure you'll be happy here. The Athertons are fine people."

"I can see that."

Hannah bristled at Deidre's notably sweet tone and overly friendly manner toward John. She didn't like her.

"Sadly, John and Hannah won't be living here much longer. They're planning to move to a place of their own."

John disengaged his hand. "Figured I'd have a go at my own farm."

"Sounds like a grand idea." Deidre's eyes remained on John. "I hope ye do well."

"God willing, we shall." John smiled.

Hannah thought his smile a bit too broad.

"There's a piece of land just north of here. I'm going to have a look at it this afternoon."

"Once you've moved, William and I will miss having you here. But we're delighted you're making a new start. I'm confident this venture will be a success." Mrs. Atherton glanced at the new housemaid. "Well, Deidre and I have some things to discuss, and I've promised to show her around. She'll start working with Lydia right away." She placed a hand on Deidre's back, and the two moved past Hannah and John, strolling toward the garden.

Trepidation felt like a strap tightening around Hannah's chest. Shaking loose the sensation, she looped an arm through John's, and the two walked toward the barn. "I wish I could go with you."

"And I'd value your presence, but Murphy Connor is the one who put me on to the property, and he's an Irishman who believes women should stay at home." He grasped Hannah's hand. "If I think it's the place for us, I'll take you there tomorrow."

"All right."

John looked more closely at Hannah. "Is something troubling you?"

Hannah clasped John's hand and stopped, facing him. "I know we've planned and dreamed of building a place of our own, but I must admit to feeling a bit frightened. I know the area and it's quite isolated. Most anything could happen—snakebite, or a raid by the Aborigines. And there are escaped criminals about. I don't know that I'll feel at ease there on my own."

"Hannah, I had no idea. But you need not worry. I'll be there. I'd die before I let anyone harm you." He caressed her upper arms. "It'll be fine. You'll see. Very few of the farmers have had trouble."

31

"I know. And I believe this is the right thing to do, but I still can't help but be a bit anxious." Sorry that she'd said anything to dampen John's spirits, she assured him, "Don't worry about me and my qualms. I'm positive I'll feel fine once we're settled."

Gently, he kissed her forehead. "I'm sure you're right."

Leaving behind the morning light, John and Hannah stepped into the barn where the heavy smell of hay and manure greeted them. He led the way to a stall in the back. "It sounds like fine land. Connor said it borders the river and that it isn't too far from the township. And he said there's good grazing."

Hannah rested a hand on the stall gate. "I can scarcely imagine what it will be like to live on a place of our own. Two months ago we were prisoners with no prospects at all." She leaned against John, hugging him with one arm.

He gave her a squeeze. "God has been gracious." He grabbed a halter from a hook on the wall, opened the stall, and stepped inside. "There you go, boy," he said, moving to a chestnut gelding. John patted the animal's neck and then slid the halter over his head, gently tucking its ears through the straps. He quickly saddled the horse and led it out of the barn.

As they emerged, Mrs. Atherton and Deidre walked across the lawn toward the back door of the main house. Hannah studied the new employee. Something about her left Hannah feeling unsettled. "What did you think of the new housemaid?"

John glanced at Mrs. Atherton and Deidre. "She seems pleasant enough."

"She's quite handsome."

"That she is." John looked at Hannah. "By your tone, I'd say you're not pleased with that."

"She's comely enough, but that's not what troubles me. There's something about her . . . something not quite right."

"Whatever could be wrong? I'm sure Mrs. Atherton wouldn't bring someone into the house who's not to be trusted."

"I suppose you're right." Hannah watched until the women disappeared inside the house. Her disquiet remained.

"I'd better be off if I'm to get back before dark." John kissed Hannah. "Look for me before dinner."

She rested a hand on his arm. "Do be careful. There was another attack on a family a few days ago."

"I know. I've got my pistol." John patted the firearm he wore at his side. "I doubt the Aborigines are concerned with a lone rider. They're more interested in keeping farmers from building on the land. I'm sure they see us as a blight."

"What's happening to them does seem a bit unfair." Hannah gazed up the road. "But what's to be done about it?"

"In time, I hope whites and blacks will live harmoniously. There's land enough for us all."

"No, there's not really. The blacks don't stay in one place. They wander. With more and more settlers taking up parcels of land, what will become of them?"

"I don't know, but progress won't be held back."

"At any rate, be watchful. I shan't rest until I know you're home safely."

"I'll be careful." Putting a foot in the stirrup, John pushed up into the saddle. "Have a good day, luv." He turned the horse toward the road and started off.

John glanced back at Hannah as he moved up the drive. They'd been married scarcely two months, but already he couldn't imagine life without her. *How grand it will be to have a place of our own. We'll have a fine house where we can build a life together and raise our children.* He allowed his imagination to embrace thoughts of what life would be like—he and Hannah working together, establishing the farm and a family. As Hannah had said, there would be danger, but then most things in life held peril of some sort or other.

"John."

John relinquished his musings and pulled his horse to a stop.

Mr. Atherton stepped out of the tool shop and walked down the drive toward him. "I'd hoped to catch you before you left."

"Good day, sir. Is there something you need done before I go?"

"I'd just like a word is all."

John climbed out of the saddle. "Is everything all right?"

"Yes. Fine. I wanted to speak with you about your plans."

"Plans, sir?"

"Your idea of raising sheep."

John knew Mr. Atherton had qualms about his making a change from machinist to farmer. "I'm sorry about leaving your employ, but I—"

Mr. Atherton lifted his hand, palm out. "No, no. That's not a problem. Perry will work out fine. You've taught him well." Using his thumb, he nudged up his hat. He seemed uneasy. "I well know the desires of a young man—hoping and dreaming of a place of his own. All men want that. And I'm not one to stifle dreams. I've had a few of my own." He grinned. "But I feel I must voice a concern . . . Your choice of vocations seems a bit unusual. You're a fine machinist and you've a good head for business. Trade or a production enterprise of some sort would seem more fitting."

34

John knew Mr. Atherton spoke the truth. He'd had similar discussions with himself. "I know I'm taking a risk. But raising sheep and attending to my own property requires good business instincts. And as you've stated, I possess those. And there'll always be a need for tools. I can craft my own rather than purchase them."

John let his eyes roam over the Atherton farm. "I spent most of my life in the city, and for years I did as my father wished—working at his side and learning the tool business. And when he died, I took over the company. But I always wanted more—adventure and an opportunity to do something of my own choosing, something more challenging. I even considered moving to the Americas. It's a place where a man can make a fine living as a farmer. I probably would have done it too, if not for my wife Margaret. London was the only place for her. She wouldn't let go of it."

He took a deep breath. Even now, the thought of her violation stabbed at him. "Of course my dreams and hers ended with her betrayal and her death." The memory of prison, Margaret's infidelity, and his cousin's treachery raised old resentments. He studied a fly darting about a dung pile. "Things like that can steal a man's spirit." John's anger drained from him and, like a breath of clean air, peace filled him. He looked into Mr. Atherton's blue eyes. "As it turns out, New South Wales was my destiny."

He removed his hat and shuffled the brim through his fingers. "This venture may not be a success. I'm a novice. What I know about country living is what I've learned since coming here." John replaced his hat on his head. "I want to try."

Mr. Atherton smiled and extended his hand. Grasping John's, he said, "I wish you well, then. I heard the piece you're looking at could become a fine farm. And there's a large property that borders it."

"Yes. I'm hoping to purchase it one day."

"It may be just what God wants for you and Hannah."

"I pray you're right, sir."

Mr. Atherton studied him a moment. "I think it's time you started calling me William. We're friends now."

"Thank you, sir, er . . . William." John smiled. "It'll take a bit of getting used to."

Mr. Atherton grinned. "You best be on your way. Don't want to keep ol' Murphy Connor waiting. He's not the most patient fellow."

"Right you are." John climbed into the saddle and, with a nod at William, headed for the road. Moving away from the Athertons' and toward what he hoped would one day be his own home, John couldn't quiet his jitters. He wanted this to be the right place for him and Hannah.

The road was empty, the forest quiet except for an occasional cry of a bird and the incessant buzz of flies. They tried to find their way into his eyes, his nose, and his ears. He swatted at them, but they were unrelenting. A lizard darted across the road and the gelding startled, then quieted under John's firm hand.

He scanned the forests and fields, watching for Aborigines. He knew it was a futile endeavor. Aborigines could well be watching him but would remain invisible unless they chose to reveal themselves. His heart leaped when, out of the corner of his eye, he thought he saw something dart behind a tree. It turned out to be a koala starting up a gum tree. The small animal climbed, reaching for a handful of eucalyptus leaves. Stuffing the morsels into his mouth, he chewed slowly and dispassionately watched the passing rider.

John chuckled. "That's quite enough of worrying."

A shrill "Coo-ee" echoed through the forest. Another answered the first, only it was farther away. John knew the cry—it was Aborigines. They used the call to communicate with one another. Watchful, he nudged his horse to a faster pace.

Although recent skirmishes had intensified John's concerns, he couldn't help but admire the indigenous people of New South Wales. In spite of severe and even ruthless challenges, they'd hung on to their way of life. They were daring and enterprising. They knew where to find food and water even in places where there seemed to be nothing. And they could walk endlessly without tiring. He remembered when he'd followed the tracker while hunting down his cousin Henry. The man's skills were myriad and unflagging. Henry hadn't had a chance of escape.

Since Henry's trial, John had given his cousin little thought. Now he wondered how severe his cousin's misery was. At Newcastle Prison it must certainly be profound.

Across the river, John spotted a disheveled-looking man he'd never seen before. The moment the stranger realized he'd been seen, he scampered deeper into the bushes and disappeared. *Why in the world would he do that? There's no need to hide.* John stopped and watched for the fellow. He never reemerged, and John finally went on his way. *Most likely an escaped prisoner. Hope he doesn't cause trouble.* John decided that on his way back through town he'd report the man.

He approached a trail that led to the property. Murphy Connor was already there. He sat on an embankment and his horse grazed beside him. When he saw John, he wiped sweat from his forehead, set his hat in place, and stood.

"Good mornin' to ye," the middle-aged man said. "It's a hot one, eh?"

"Indeed." John dismounted and shook Mr. Connor's hand. He scanned the acreage.

"Fine piece of property," Connor said. "Even if it is a bit small."

"Thank you for taking time to meet me."

"When I heard it was one of the government properties, I thought of ye. It would give ye and the wife a first-rate start. My land borders this piece and I figured ye for a good neighbor." He smiled.

"Thank you." John could feel excitement build inside. "It's fine land, indeed."

Connor gazed over the landscape. "Property runs down t' the river on one side, and there's a pond, and a stream runs through it. Course when things dry up, there'll not be much water."

He nodded at the Parramatta River. "If it was me, I'd build me a house down there. Having water close to your place will make yer wife happy." He pushed a wad of tobacco deep into his cheek. "The Parramatta will see ye never go without water for the house and garden."

"Ye plan on raising cattle?"

"No. Thought I'd try my hand at sheep."

Connor glanced at the sun. "Ye sure, lad? Cattle's a lot easier. Not as much of a market for sheep."

"Not yet, but there will be." John smiled. "You just wait and see." He nudged his hat back off his forehead. "I'd like to have a look 'round. I heard there's a large piece bordering this one."

"There is, indeed." Connor grinned. "That was me thought too. Figured one day ye might be able to buy it."

"You know the property well?"

"That I do. I'd be happy t' ride 'bout the place with ye." He climbed onto his horse and settled in the saddle. "The ground and grass is the best ye'll find for grazing."

The two men looked at the small portion of land available through the government and then explored the larger property. John's enthusiasm grew. The land was mostly made up of broad grasslands, golden and heated beneath the summer sun. Trees dotted the sprawling landscape, and John figured there'd be plenty enough for building a house and barn. This was it. This would be his and Hannah's home.

<hr />

John rode into the yard, excited to tell Hannah what he'd discovered. When he didn't see her right off, he dismounted and led the horse into the barn, relieved it of the saddle, and then tied him outside his stall. After a quick brushing and a handful of grain, he led the horse into his stall. Anxious to get to the house and talk with Hannah, he grabbed an armful of hay and dropped it into the crib.

The gelding pushed his nose into his feed and snatched up a mouthful. John gave him a final pat and headed for the cottage.

Stepping inside, he was hit by stifling heat. Hannah knelt beside the hearth, using a large wooden spoon to stir a pot of stew. Damp hair plastered itself to her moist face. She smiled, replaced the lid, and moved the pot back over the fire. "You're home just in time." Moving to John, she stood on tiptoe and planted a kiss on his cheek. "You look hot."

"I am. And it's stifling in here. Wouldn't it have been wiser to build a fire outdoors?"

A wounded expression touched Hannah's eyes. Immediately John wished he could take back the words.

"I'm not good at outdoor cooking."

"It's fine, luv, really. The stew smells good and I'm starved." He studied her, wearing a half smile. "Would you mind if we ate on the front steps?"

Hannah grinned. "That's a fine idea. Perhaps there'll be a breeze." Using the back of her hand, she wiped a strand of hair off her face. "I'll spoon us each a bowl. Then we'll sit and talk." She moved to the cupboard and took down two wooden bowls. "I daresay, I've been watching for you for more than an hour. I can scarcely wait to hear about the property."

John removed his hat and hung it on a wooden peg near the door. "And I want to tell you about it." He moved to the porch, dipped water out of a wooden cask and drank a ladleful, refilled it, and drank it down as well, and then sat on the top step.

Hannah emerged with the bowls of stew, and after handing him one, she sat beside him. Closing her eyes, she blew out a breath. "This is better. Cooler." She glanced about. "But a bit embarrassing. Everyone will know how foolish I've been, building a fire on such a hot day."

"They don't care a whit about where you cook." John leaned close and kissed her temple.

"I've never cooked well outdoors. I'm quite clumsy at it. In London it was rarely too hot to use the hearth. Perhaps Lydia will help me . . . again." She took a bite of stew. "I suppose I could have made cold meat sandwiches."

"Hannah. Stop. This is fine. I love your stew. And the fire will die down."

"It'll take hours."

John took a bite and chewed. "Delicious. Much better than a sandwich."

Hannah set her spoon in her bowl and focused on John. "All right. Tell me all about it."

"Tell you about what?" John teased.

"The land."

He smiled. "It's exactly what we've been hoping for. It's ours if we want it."

Hannah's eyes widened. "Just like that?"

"We'll have to file, but Murphy Connor was sure no one else had put in for it yet." He smiled broadly. "You'll love it. It's grand. Good grazing and plenty of timber for building. And a perfect spot for a house near the river." John remembered the man he'd seen hiding in the deep grasses on the banks of Parramatta, and the perfect spot seemed less perfect.

"Really? It's just what we want, then?"

"It is indeed. With irrigation from the river, we can have a garden, and when I've got our house built, I'll see to it that we have a pump in the kitchen." He sat up straighter and looked out, seeing in his mind what he'd seen that day. "Connor took me to look at the adjoining piece. There's a hillside that overlooks a great deal of the property—you can see for miles—it's quite scenic. I thought perhaps we could picnic there."

"I can't wait to see it. But, John, we don't know if we'll ever get the other piece of property."

"We will. I'm determined to have it."

Hannah rested a hand on John's arm. "Then I'm sure it will happen."

"If Mr. Atherton can spare me, we'll go tomorrow. Will you be needed in the house?"

"I'm sure everything will be fine without me. Deidre's quite proficient. I might as well have been gone today."

"You don't sound happy about it."

41

"Deidre seems to be good at everything."

"And that's bad, eh?" John grinned.

"No. Of course not. But . . . well, it feels strange not being needed."

"I need you." John pressed a kiss to her temple.

Hannah smiled at him. "I know."

She returned to her meal. "There's something not right about Deidre. She's too eager, too devoted. I don't trust her."

"Are you sure you're not just jealous?"

"Jealous?" Hannah snapped. "Absolutely not." She shrugged. "All right. Perhaps I am a little. It's just that everyone seems so taken with her. Even Lydia. Since we married, things have been different between us, and now she seems even more distant."

"You can't expect them to be the same. Lydia's not married and you are. And soon you'll be moving to your own place. Plus you're free and she's not. You can't forget she's taken over the housekeeping duties. She has more to do. A lot has changed."

"I know. I just hoped we could remain good friends. Now with Deidre . . ." Hannah stirred her stew.

"It's not Deidre's fault. Perhaps you're being too hard on her."

Hannah flashed John a look of irritation. "I suppose you're smitten with her too."

"I'm smitten only with you." John leaned close and kissed Hannah on the lips. "Only you."

Hannah leaned against him and then straightened. "I don't know how word got out so quickly, but there were a number of men who seemed to have errands of one kind or another that required they speak to the housemaid. And Deidre was clearly pleased by all the attention." She rubbed her temples. "I know she's not who she seems to be. I can feel it. I don't trust her."

"I'd say it's time to talk about something else."

Hannah sighed. "You're right. My fretting won't help." She managed a tight smile. "So, shall we plan to visit our property tomorrow?"

"Absolutely."

4

With one final swing of the ax, the acacia wood popped and split. John pulled the blade free and then pushed against the smooth bark of the young tree. Stepping back, he watched it fall. He used his shirtsleeve to wipe sweat from his brow and moved to the downed tree and began the job of cutting away branches.

Finally, John hauled the limbless acacia to a pile of other logs. "That ought to do it." He grabbed a flask hanging from the mule's harness, unscrewed the top, and took a long drink. After replacing the lid, he draped the flask over the yoke and stroked the animal's neck. "You ready to get to work?"

Chaining logs together in a bundle, he attached the main line to the harness, and then, giving the mule a friendly pat on the hindquarters, he lifted the reins and stepped around behind the logs. John clicked his tongue and slapped the lines gently, and the animal plodded forward, straining in its yoke. When he reached a partially completed cabin, John pulled back on the reins and the mule stopped.

Using a handkerchief to mop sweat dribbling down the back of his neck, John studied the small cottage that stood fifty yards from the Parramatta River. There was still a lot to be done before it was finished. Only three walls were up. They were made of small logs standing upright side by side and tied firmly together with twine. There were gaps he'd need to fill, but that would come later.

The more John stared at his work, the more frustration he felt. It was a pathetic dwelling and not remotely fit for someone like Hannah. But it would have to do. He didn't have enough funds to build a proper house. For now, this would shelter them.

He glanced at a pale blue sky and a blazing sun that baked him and the hard ground. He longed for clouds and a cool rain. His stomach felt hollow, and he wondered if Hannah would arrive soon.

The jangle of harnesses gave him his answer. He turned to see her driving a buggy up the rough path that led to the house from the road. He smiled. *How like her to arrive at just the right time.* Although pleased to see her, John worried about her being out on the road alone. It wasn't safe. Again, he glanced at the cabin and wished she didn't have to live in such a primitive place.

Smiling, Hannah pulled the buggy to a stop and lifted a basket. "I thought you might be hungry."

"That I am." John grasped her hand as she stepped down, dropping a kiss on her cheek. "You know me so well; my stomach's rumbling." John fixed her with a stern look. "I don't want you out and about by yourself. It can be dangerous."

"I understand, but if we're to live out here, it's something we must deal with. I'm not about to allow fear to keep me trapped in my house. We'll have to trust the Lord for our safety."

She shaded her eyes and turned to look at the cottage. "You've done quite a lot. We'll be moving in soon, won't we?" If she felt any disappointment at the dismal construction, she showed no hint.

"Soon. I'm sorry. I know it's not much. But when it's finished it'll serve us well." Inadequacy grinding at his insides, he added, "You deserve better."

Hannah grinned. "That I do, but this is just a beginning. It will do nicely for now." She draped an arm about John's waist. "Can I look inside?"

"I'll give you a tour," he said in a teasing voice.

Hannah grasped John's hand and the two stepped into the tiny one-room house. A rock hearth took up most of one wall. Hannah moved to the stone fireplace. "You've done a grand job. It's sufficiently wide and quite suitable for cooking." She planted her hands on her hips. "And when the cold weather comes, it will keep us snug and warm."

At that moment standing in the midst of the hovel he'd built, John couldn't recall ever loving Hannah more. He pulled her to him. "Have I told you recently how much I love you?"

"Indeed you have, sir." Hannah leaned in closer to her husband.

Gazing into her dark eyes, John admitted, "It's going to be dreadful. While the heat lasts, it'll be stifling hot in here and the flies will be appalling. And when the rain comes, we'll be living in a sea of mud."

"It won't be dreadful at all." She gazed about the tiny house. "The heat can't be worse than where we are, and we can put shutters on the window to keep out the flies." She leaned against him. "I heard there's to be less rain than usual this year. That will help with the mud." Her expression turned serious. "No matter the difficulties, I will be content. This is our home on our own land. Ours." She draped her arms about John's neck. "Not so long ago a life of servitude and chains was all we had before us. This place—you—it's all a miracle."

John felt renewed anticipation. "It is indeed. And I *will* build a proper home, but I can't do it straightaway. There's too much that must be done first."

"We'll manage." Hannah gave him a squeeze and then stepped outside to the buggy. "Shall we eat?" She took the basket from the seat. "I brought cheese and bread, apples, and custard."

"Mmm. Sounds perfect."

"I brought something to sit on. It's on the seat." Hannah walked toward the river.

John retrieved the quilt, but before following Hannah he also grabbed his musket, which rested against the cabin.

Hannah stopped beneath a gum tree. She turned to John and looked at the gun. "Will we need that?"

"Just in case." John rested it against the tree. He swept away twigs and gum nuts that had fallen from the branches and then unfolded the blanket and spread it out on the ground.

Hannah sat and arranged her skirts so they wouldn't crumple and then opened the basket. "We are isolated here. I must admit to still feeling a bit unsettled at the thought of being so alone. I feel it especially when I travel the empty road between here and the Athertons'. Lydia made me bring a pistol. But it would do me little good. I have no notion of how to use it."

"I doubt there's much for you to worry about. There's been no trouble in recent days. And I daresay, we're safer here than we were on the streets of London."

"You're right on that count." Hannah looked up the empty road.

John grasped her hand. "Try not to worry."

"I'm fine. Really." She opened the basket and took out sliced bread and cheese and a flask of water. Placing the cheese between two pieces of bread, she handed the plain sandwich to

John. "This is quite a pleasant spot. I love the tangy scent of eucalyptus." She breathed deeply. "And the river here is nice, it's a bit more lively. After we move in we can picnic often." She gazed out on the quiet river. "Look there." She pointed at a large white bird standing among the rushes along the bank. It had sticklike legs and a long narrow beak it dipped beneath the surface of the water to probe for food.

"It would seem he's hungry too." John bit into his sandwich.

The bird moved slowly along the river's edge. Without warning, it spread its wings and launched itself into the air. With its legs trailing behind, the bird flew slowly and gracefully and then disappeared beyond the trees.

"I never tire of watching the birds and animals," Hannah said. "They're interesting and beautiful. I look forward to the day when I can sit on my veranda and simply gaze at the wildlife and the incredible landscape."

John leaned back on one arm. "And on a hot day we can cool ourselves in the river."

"I don't know how to swim."

"It's not difficult. I'll teach you. And our children." John studied a quiet pool in the shallows and imagined the good days ahead.

"Of course," Hannah said, her voice stiff.

John looked at her. "Are you afraid, luv?"

"Of what? Swimming?" She chuckled. "No. I've just never learned. In London the Thames wasn't far from where I lived, but it was too ghastly a place to swim. And it would have been indecent of me anyway."

"Not here. We've our privacy." John closed his eyes for a moment, remembering. "I recall there being some grand places for swimming outside the city."

"Mum and I rarely ventured out of town." Hannah took a bite of her cheese. "Do you think we can move into the house soon? Lydia has taken on the position as housekeeper, and she's quite competent. Mrs. Atherton has no need for me." She looked at the tiny cottage. "If we lived here, we'd have more time together. And I could lend a hand."

"I've the floor and roof left to do yet. And we can't move in until there's a door."

Hannah broke off a piece of bread and put it in her mouth. "Perhaps if we lived here, we could finish more quickly because I could help. I don't need a door." She glanced at the sky. "And I doubt we'll have any rain soon."

"No door or roof?" John shook his head. "Doesn't seem fitting. I don't want my wife living in such a state. It'll be spare enough as it is." John ate the last of his sandwich and talked around the mouthful. "I've hired a man, Quincy Walker. Well, not exactly hired. He said he'd work for food and shelter."

"We've no shelter, but I'd be happy to feed him." Hannah met John's eyes. "If he comes to work for you, then you'll need a cook."

"I suppose you're right."

"I don't see why we can't move in as soon as the floor is in place." Hannah drank from the flask. "Could Quincy live in a lean-to?"

"He might be all right with that, at least until we can put up something more substantial." John studied Hannah. "You'd truly not mind living without a roof or a door?"

"Well, if Quincy is going to be here, a door would be nice for privacy. We could use a blanket for now." Hannah leaned back on her hands. "But I'd rather be here and get the house finished. And I'm not afraid when you're with me." She leaned toward him. "I just want our life here to begin."

Lying beside John on a bed of woven rope, Hannah gazed at a night sky bejeweled with stars. "It's a perfect night, isn't it?"

John clasped his hands behind his head. "I'd say nearly so."

"Our first night in our own home."

"As humble as it is," John said sardonically.

"It's only temporary."

A dingo howled, cutting into the quiet of the night. Another cry followed the first.

"Tomorrow I'll put in a door."

Hannah cuddled closer to John. "I'm not afraid. Really I'm not. When I'm with you I feel completely safe."

"I won't always be here. I'll need to make trips into Sydney Town for supplies and I'll have to travel to buy sheep."

Hannah knew. She'd thought about the days and nights she'd have to spend alone. The idea frightened her, but with as much confidence as she could muster, she said, "There's nothing to be done about it. I'll simply have to learn to be more independent." She rested her cheek on his chest, feeling comforted by the steady thump of his heart. "I like the open roof and not having a door." She yawned. "It makes the house cooler."

"Well and fine on a hot day, but there'll be wet and cold ones to come. And cooler or not, the door will be set in place tomorrow."

Hannah barely heard him. She was exhausted and could scarcely keep her eyes open. John pressed his lips to the top of her head and caressed her back. Secure, Hannah drifted into sleep.

When morning light awakened her, it was as if the night had passed in a moment. John was already out of bed. She sat up and her muscles complained. For several days, she'd worked alongside him, helping to finish the walls, laying wood planks in place for a floor, and moving in their few furnishings. They didn't have much, but she'd managed to make the cottage look homey.

She let her eyes roam over the house. It was small but clean, and the hearth was a good one. A hook for managing cooking pots rested against one side of the fireplace, and a heavy iron teakettle sat on an iron stand in the coals. John had built two benches. One sat beside the hearth and the other had been placed just inside the door. He'd also made a rough-sawn table with two chairs and a wooden cupboard that held basic necessities. A row of hooks for clothing stood in line on the wall next to their bed.

Hannah set her bare feet on the rough-hewn floor. The coarse boards felt prickly, but it didn't bother her. She knew that after several scrubbings the floor's surface would become smoother. She moved to the window and watched John carry an armload of boards to the house. After a long yawn and a good stretch, she stepped to the doorway.

"These will do fine for a doorframe," he said. "I'll have it finished in no time."

"I can see you've been up a good while."

"That I have." John offered Hannah a smile.

She hurried outside and walked several paces from the house where she found privacy behind a tree.

Just as she put her skirts to rights, she saw movement across the river. Her heart thumped. An Aborigine stared at her from the shadows. Hannah sucked in her breath. What was he doing there? Had he been watching her? Humiliated and frightened, she hurried back to the house.

"As soon as I get the roof on, I'll see to it that we have a proper facility."

"John." Hannah's voice trembled. "There's an Aborigine across the river."

"Is he still there?"

"I don't know. I hurried back."

John grabbed his musket and moved toward the road. "Stay in the house," he commanded and made his way to the edge of the property.

Fear thrumming through her, Hannah hurried indoors and went to the window to watch. Her eyes moved over the land-scape, but there was no sign of the man.

John cautiously approached the river and walked the bank, first heading downriver and then upriver. Finally, he made his way back to the house, occasionally glancing behind him.

Hannah met him at the door. "Did you see him?"

"No. I'm sure he was just curious and has gone on his way."

"He startled me so." Hannah pressed a hand against her throat. Her pulse raced. "I wasn't expecting to see anyone, es-pecially not while I was . . ."

John chuckled. "As soon as I finish the door, I'll get an out-door convenience built."

"Thank you." Hannah stepped inside. "I'll make breakfast."

John and Hannah sat on a bench at the front of the house, munching on scones and dried beef. John kept an eye on the river. "I need brackets for the door. I can get some at the Ather-tons'. Would you like to come along?"

"Yes. I'd love it." Still frightened over the Aborigine being so close to the house and watching her, Hannah was thankful for the invitation. "It would be lovely to see Lydia and Mrs. Atherton."

John finished off his scone and leaned forward on his thighs. "I made a deal for our first batch of sheep."

"You did? You didn't say anything."

"Sorry. In the midst of all the work, I guess I forgot. The man who has them lives near Sydney Town. He said I could get them anytime. I'd like to go next week." His face tensed and he lifted his eyebrows slightly. "I'll be away a few days."

Hannah had just taken a bite of scone. She chewed and managed to force it down. "So we'll truly begin, then." She gazed at the property.

John smiled. "Today we'll have a door, tomorrow a roof, and even a stock pen before I go. We've truly begun."

"That's an awful lot for you to do before next week."

"I talked to Quincy, and he said although he's still working for Mr. Atherton, he'd be glad to help out. We just need to keep his stomach full."

"I can do that for him." Hannah smiled, but her mind was still on the news that in a few days John would leave her here alone. Fear spiked through her. "Perhaps I should know how to shoot a pistol."

"That's a good idea."

⬛

Hannah watched as John poured black powder into the pistol muzzle.

"Be careful not to put in too much," he said, and then pulled the string on a pouch closed with his teeth. He fished out a lead ball from another small bag and pushed it into the barrel. Using a rod attached to the underside of the gun, he stuffed the powder and ball in tightly. He looked at Hannah. "You think you can do this?"

Hannah hated the idea of firing a weapon, but she needed to know how. "It doesn't seem too difficult. I'll have to practice a few times."

"Right." John turned his attention back to the gun. "The next step is to pull the striker back, but just halfway. After you've done that, you need to prime it with a bit of gunpowder." He poured some into the flash pan and then closed the lid. "Now it's primed and ready to shoot. If you're carrying it or keeping it on the shelf, you can leave it primed so it's ready to fire when you need it."

He glanced at a target he'd set up. "I'll see to it that you always have a pistol primed. There's a safety notch here to keep it from firing until you're ready." He showed her how to put the safety on and then asked, "So, you think you can remember all that?"

Hannah nodded, but she wasn't truly sure. There were so many steps.

"Now, when you want to shoot, you pull the striker back like this." He demonstrated. "Then grasp the pistol with both hands to keep it steady." He held the gun out in front of him and aimed at a wooden slab leaning against a stump. "And then you pull the trigger, right here." He squeezed the trigger.

The gun discharged with a loud explosion and seemed to jump in John's hands. Hannah flinched. "Oh my Lord! I shan't be able to do it."

John smiled at her and lowered the pistol. "Of course you can. You must."

Hannah knew he was right. "I'll give it a go, then." Hands trembling, she took the gun and did just as he'd shown her. When it was loaded and primed, she cocked it and grasped it between both hands. She fired, missing the stump completely.

"Not bad for your first attempt," John said.

Swamped in a cloud of smoke and her hands tingling from the kick of the pistol, Hannah was certain she never wanted to fire a weapon again. "Oh, the stink is awful. What is that smell?" She fanned the air with her hand. "It's like cooked eggs."

"Just the burned powder."

Quaking and frustrated, Hannah lowered the pistol. "I was terrible."

John chuckled. "You'll do better. Try again."

Hannah didn't want to, but she made two more attempts. The last time she managed to hit the target, but the noise, smoke, and pain in her hands begged for her to stop.

"Well done. We'll practice more another time." John rested a hand on her shoulder and gave it a gentle squeeze

---

"Are you certain you wouldn't rather stay at the Athertons'?" John asked as he headed for the door.

"No. I'll be quite all right. I'd best get used to spending time alone." Hannah managed to smile. She would have preferred staying at the Athertons', but that was foolishness. She was a farmer's wife and must become self-reliant.

She glanced at the wall where two pistols hung. "I'll do fine. You're not to worry." She rested a hand on John's arm. "Just bring back our sheep."

John kissed her. "I'll think about you every moment."

"I'll be thinking of you too."

John stepped outside. Quincy, already sitting atop his horse, nodded at Hannah. "G'day."

"Good day, Quincy."

John pushed up into his saddle, lifted his hat slightly, and then turned the horse and moved away from the house. The two men cantered toward the road. Hannah watched until she couldn't see them any longer. Taking a deep breath, she closed the door and turned to her morning tasks. She tried not to think about what could happen while John was away. They'd not seen any Aborigines since the one incident, but she still worried that they were out there . . . watching and waiting. Plus there'd been an unsuccessful search for an escaped prisoner. Desperate escapees were always a danger.

The day passed uneventfully and, surprisingly, Hannah slept well that night. When she awoke the next morning, however, she felt very much alone. John would be gone at least three more days.

She pushed aside her melancholy. There was work to be done. The Athertons had made a gift of a milk cow. Hannah was clumsy at milking, so the cow was sometimes disagreeable. She had named her Patience, hoping the name might bring out the best in the animal. Thus far it had done little good.

Now the bovine bellowed, letting Hannah know she needed to be milked. Carrying a wooden bucket and a stool, she walked to the corral where the small cow waited, still mooing her distress. As difficult as this task was for Hannah, she was thankful for the fresh milk, cream, and butter.

She let herself into the pen and patted the bovine's side. "Good day to you. I hope you'll have patience with me this morning." The cow looked at Hannah from behind brown eyes lined by long lashes. Hannah caressed her soft nose. The animal snuffled her palm, searching for grain.

Hannah set her bucket and stool beside the cow and then

grabbed an armful of hay from a lean-to and spread it out in the crib. Patience pushed her nose into the fragrant fodder and was soon grinding hay between her teeth.

Apprehensively Hannah moved the stool closer to the cow and placed the bucket beneath her. Gwen had shown her how to milk, but Hannah had yet to master the task. Often, before she could finish, Patience would grow frustrated with her and with a swish of her tail would move off, sometimes knocking over the pail. Most days John took care of the milking, but that did her little good now.

She rested a hand on the cow's bulging side. A calf was expected in the spring. Although eager for the birth, the thought produced a pang of longing in Hannah. If only she were expecting a child.

Using a damp cloth she'd draped over her shoulder, she wiped the udder clean and then pressed her forehead against the animal's fragrant warm hair and gently tugged on the teats. Milk splashed into the bucket.

Her mind returned to the expected calf. John hoped for a heifer so there'd be enough extra milk and cream to sell, but Hannah wanted a bull calf. That way they'd have beef for eating instead of chicken, rabbit, and kangaroo. She was tired of chicken and rabbit and didn't like eating kangaroos. The large golden-haired animals were lovely, playful creatures. And the mothers were nurturing to the delightful joeys. She hated killing them.

Hannah worked steadily, but the bucket was only half filled when Patience decided she'd stood still long enough and started fidgeting, swishing her tail furiously. Hannah tried to work faster. Perhaps more hay would help. She straightened, moving the stool back and setting the bucket aside.

Her eyes locked with those of a black man who stood no

more than ten yards away. Her pulse jumped and she gulped in a quick breath. There were two of them, their black skin dusted with summer dirt. She backed away.

"What do you want? Would you like some milk?" She picked up the bucket and extended it toward them. She received no response.

Quaking inside, but trying to look calm, Hannah walked toward the gate chatting amicably all the while. "I'd be more than happy to share my bread and cheese with you. There's cheese down at the river." She pointed at the makeshift springhouse.

The men remained silent.

Hannah stepped through the gate and closed it. "I can pour you some milk. Just a moment." Hurriedly she walked toward the cabin. When she glanced back the men were gone. She stopped. Where were they?

Her heart thumping wildly beneath her ribs, she looked all around. What had become of them?

Milk sloshing over the sides of the bucket, Hannah hurried to the cabin, stepped inside, and pushed the door closed, slamming down the latch. Setting the milk on the table, she moved to the window and peered out. She couldn't see them.

Hands shaking, she grabbed both pistols from their places on the wall and then returned to the window. Still no sign. Setting the guns on the table, she closed the shutters and bolted them. She tried to quiet her breathing. If only she could go to the Athertons', but John had taken the horse, and the mule was trained only to the plow. There was nothing she could do.

Hannah picked up the pistols and moved to a chair and sat. Quaking, she held the guns in her lap and prayed.

5

Hannah pressed her hands down on the sill of the window and gazed out. "Where is he? He should be home."

It had been three days since Hannah's encounter with the Aborigines. They'd not returned, but she was still afraid. Glancing at the primed pistols she'd left on the table, she crossed to the hearth. Using a hook, she moved a pot of stew from the lug pole to a trivet. Lifting the lid, she stirred the vegetable mixture and then hefted it back over the heat. John would be hungry when he got home.

An ache jabbed at Hannah's lower back. She straightened and rubbed at the sore muscle. Using a corner of her apron, she wiped perspiration from her face. A peculiar noise carried in from outside, and her nerves leaped. She hurried to the window and listened. A murmuring, complaining sound filled the air. What was it?

Suddenly she knew. "It's sheep! John!" She ran to the door, gathered up her skirts, and sprinted down the drive.

A burst of wind swirled dust into an eddy. Hannah gazed through the earthen cloud. Where was he? A breeze caught at her hair and billowed her skirts.

She saw the first of the sheep and then more. They moved

placidly through a dirt cloud. John appeared, sitting confidently atop his dark bay. He spotted Hannah and waved, smiling broadly.

She waved back and fought the impulse to run to him. She dare not startle the sheep for fear of scattering them. "Lord, thank you for bringing him home to me," she whispered.

Bleating and searching for mouthfuls of grass, the mob moved past. They barely seemed to notice her. When John reached Hannah, he stopped and caught hold of her outstretched hand. "Hannah," he said, his voice full of devotion.

"Thank the Lord, you're home. I was worried about you. Now my heart can rest easy."

Gazing at her, he clasped her hand more tightly, then returning to a more businesslike demeanor, he asked, "Can you open the corral gate?"

"Of course." Hannah moved cautiously past the sheep, then hurried to the stock pen. After opening the gate, she lifted a lead rope from a post and moved to Patience. Snapping it to her halter, she led the cow out of the pen and tied her.

Returning to the gate, she swung it wide open and stood between the enclosure and the house, wondering just how John and Quincy planned to steer the flock through the gate and into the pen. Hannah spotted a broom on the porch and ran to get it, hoping it would provide her more than an extra arm's length. She quickly returned to her post and extended the broom to block any attempts at defection.

Quincy kept his horse on the other side of the mob, and John continued to herd from behind. The animals seemed content to remain together and ambled into the enclosure. They crowded around a water tub, burying their noses in the blessed liquid, while John climbed down from his horse and closed the animals in.

He removed his hat and leaned against the fence. Hannah joined him, tucking herself in beneath his arm. He turned a warm smile on her. "It's grand to see you." Enfolding her in his arms, he buried his face in her hair. "You smell good."

"I've missed you." Close to tears, Hannah pressed her face against his neck and tightened her hold. "I'm so glad you're home."

"How good it is to be here. All I've done is think about you." Keeping one arm around her, John turned to study the sheep. "We've had long, hard days, but we've done it." He looked at Quincy and chuckled. "These are not the smartest animals. I daresay a chicken has more brains than a ewe."

"Intent on getting themselves killed, I'd say." Quincy grinned.

"We need a good herding dog."

"A dog?" Hannah asked.

"If we're going to raise sheep, we have to get one. Not just any will do, though. Mr. Jones has three he uses for herding. They're smart and know how to round up sheep and how to keep them from becoming unruly. They're born that way, knowing what to do. They only need a bit of training. Jones has a female ready to whelp any day. Told me I could have my pick out of the litter for a bit of machine work that he needs done."

"A dog, eh?" Hannah grinned. "I'd like to see one that knows how to watch over sheep."

John laid his arms on the top of the fence and rested a foot on the bottom board. "These animals might be stupider than a rock, but they're sturdy—Merinos from South Africa. Good for mutton and for wool. And in a few months there'll be lambs."

Hannah gazed at the shuffling, bleating animals and suddenly felt overwhelmed. How were they going to do this? They knew nothing about raising sheep.

"We'll be busy come late April, early May. We can expect a lamb from every one of them. And I'm hoping to have more ewes by then too. Mr. Jones said he'd have more when I'm ready."

"Will the new ones also be carrying lambs?"

"I should hope so."

"That sounds like a lot of sheep. Do we have enough land?"

"I was told that Mr. Jones might allow us to run our sheep on his land since he's living in Sydney Town and not using it. I'll ask him."

"He's a good man." Quincy leaned against the fence and eyed the ewes. "Ye can count on losses. Sometimes it seems lambs are born trying to die. If they make it, there are dingoes to think about and disease. And ye'll need a warm dry place for the ewes to drop the lambs."

"We'll have a shed up by then." John lifted his hat and resettled it on his head. "We'll do all right." He turned to Hannah. "How did you fare, luv? Any trouble while we were gone?"

"No." Hannah said, deciding not to tell him about her fright, at least not just yet. It would only worry him. "Except for Patience. I'm still dreadfully slow at milking, and she won't stand still long enough for me to finish. I'm worried that if she's not milked thoroughly, she'll dry up."

John dropped an arm over Hannah's shoulders. "Tomorrow, first thing, I'll get the stanchion built."

"First thing, you'll milk her."

John smiled and nodded, then glanced at the sky, its blue color deepening as the sun perched on the horizon. "It'll be dark soon. Figure I'll take a bath in the river."

"I've stew cooking."

"Good. I'm starved."

Hannah moved toward the house. "You'll need clean clothes." She glanced at Quincy. "You too. I washed your trousers and shirt, as well."

"Ye did? Thank ye." Grinning, Quincy followed John and Hannah to the house.

⊷⊶

Hannah shook out an apron, draped it over the clothesline, and then reached into her pocket for a wooden pin to secure it. A wind gust picked up dirt and leaves and swirled them into the air. She groaned. If the wind kept up, the clothes would only get dirty again.

She heard the sound of some sort of conveyance down at the road. She stopped and listened, hoping it wouldn't pass. Visitors were rare. The jangling of bridles and harnesses quieted and then grew louder as the vehicle moved closer.

Hannah gazed at the road. A wagon approached. There were two people sitting on the front bench—Lydia and Lottie! She'd not seen Lottie for a long while. When they'd crossed from Britain on the prison ship, they were nearly inseparable. Lottie had seemed like her own child.

"Oh," Hannah exclaimed, running to greet her friends. "I can barely believe my eyes," she said as Lydia pulled the horses to a stop. Hannah reached up and helped Lottie down. She hugged the little girl. "What a grand surprise." She turned toward Lydia. "How wonderful to see you."

Lydia moved around the horses and opened her arms to Hannah. "I've missed ye. How have ye been getting along way out here?"

"Good." Hannah glanced to the north. "John and Quincy are working with the sheep. There's always so much to do. And they spend a goodly amount of time trying to keep the roaming creatures from straying too far."

"Too bad ye don't have a sheepherder," said Lottie. "They'll keep watch over them for ye." When she talked she bobbed her head, tousling her auburn curls.

"Indeed, that would be grand. But we've no money for such a luxury. Perhaps one day." She smiled at Lydia. "I can still barely believe you've come."

"We were worried 'bout ye. We've not seen ye at church for two Sundays, now."

"John's been working hard. Most days we labor from light 'til dark. He didn't feel he could take even one day away." Hannah frowned. "I've missed church but didn't have the heart to leave him. He promised this week we'd go no matter what." She returned to the basket of clothes. "Let me finish hanging these and then we can go inside for tea."

Lydia and Lottie helped Hannah hang up the remaining clothes and then the three walked toward the house.

"It's blistering hot," Lydia said. "And I went off without my bonnet." She glanced at the hazy sky. "This wind isn't a help. Only makes things worse."

Hannah stepped onto the cottage porch. She smiled down at Lottie. "Would you like a biscuit? I have some fresh baked."

"I'd like that." Lottie grasped her hand. "I've missed ye, mum. Why don't ye come to see me more?"

Hannah leaned close to Lottie and gently brushed a loose

lock of hair off her face. "I wish I could, sweetie. But since John and I moved here, there's always something that needs my attention." She nodded at a garden patch. "I managed to get the garden in, but it was a bit late. The vegetables don't like the heat, so I doubt we'll get much from it. But next spring will be different."

Lottie made a face, her freckles crinkling. "I don't like vegetables much anyway."

Hannah stepped inside the door. "Please, come in." She took three cups from the cupboard and set them on the small table near the window. "John made this table, and the chairs to go with it."

Lydia ran her palm over the surface. "It's well done and feels sturdy."

Hannah lifted a kettle out of the hearth and poured brewed tea through a strainer and into a teapot, and then she filled the cups with the hot beverage. When she'd finished, she returned the soaking tea leaves to the water and set the pot on the hearth. "I haven't any sugar."

"I don't mind." Lydia accepted the warm drink.

After climbing onto another chair, Lottie daintily picked up her cup.

Hannah smiled. She was obviously trying to behave like a grown-up. "You're becoming such a young lady, Lottie."

Her eyes brightened and her face flushed pink. "I've no need for sugar." The ten-year-old took a sip. "This is quite good."

"Thank you." Hannah set a plate of biscuits on the table and joined her friends.

"So how do ye like living out here?" Lydia asked. "It's a bit isolated."

"It is, but I like it. Except I don't see my friends often enough.

John works hard, but he's not had time to build a better house. He will, though, just as soon as some of the necessities are completed."

Lydia glanced about. "I think ye've made it look real homey."

Hannah knew the house looked dismal, but there was nothing to be done about it. Changing the subject, she said, "I've learned something new." She pressed her lips together as if holding back a secret. "John taught me how to load and shoot a pistol and the musket."

"Did he really?" Lydia leaned forward on her arms. "Ye need to know that, living way out here."

"And I've learned to ride too," Hannah added.

"You mean a horse?" asked Lottie.

"Yes. It's splendid fun." Hannah gazed at her tea and quietly added, "I ride astride."

"Really?" Lydia giggled. "Oh, wouldn't Mrs. Goudy be in a dither over that. And so would Mrs. Atherton, I should think."

"It's a necessity. I've no sidesaddle. And I decided if I was to be of any help to John, I'd best learn."

"He doesn't mind?"

"I don't think so, at least not if I stay close to home. But he did say that the next time he goes for sheep, he'd like to have my help."

Humor in her eyes, Lydia looked at Hannah from beneath her lashes. "It's scandalous. What will people say when they see you?"

"I'm not certain I have the courage to ride off the property, but I suppose I'll have to, at least if I'm to help with the sheep."

"When will that be?"

"Soon. John's doing some extra work for Mr. Atherton so we'll have enough money for another horse plus the sheep."

"I've seen him 'bout from time to time."

Hannah picked up a biscuit. "John told me he's seen Dr. Gelson there on occasion."

Lydia's face reddened. "He drops in now and again."

Lottie leaned her elbows on the table. "The last two Sundays he sat with Lydia in church. And he's always smiling at her."

"Really?" Hannah raised her eyebrows.

Speaking through a mouthful, Lottie said, "I heard he comes 'round all the time, mostly to see Lydia. He was there today."

"You were at the Athertons'?" Hannah asked.

"Yes, me and Mum went to visit."

Hannah felt a pang of envy. She wished Lottie were her child. She had been once, sort of.

"I asked Lydia if she'd bring me out to see ye." Lottie smiled. "But then Dr. Gelson came by. I don't think he was happy Lydia was leaving."

"So, you're a pair, then?" Hannah asked.

"He's not announced any intentions. But we do see each other." Lydia's golden skin turned a deeper bronze.

"And what of Perry? Has he found anyone?"

"Perhaps. He and Gwen seem to be getting along well."

"Good."

Lydia gazed about the tiny cabin. Her eyes settled on the ceiling made of tree bark and sod. "Will you be putting up a new roof?"

"In time. But not right away. We've very little capital."

Lydia continued to study the ceiling. "I doubt it will hold if we get much in the way of rain."

Hannah understood they needed a stronger roof, but there

67

was nothing they could do about it now. "I'm sure we'll be fine. The barn still needs to be built. And we've need of a lambing shed as well." She drank the last of her tea. "John refuses to borrow any money."

A furrow cut across Lydia's forehead. "There must be something that can be done. I can't bear the thought of you spending the winter in this cabin."

"It's better than what we knew on board ship and at the factory. And we managed well enough."

"I don't know how well we managed, but we did survive."

***

Grinding and dredging noises woke John. And there was a jangle of harnesses mixed with the sound of voices. It was all coming from down by the road. Sitting up, he threw back his blanket and clambered out of bed. "Good Lord, what is that racket?" He moved to the window. A parade of wagons, horses, and people rattled up the drive.

Bewildered, he stared at the menagerie. "What's this?"

Hannah catapulted out of bed.

"Looks like the whole blooming town is here."

Hannah joined John at the window.

Perry drove a dray loaded with stones. Gwen sat on the seat beside him. Lydia walked alongside a pair of draft horses that pulled the heavily loaded cart. She smiled and waved at Hannah and John.

"Do you know what this is about?" Hannah asked.

"I've not a clue." John pulled on trousers and a shirt and pushed his feet into boots. Combing back mussed hair with his fingers, he stepped outside.

Mr. Atherton drove another cart loaded with lumber. John

approached him. "Good day, William. What is all this?" He looked at the collection of people and beasts.

William Atherton climbed down from the wagon. "It seems you've a number of friends who don't like the idea of your spending the winter in a hut."

"We've come to build you a proper house," Lydia said, striding up beside Mr. Atherton.

His mind still muddled from sleep, John couldn't grasp the truth of the situation. "I've not even ordered materials."

"True enough," William Atherton said, wearing a playful expression. "But we did." He turned to look at the people and the wagons loaded with building supplies and then back at John. "If you could kindly show us where you want the house to stand, we can begin working."

John didn't know how to reply. He took a step closer to Mr. Atherton and whispered, "I've no money."

"That may be true, but you've a great deal of skill. You can count this as a loan against the work I'll need from you." He cocked one eyebrow. "Is that acceptable?"

Still perplexed and overwhelmed, John stared at William for a long moment and then looked at Hannah who stood in the doorway. Her expression of shock transformed into a grateful smile. John turned back to Mr. Atherton. "That would suit me fine, sir." He held out a hand to his former employer. "Thank you."

"You're welcome."

John looked at the people who had gathered. "Thanks to you all."

"So, where would you like the house?" Mr. Atherton asked.

John pointed at a piece of ground he'd leveled where he'd hoped one day to construct a home. "I believe that will do nicely."

"It will at that." Mr. Atherton and the men went to work unloading the wagons. The dray was maneuvered into the center of the building site, and a group of men hefted stones that would be used for the fireplace. Others carried lumber and a myriad of other building materials.

Hannah stood beside John. He slipped an arm about her waist. "I can hardly believe it." She leaned against him, and John kissed the top of her head. "I'd best get to work," he said, barely able to speak around the lump in his throat. He blinked back tears and hugged Hannah more tightly. He'd prayed and God had answered.

The next few days John and Hannah's place was a frenzy of activity as the hearth was built and the house around it. The women kept the men fed and managed to see to the farming chores. As the house grew, they helped Hannah with the tasks of washing and scrubbing, and in the quieter moments they worked on a quilt Mrs. Atherton had started many weeks before.

The day the home was finished, a feast of roasted pig, potatoes, string beans, turnips, and an assortment of desserts was prepared. The furnishings were moved into the house, and Catharine Atherton carried in the finished quilt and placed it on John and Hannah's bed. "Something new for your home."

"Thank you," Hannah said, her voice barely more than a whisper.

With the house finished, John and Hannah stood in the yard, arms intertwined, and gazed at their new home. It was a fine house, with three rooms downstairs, a loft upstairs, and a solid roof. Plus there were windows with glass panes.

John clasped Hannah's hand and led her indoors. The sound

of their footsteps echoed on the new wood floor. Hannah walked to the hearth and rested her hand on an oven that had been built into the stone face. "It's too much." She looked at her friends. They'd crowded into the room behind them. "I couldn't imagine a finer home."

John pulled Hannah in close to his side and turned to face his friends. "There are not adequate words to thank all of you."

"We consider ourselves thanked," Mr. Atherton said.

Catharine moved to Hannah, and taking her hands in hers, she looked intently into the younger woman's eyes. Gently she said, "To William and I, you and John are like our own." Her eyes were awash with tears.

Hannah squeezed Catharine's hands.

"All right, then. How 'bout a bit of music?" Quincy slipped a mouth harp out of his front shirt pocket and put it to his lips.

Lanterns were lit as the sun set. Music echoed across the farm. Friends and neighbors feasted, danced, talked, and laughed. It was a perfect night.

"I'm almost too full to move," John said, resting a hand on his stomach. "But I dare not pass up this opportunity to dance with my wife." He led Hannah to a level piece of ground and took her into his arms. "I haven't felt so carefree since . . . well, since forever." Gazing into his wife's brown eyes, he said more seriously, "I wanted to give this to you, but . . ."

Hannah put a finger to his lips. "I know. And God knew your heart." Her hand moved to his neck. "I would have been happy living anywhere with you."

"God has blessed us." He gazed at the house.

"And you deserve it, John. You've worked so hard and you've trusted in the Lord."

"It's you who deserve the best of everything."

Doubt touched Hannah's eyes. "Certainly not everything."

John wondered what he'd seen there, but he didn't want to spoil the mood, so instead of saying anything, he surveyed the house. "It's a good sturdy home, a fine place to raise a family. When the children come, we'll use the extra room downstairs, and as they grow, the loft will serve them well." A stricken expression flashed across Hannah's face. He pulled her close. "Don't worry, luv; we'll have children. We've not been married that long yet."

Hannah grasped him tightly and pressed her forehead against his shoulder. John was almost certain she was crying.

Her eyes wet, Hannah looked up at him. "We've been married long enough. And I'm afraid. What if it never happens?"

"It will. Trust in the Lord." John smiled, but fear tugged at him as well. "Perhaps you're already with child and just don't know it yet."

"Perhaps." Hannah didn't sound convinced. "It's been six months since our wedding."

A musical laugh carried across the yard. Deidre stood happily amidst a group of men, each waiting for a turn to dance.

"She certainly turns heads, doesn't she?" John said with a laugh.

"She does at that. But I doubt her charm touches the inside."

"Why do you feel that way? From all I've heard she works hard and she seems to have an agreeable disposition." He leaned back and looked intently at Hannah. "You said you're not jealous. Are you? You're much prettier than her, you know."

"You're overly kind, husband."

"I'd not give Deidre a thought. I'm sure she's innocent enough."

Hannah studied the blonde beauty. "Innocent? I think not."

6

Looking through a blur of tears, Hannah swept hot ashes out of the oven and into a metal firebox. Grasping the handle, she headed for the door. As she reached for the latch, it lifted and the door opened. John stepped in.

"I'll take that," he said, reaching for the handle. "My stomach's already grumbling. Hope dinner's nearly ready."

"Nearly." Hannah released the box.

"Good. I can smell fresh hot bread already."

"That you'll have to wait for until morning." Without meeting his eyes, she moved to the hearth where a flat wooden shovel rested against the stone face. She carried it to the table and set it beside rising bread.

"Hannah?"

Still not looking up, Hannah sprinkled cornmeal on the peel and placed two mounds of bread dough on the shovel. "What?" She glanced at John.

"You look a bit down."

"No. I'm well." She carried the bread to the oven and set it inside, carefully sliding it off the wooden peel.

"Hannah."

"I'm fine." Hannah set the oven door in place and returned

the paddle to its spot beside the hearth. *How can I tell him?* She took in a breath and forced herself to meet her husband's gaze.

"Is everything all right?"

"Of course," she said. But everything wasn't all right. Her menstrual flow had come. *No baby. I know I'm not meant to have babies.*

"You're certain?"

"Yes. I'm just busy." She made an effort to lighten her tone and managed to smile.

"All right, then. I'll dispose of this, and then I've a bit of work still to do. Plus Patience needs milking before I can put her away for the night."

"That's fine." Hannah turned to the hearth where a pot of beans hung from a pole above the fire. Careful to hold her skirt away from the embers, she used a wooden spoon to stir the meal. "Dinner is nearly ready. I'll set it on the table." Hannah didn't look at him; she didn't want him to see her grief.

Holding the firebox at arm's length, John leaned close to Hannah and peered over her shoulder. "Looks good."

He rested his hand on her back, and she kept stirring. Abruptly, he straightened and said, "All right, then. There'll be fresh milk for dinner."

"Can you fetch butter from the springhouse?" Hannah asked, trying to keep her voice cheery. She set a lid on the pot.

"Right." John opened the door and stepped onto the porch. "It seems we have visitors."

"Who would come out so late in the day?" Hannah joined him on the front step and watched a buggy bounce up the drive. Having callers would normally have delighted her, but today she had no heart for company. All she wanted was to climb into bed and sleep away her misery.

"Good day," John called jovially as David Gelson pulled his buggy to a stop.

Lydia sat beside David. "Good day to ye," she called.

David climbed down and then assisted Lydia.

Stepping from the porch, John held out a hand to David. "This is a fine surprise."

With a glance at Lydia, David said, "Lydia wanted to see Hannah and insisted she couldn't wait." His sapphire blue eyes crinkled at the edges when he smiled.

Hannah put on her best greeting face. "So glad you've come." She moved down the steps and hugged her friend. "I must say, I'm surprised to see you out this late in the day."

"I know, but the weather is fine, and there'll be a full moon to see us home."

John placed an arm around Hannah's waist. "I'd fancy a drive by moonlight with my lady."

Hannah couldn't resist his charm and leaned in close to John. "It does sound nice."

Lydia glanced at David, her cheeks looking pinker than usual.

"Please, come in." Hannah led the way up the steps.

Lydia followed Hannah inside and glanced about the room. "It looks grand. You've made this look nice and homey."

"There's still a lot to be done, but John's working hard." Hannah smiled at John.

"We're doing it together." He smiled down at Hannah. "We were just about to have dinner. Will you join us?"

"We'd love it if you could," Hannah added. "It's nothing much, just bread and beans, but there's more than enough."

David glanced at Lydia. "We didn't mean to intrude."

"No intrusion. It's a pleasure to have your company," John said. "Please, stay."

"I'd love it . . ." Lydia looked at David. "As long as ye don't mind."

He smiled. "I didn't realize it, but I'm starved."

"Fine, then," John said. "I was just on my way out to milk the cow and to fetch some butter."

Now that Lydia was here, Hannah warmed to the idea of company. She needed someone to talk to, and Lydia's cheerful countenance was a pleasant distraction.

Lydia smiled over her shoulder at John. "I think ye ought to give David milking lessons. I doubt he's ever done any farmwork."

"Is that true?" John asked.

"Afraid so."

"Well then, I suppose I can teach you if you've a mind to learn." He grinned.

"I suppose it's not a bad idea." He shot a glance at Lydia. "My family always had servants, and they did that sort of thing."

"Milking might be something you'll need to know. One day you may receive a cow as payment." John laughed. "It's not so difficult, especially now that I have a stanchion for Patience."

"Patience?" David asked.

"That's what Hannah calls the cow."

"You're naming the cows now, eh?" Lydia grinned.

"And what's wrong with that?" Hannah folded her arms over her chest, submitting a friendly challenge. "She's a bit difficult, and I thought the name might help."

"And has it?" Lydia's smile widened.

"No. Not at all. But with the stanchion, she's forced to remain in one place until I've finished."

John opened the door. "We best get to it if we're to have milk with our meal." He held the door for David and the two stepped outside.

"Dinner will be ready by the time you return," Hannah called after them.

"Good. My stomach's grumbling." John gave Hannah a crooked smile and then closed the door.

Lydia sat at the table and gazed about the room. "This is a fine house." Her eyes moved to the oven. "And to think ye have yer own oven. What a pleasure that must be."

"Indeed." Hannah suddenly felt gratitude rather than disappointment. "If not for you and all the others, we'd still be living in that tiny cottage. Thank you for all you did."

"I didn't do much."

"No. You did. I remember how much you hated the cabin. I'm certain you had a lot to do with all the assistance we received."

"Me and some others."

"There are still mornings that I awaken and am startled to realize I live in such a grand house." Hannah sat across from Lydia. "I'll always be thankful to you and for everyone who helped us."

"It was great fun, especially the planning. But I must say I had some difficulty keeping the secret." Lydia smiled. "I wanted to tell ye so badly."

Hannah nodded, still unable to completely shake off her doldrums. "How are things for you and David?"

Lydia didn't answer right away. She glanced out a front window. "All right, I guess."

"You sound as if there's some sort of trouble."

Lydia took in a deep breath. "I'm a bit worried."

"Can you tell me?"

"I just don't know that it's going to work out between us." Lydia's voice quaked.

"You seem so happy."

"Do we?" She closed her eyes for a moment. "He's not been himself lately. Or perhaps he's more himself than before." She glanced at Hannah and then at the tabletop. "He grew up in a fancy house with servants and all that sort of thing. And he's well educated, obviously. If he were in London, he'd not be seen with the likes of me." Lydia smoothed the surface of the wooden table with her index finger. "I think he wants me to be someone I'm not."

"What do you mean? I thought he liked you quite well."

"And he did—anyway, I thought he did. But the last few times we've been together, he's been impatient with me, wanting me to behave more genteel. I don't think I'm refined enough for him."

"I like that you don't put on airs." Hannah smiled. "And I'm glad you speak your mind and use plain language. I wouldn't want you to be any other way."

"Thank ye. But yer not David."

"I'm sure he likes you just fine as you are."

"No. He doesn't. And I don't know any other way. Acting genteel . . ." Lydia's eyes welled up with tears, something Hannah had rarely seen. "I'm afraid if I don't change, he'll not want me and . . . I love him. To lose him would be an unbearable wound."

"Oh Lydia." Hannah reached across the table and grasped Lydia's hand. "I'm sure you've nothing to worry about. Of course he loves you."

Lydia stood and walked to the front window. With her arms

folded across her chest, she watched the men. "I think in the beginning he liked me because I wasn't like the women he'd known in London. And perhaps it was exciting to spend time with . . . with someone like me. But I have to be honest with myself. I'm nothing more than an ill-used convict."

"Stop it. That's enough of that kind of talk." Hannah pushed away from the table and moved to her friend. She rested a hand on Lydia's arm. "You're a fine person, and if David Gelson can't see that, then he doesn't deserve you."

"I doubt he thinks so. He's always asking me 'bout the way I dress. He even offered to purchase fabric for me. And he's forever correcting my speech. Not just the words, but the way I say them. He tells me I ought to speak more gently and less often."

"Perhaps he believes life would be easier for you if you were more refined. He might be thinking about your well-being."

"I doubt he's thinking 'bout me. It's himself he's thinking of. I'm probably an embarrassment to him." Lydia twirled a lock of hair that had fallen out of place. "I've seen him . . . with Deidre, more than once."

"Where?"

"At the Athertons'."

"Why was he at the Athertons'?"

"The first time, a fellow fell out of the hayloft and broke his shoulder. And the last time a chap was sick with a fever and chills." Lydia squared her jaw and her eyes turned hard. "He didn't even come to see me. But I saw him with Deidre."

Hannah searched her mind for a plausible explanation. She stepped in front of Lydia, blocking her view. "Perhaps he couldn't find you. And you know how Deidre can be. She's forward, always seems to be hunting for a man."

"I trusted her. I thought we were friends."

"I don't know that Deidre has any real friends, especially when it comes to competing for a man."

"I should have known not to trust her." Lydia turned and faced the room. Her voice hushed, she said, "She's no more genteel than me; she just pretends to be. But she is a lot prettier."

"David must care about you. He's here with you now. He drove you all the way from the Athertons'. He'd not do that without good reason. I'm sure he fancies you."

"Coming to see you was my idea. He only offered a ride after I told him how much I was missin' ye."

"But he offered." Hannah moved to the hearth and stirred the beans. "You're not usually so pessimistic." She set four bowls on the table. "You've always been the one who had faith."

"It's different this time." Lydia chewed a nail. "From the beginning I've wondered why he was interested in me."

"Lydia—you're being too hard on yourself. You'd make a fine wife for any man."

"Ye think so? Then why is it I'm not married?"

"Perry would have married you."

"Perry? He's not for me." Lydia moved to the cupboard. "I hope yer right 'bout David and I'm fretting over nothing." She picked up a partial loaf of bread. "Would ye like me to slice this?"

"Thank you."

"A knife?"

"There, on the shelf."

Lydia took the knife, sliced the last of the bread and set it on a plate, and then placed it on the table. "And how 'bout ye? How have ye been?"

"I'm fine. Happy."

"Oh? Ye didn't look fine when I arrived. I saw something else, something not right."

"I'm well. What have I got to be gloomy about? I've a splendid home and a wonderful husband." Hannah tried to sound cheerful, but a lump stuck in her throat, nearly choking off her words.

"All right, then. What is it?" Lydia moved to Hannah. "Tell me what's troubling ye?"

Using the corner of her apron, Hannah dabbed at unbidden tears. *Oh, why can't I control my emotions?* "Nothing really. Nothing at all."

"Then why the tears, eh?"

Hannah lifted the beans and set them on the table. "I'd hoped that maybe this month . . . but . . ." She looked at Lydia. "I'm afraid I'll never have a child."

"Ye will. It takes longer for some than others." She hugged Hannah. "Babies happen when God decides the time is right."

"That's what I'm afraid of."

"Why would ye be afraid of that?"

Hannah glanced outside to make sure the men weren't near the house. They walked along the river, hands in their pockets, looking as if they were deep in conversation. The pail of milk had been left by the barn.

"I know God's forgiven me for what I did."

"What ye did?"

"The baby and all of that." Hannah pressed the palms of her hands together. "But sometimes, even though we're forgiven, there are penalties to be paid. I'm afraid God's decided not to bless me with children. He gave me a child once, and I wanted it to die."

81

"God knows our hearts. Ye were in trying circumstances, living in torment. I don't believe for a moment he's punishing you." She gently held Hannah's shoulders. "Having a baby doesn't always happen right away. Why, there's a woman I know in Sydney Town who waited three years before she and her husband had their first. And now they've four."

"Really?" Hannah felt a glimmer of hope. She pressed a hand to her mouth, trying to quell her fear and heartache. "I'm so afraid. Every month I wait and I pray, but each month there's no baby. Why would I conceive a child with Mr. Walker when . . . it was only that one time? And it was so brutal, so awful."

"I don't know. Sometimes it happens like that." Lydia folded her arms over her chest. "Have ye told John 'bout the rape and the baby?"

"No. I can't tell him. He'd never forgive me for keeping such a secret." Hannah set out flatware. "And now that there are no babies . . . he'll know it's my fault."

"I thought ye would have said something by now." Lydia set a hard gaze on Hannah. "Yer not honoring him. He's a better man than ye give him credit for. Ye've been dishonest with John and it's time he knew the truth."

"I can't. And it's not that I don't honor him. I do."

"Ye married him under false pretenses, Hannah. Ye didn't trust him." Lydia softened her tone. "John loves ye. When ye tell him, he might be a bit angry at first, but he'll come 'round."

Hannah tried to envision what it would be like to confess to John. She could see the disappointment and revulsion in his eyes. She couldn't bear that. "I'm afraid."

"Tell him. He's yer mate. He'll support ye."

"You really think so?"

"I do."

Hannah wanted to believe Lydia. John was kind and he loved her. Did she dare speak up?

"All right. I'll tell him. But I'll have to wait for the proper time."

7

Hannah did her best to stuff her petticoat and skirts into stirrup stockings John had purchased for her. They were the most uncomfortable and most unattractive thing she'd ever worn. Barely managing to get her skirts inside the unwieldly, thighhigh leggings, she looked at John. "Must I? They're hideous and awkward."

"I'm sorry, luv, but I won't have my wife riding astride without them. There's decency to be considered." John studied the loose-fitting stockings. They were two yards wide at the top and truly ungainly looking. He tried not to smile.

"I shan't wear them. They're antiquated and unnecessary."

"You'll stay home, then. It's improper for a lady to ride astride without some type of covering."

"Where did you find these?"

John grinned. "A fellow I know in Sydney Town had them in his storeroom."

"They must have belonged to his mother." Hannah's voice dripped with sarcasm.

John had no doubts about Hannah's decency, but he couldn't allow people to talk. He rubbed his chin and tried to think of a way to convince her of the appropriateness of wearing the garments. "I admire your riding ability and your desire to help drive our flock of sheep home. And it will be splendid sharing your company. But I won't have you disgraced."

Hannah took in a deep breath. "All right, then. I'll wear them, but under protest. You know as well as I that they're utterly ridiculous."

Quincy moved his horse closer. "It might be better if you rode sidesaddle." He didn't look directly at Hannah, but kept his eyes on the reins in her hands.

"That's nearly as ridiculous. For a woman to balance herself atop a horse in such a fashion puts her life in jeopardy. And even if I were so inclined, we've no money for another saddle. It's only because of Mr. Atherton's generosity that I have this mare."

Quincy simply offered her a nod and rode down the drive toward the road.

John watched Quincy's back and then turned to Hannah. "You sounded a bit shrewish. He didn't deserve that."

"You're right. I'm sorry. But . . ." She looked down at her garments and threw her arms wide. "These are so disconcerting. I couldn't restrain my frustration." Looking defeated, she added, "I'll apologize to him."

"Good. We better be off. The Langtons' estate isn't too distant, but if we dally we'll not make it home before nightfall." He glanced at the musket in his saddle holster and for a moment rested a hand on his pistol. He hoped there'd be no need to use either.

"Is it dangerous to be traveling?" Hannah's voice was laced with apprehension.

"No more than usual. But it's wise to be prepared."

"I heard Aborigines attacked a family west of here."

"They did, but there was no loss of life."

Hannah pulled the reins tighter, and the horse tossed her head in an unhappy response. "That's true, but it could have been much worse."

John knew there was reason to worry, but he didn't want Hannah troubled. "There is always danger; no life is free of it. But all I expect today is an uneventful and pleasant ride with my wife and a successful outcome as we guide a contented flock of sheep home."

A gust of wind whistled across bare ground and whipped debris into the air and up beneath the eaves of the house. John studied a gray sky. "Smells like rain. Might get wet before the day's through."

"We need rain, but I hope it holds off until we get home."

"Right." John kicked his heels into his horse's sides and trotted after Quincy. Hannah followed.

By the time John, Hannah, and Quincy approached the Langtons' home, rain had started to fall in large droplets. Undisturbed by the moisture, John pulled back on the reins and stopped. Leaning on the saddle horn, he admired the house and outbuildings. "Fine property. Large home."

"Not as big as the Athertons'." Hannah pulled her horse up beside John's.

"No. But I'd say they've done quite well for themselves." John let his eyes roam from one barn to another and to a row of three cottages and a work shed. He nodded at a large, long building. "That's the shearing barn. We'll be needing one soon." He pulled his hat down in front, shading himself from the increasing rain. "Charles has done well for himself. And he only began five years ago." He glanced at Hannah. "With a bit of luck, in a few years, we'll have a grand place like this." Feeling the swell of ambition, he moved forward.

Charles Langton, a stocky, redheaded man, stood beside a small stock pen crowded with bleating, jostling sheep. He was known for his good business mind and hard work. Two little boys who looked just like him darted from the house and joined their father. Standing on either side of him, they leaned against the fence in the same way Charles did, with one arm resting on a railing.

John looked over the sheep as he rode up to the stock pen, then turned his attention on Mr. Langton. "Good day to you," he said, dismounting. He extended a hand in greeting.

Charles Langton shook John's hand heartily. "Good day. And a fine one it is too. This rain means better grazing."

"It doesn't appear we'll have a deluge." John turned to Hannah and assisted her from the horse. She managed, but in a clumsy fashion because of the stirrup stockings. Once on the ground, Hannah nodded at Mr. Langton and awkwardly removed the protective leggings.

Charles remained straight-faced, but a smile hid behind his eyes.

Free of the ungainly garments, Hannah straightened her spine and pushed back her shoulders. "Good day, Mr. Langton. It's a pleasure to see you again."

"Good day to you, Mrs. Bradshaw. You're looking well. Have you come along to assist your husband?"

"I have, indeed."

John nodded toward Quincy. "You know my man Quincy?"

87

"That I do." Charles smiled and touched the brim of his hat. "Good to see you."

Quincy nodded.

Charles rested a hand on each of his son's heads. "My sons—Ryan and Lewis. Ryan's the younger one here, just six." He mussed his hair. "And Lewis is two years older."

"Nice-looking lads."

"They're good boys." Mr. Langton turned to face the pen. "Well, this is the lot of them. They're fine Merinos. They'll give you quality lambs and superior wool."

John leaned on the fence and studied the animals. His eyes moved from one to another, searching for defects. "Mind if I have a closer look?"

"Go on ahead. You'll find them all in good condition."

With Quincy beside him, John stepped inside the pen. They moved among the sheep, studying each and checking for disease or faults. Finally John turned to Charles. "They look fine, indeed. I'm surprised you're willing to part with them."

"Need to do some thinning out. I can only handle so many." Langton opened the gate for John and Quincy.

John reached inside his coat and lifted out a leather purse heavy with coins. "The amount we agreed upon." He set the coin purse in Charles's hand. "You may count it if you like."

"No need." He grinned. "But if you've shorted me, I'll know where to find you." He laughed. "Have ye a dog?"

"No. But I've been thinking I'll be needing one."

Langton eyed the sheep. "It'll be tough driving them home without one. I've got a dog I can throw into the deal. He's young, but he's smart and good with the sheep."

"That would be fine by me."

"Good then. His name's Jackson. I'll introduce ye after lunch.

That is, if ye'd care to share a meal with me and my family before ye drive this mob of mutton home."

John glanced at Hannah who gave an affirmative nod. "Sounds grand."

———

Rain came down in a soaking drizzle as John, Hannah, and Quincy headed toward home. The sheep ambled along while Jackson, a long-haired, black dog, skillfully padded along beside the flock. He nipped and barked as needed to keep the animals in place and moving forward.

"It was good of Charles to include Jackson." John watched the dog. "He's clever."

"Lucky for us he's got a new litter of pups."

"And he's got another five working dogs," Quincy added.

Hannah leaned forward slightly and pulled up on the stirrup stockings. "Having a good dog will be of great help."

Jackson seemed well acquainted with the sheep. He knew which ones to watch out for, and some of the ewes obviously disliked him and took every opportunity to kick or butt at him.

Water rolled down Hannah's hat and dripped onto her face. She'd been waiting for the right time to tell John about Judge Walker and the baby. He seemed in a fine mood. This might be as good a time as any. She studied John, and her stomach tightened at the thought.

John smiled at her. "You're good and wet."

"This hat is almost of no help," she said, eyeing the sheep. "Even they're having difficulty." Water didn't penetrate their dense wool coats, but it did manage to get into their eyes and noses. "I ought to have a wool coat, eh? Or a wool hat."

She chewed on her lower lip and considered speaking to John. It had been such a good day. She hated to spoil it. *I'll wait. It's not quite right yet.*

The wetness and cool temperatures had penetrated Hannah's coat. She was cold and longed for the warmth of her home.

John and Jackson took off after two mulish ewes that seemed determined to go their own way. When John came back around, he said, "That was a fine meal Mrs. Langton served, but I'm already hungry."

"I quite like Ella. She's very nice and friendly. I hope we'll have an opportunity to visit again."

"I'm sure you will. I'll most likely be doing business with Charles in the future, especially now that we have use of the adjoining property. Good of Mr. Jones to lease it to us." John rested a hand on his stomach. "What did you plan for dinner?"

"I've fresh bread and a stew warming over the fire. That should see to your chronic hunger." She smiled. "I don't know where you put it all."

The drizzle had slowed and a breeze parted the clouds, exposing a deep blue sky. "Perhaps it will warm up a bit," Hannah said.

"I'd rather have the rain. We've a need." John glanced up at the brim of his hat where droplets dripped onto his face.

Quincy rode up alongside John. "There's a stream just ahead. Ye want to stop and let the sheep drink?"

"Good idea."

Quincy rode off and with Jackson's help headed the sheep toward the stream.

Hannah and John separated and rode along either side, helping guide the flock. As if knowing their way, the animals waded into the calm stream, put their noses into the water, and drank.

Hannah and John dismounted and led their horses to the water. *This would be a good time,* Hannah thought. Quincy was farther downstream. They were alone.

She glanced at her stirrup stockings. "We've not seen a soul. Do you mind if I take these things off?"

John glanced about. "I don't see any harm. I doubt anyone will be traveling this way today."

Hannah gratefully removed the hideous attire and handed the leggings to John. He rolled them up and tied them behind her saddle. "Thank you," she said. "I'm glad to be rid of them." Her gaze fell over the mob. "These Merinos seem a bit more gentle than the last ones you brought home."

"They're good stock. And with these we'll have fifty—long as they stay healthy. Quincy said he spotted a couple of dingoes eyeing the flock a few days ago. They could do some damage, especially when the lambs come."

Hannah's mind wandered to what she ought to say to John. How could she phrase her confession so that he'd understand?

"Where are you, luv?"

"What do you mean? I'm right here."

"I've been talking to you, but you've not heard a word I've said."

"I'm sorry. I was just thinking about something Lydia said when she came to visit."

"Any sort of trouble going on?"

Now. Tell him now. "No. No trouble. Except that David wants her to be more genteel. And she's worried that he's spending time with Deidre." Hannah's horse yanked up a mouthful of grass, pulling on the reins. "Do you think she has reason to fret?"

"Can't say, really. David didn't mention anything. But Deidre might be a temptation to a single gent like him."

Hannah suddenly felt angry. "Why?"

"She's comely." John looked at her with a puzzled expression.

"Why is it men care only about a woman's outer beauty?"

"That's not true. There are a lot of other things that matter to us."

"There's so much more to a person than their appearance."

"I agree." He took Hannah's hand. "But beauty is of some consequence. I fell in love with you, but as a man I can't help but appreciate your beauty." He smiled devilishly. "And would you want it any other way?"

Hannah's anger dissolved, but she didn't answer John's question. Instead she returned to Lydia and her troubles. "I do hope he doesn't break Lydia's heart. She truly loves him."

"I'm sure he must see what a fine woman she is." John's eyes settled on something in the distance.

Hannah's heart picked up. "What is it? Aborigines?"

"No. A kangaroo. Looks like a fine one too. We could do with a bit of fresh meat."

"Must you? I'd rather eat rabbit. Or perhaps we could butcher a sheep."

"You don't like kangaroo?" John shot her a surprised look. "You've never said anything."

"It's not that." Hannah followed her husband's gaze. "Sometimes they seem almost human. They're intelligent and . . . well, I find it hard to look into their eyes and then kill them."

"You don't have to do any killing. That's my job. And it makes more sense to take something wild than to butcher one of our ewes. I paid dearly for them and can't spare a one. When the lambs are born, we'll slaughter some of the tups, though."

"Lambs are so dear. Must we kill them?"

"We don't need a flock of rams. And no sheep remains *dear* forever. By the time they're big enough for butchering, they'll have lost their cuteness."

His eyes remained on the kangaroo. "You stay here." John moved to Quincy, spoke to him a moment, and then set off in the direction of the kangaroo. He slipped into a grove of gum trees and moved closer to the unsuspecting animal.

Hannah knew John was doing what he must, yet her stomach ached as she watched him. He disappeared inside the grove. An excellent hunter, Hannah knew he'd manage to get off a good shot.

She heard the blast of the musket and saw the animal fall. She ought to be thankful for the meat, but the sight of the motionless creature only made her feel sick.

This is foolishness. A kangaroo is only an animal and good for our table. I ought to be helping my husband. Tying the horses to a tree alongside the creek, she hurried toward Quincy. "I'm going to give John a hand. Watch over the sheep."

"Glad to, ma'am."

She moved toward John. When she was close, she thought he looked distressed. "What is it? What's wrong?" She ran toward him.

John stood. "No. Stop. Best you don't come near."

"Why? What's happened?" Ignoring his order to stop, Hannah rushed to him. "What is it?" She looked at the animal and

93

then saw what John had seen—a joey, its head draped over the edge of its mother's pouch.

"Oh no!" Hannah knelt beside the kangaroo and lifted the baby out of the warmth of his home. He struggled and kicked at her, but she bundled him inside her petticoat and held him close. "Calm down, now. I'll not hurt you." She stood, still holding the little one close. He quieted. "What shall we do with him?"

"There's nothing to be done."

"What do you mean? We can't just leave him to die."

"Put him down. I'll end it." John's voice was heavy.

"No. You can't. He's a baby."

"He's an animal with no mother. There's nothing to be done."

"If it was a lamb or a calf, you'd do everything you could to save it." Hannah held the creature protectively.

"He's a wild animal. And too little to live without his mum."

"I'll take care of him."

"You can do all you know to do and he'll still die. I've never heard of anyone who has successfully tended one this young. He needs only what his mother can give him."

Hannah looked at the tiny creature in her arms. "We can't just give up. I'll give him milk and keep him warm." She cradled the little thing the way she would an infant.

John's expression was somber. With a heavy sigh, he surrendered. "I suppose it won't hurt to try." He turned back to the mother. "I'll take care of her. You go on."

<hr>

Hannah kept the tiny kangaroo bundled tightly against her the rest of the way home. That evening, she tried to feed it, but each attempt was refused. As the hours passed, the poor creature became weaker and less responsive.

"I don't know what to do," Hannah told John. "He's dying."

John spoke quietly. "I tried to tell you. They don't live without their mums."

Hannah made a bed out of a box, putting wood chips and hay in the bottom and settling the joey inside. She placed him near the hearth and then sat up and watched over him. She tried to coax him into eating, but he wouldn't accept even a drop of milk. In the early morning hours, the joey stopped breathing.

Hannah hugged it to her and sobbed, wondering why she felt such heartache for an animal.

John climbed out of bed and kneeled beside her, laying an arm over her shoulders and pulling her close to him. "I'm sorry, luv."

"It's gone. I couldn't save it." *I can't save anything.*

John took the limp creature out of Hannah's arms. "I'll take care of it." He carried the joey across the room, opened the door and stepped outside, quietly closing the door behind him.

Hannah stared at the dying embers in the hearth. She'd not wanted her own child. Perhaps it had been her wish for its death that had killed it. Now this creature had been placed in her care, and she'd been unable to save it. How could God trust her with a child of her own?

There'd be no babies for her. She squeezed her eyes shut. *Why, Lord? Why can't I have a child? Please, please don't leave me barren.* She covered her face with her hands and sobbed, knowing that no matter how much she longed for a baby, she'd never have one.

8

Hannah set a plate of sliced bread on the table and then moved to the hearth. She hooked a cooking pot and lifted it away from the fire, then grasping the handle with a heavy cloth, she carried it to the table and set it in an iron trivet. She lifted the lid and steam carried the aroma of vegetables and cooked meat into the air. Rather than kindling her appetite, the aroma served only to remind her of the previous day's distress. Using a wooden spoon, she stirred the stew and replaced the lid.

John will be hungry. It certainly won't trouble him to eat this fare. Although Hannah knew she had no valid reason for being angry, she could still feel it stir in her belly. Every time she thought about the joey and how it had died, the hurt she felt over the innocent's loss was renewed and an ache rose in her throat.

You're being foolish. John didn't purposely kill that little joey, so why am I so angry about all this? Her next thoughts came unbidden. She closed her eyes. It wasn't John she was upset with—it was herself. She hadn't killed her child, but she'd wanted it to die, which was utterly wicked and deserved punishment.

She moved to the door and opened it. John had gone to the barn to milk Patience. Nightfall had draped itself over the land, and all she could see was a small light penetrating the darkness from inside the barn. She took a wrap down from the hook near the door, pulled it about her shoulders, and bundled inside the wool shawl as she headed down the steps. Holding her skirts up out of the mud, she walked into the darkness. It pressed in on her from all sides and she suddenly felt afraid. Was she being watched? She glanced about. *There's nothing. Stop being foolish.* She hurried to the barn.

Stepping inside, the familiar smells of animals and hay welcomed her, and she felt protected. Patience stood passively in a stanchion, chewing contentedly. Hannah leaned on a railing and watched her husband.

Intent on his work and unaware of her, he kept his forehead pressed against the animal's rounded side while his strong hands brought forth milk. When he'd finished, John straightened and patted the cow's side. "Good girl." He grasped the pail handle and then stood, grabbing the stool with his other hand. When he turned, his eyes fell upon Hannah. They lit up with appreciation. "Hannah. I didn't know you were here."

"I wanted to tell you dinner is ready. Might I help?"

"If you'll take this, I'll get her into a stall." John handed Hannah the pail and set the stool against the wall. After releasing the cow from the stanchion, he led her to a stall and tossed hay into a crib.

Doing all she could to keep her voice and spirits lively, Hannah said, "She's producing a good deal of milk, don't you think? More than we can use."

"I was considering taking some of it down to the Female Factory. I'm sure they could use it."

"I daresay they could, but I doubt they'll get any. Most likely the gaolers will take it home with them."

"I doubt that. The chaps I know would rather have a pint than milk." John tilted his lips in a sideways smile.

"Perhaps we should take some butter, then, too."

"We've more than enough in the springhouse."

With the quiet of the night surrounding them, John and Hannah silently walked back to the house. The previous day's hurt still lay between them. The warmth of the fire and the smell of stew met them when they stepped inside the house.

"Mmm. Smells good." John helped Hannah with her wrap and then took off his hat and coat and hung them on a post. "I'm starving."

Hannah set the milk on the counter and poured it through a cloth to strain out impurities.

"I'll take that down to the springhouse after dinner," John said, settling into a chair at the table. "But I'd quite like some fresh milk with my meal."

Using a dipper, Hannah filled two glasses with milk. "There's a lot of cream." She set the tumblers on the table.

"I like the cream." And as if to prove his point, John downed half the glass of warm milk. Wearing a satisfied smile, he set down the beverage.

Hannah sat across from him.

"Shall we give a word of thanks, then?" He reached for Hannah's hands and held them as he said, "Lord above, we thank you for these blessings. May we use them in a way that will be pleasing to you. Amen."

"Amen." Hannah released John's hands. As much as she knew she ought to feel blessed, she felt despair—over the joey's death and her barrenness.

She lifted the lid off the pot and dipped stew into John's bowl. He grabbed a piece of bread and spread butter over it. Taking a bite, he chewed thoughtfully. "How are you, luv? Feeling any better?"

"I am." Hannah dished out her stew and set it in front of her. She stared at it, though, unable to eat. She kept seeing the helpless joey and its dead mother. *You're being foolish. Stop it.*

Hannah buttered a piece of bread. Biting into it, she set her spoon in the stew but didn't ladle any out. Instead she stared at it, a lump in her throat. Taking a drink of milk, she forced down the bread. Finally, picking up her spoon, she filled it with stew, but she was unable to carry it to her mouth. *It was only a kangaroo. Good, honest food.* She took a bite and chewed.

John rested his arms on the table and leaned forward. "Delicious. Good bread. Good stew." He smiled and took another bite of bread. "You're a blessing to me, Hannah."

She barely nodded, tormented by guilt.

"You're quiet. Are you still troubled over what happened yesterday?"

Hannah couldn't look at John. She set her spoon in the bowl. "I'm fine," she said, but she wasn't—she needed to speak the truth.

"You're not. Why is this upsetting you so? I've never known you to be distressed without good cause."

"It was an innocent. The poor thing shouldn't have died."

John sat back in his chair, resting his hands on the table on either side of his bowl. "It was a kangaroo. And there was nothing could be done about it. I didn't mean for a joey to die. I didn't know it was there. And you did all you could to save it."

"I know. I'm being foolish. I'm sorry." Hannah made another attempt at eating.

John reached across the table and took one of her hands. "I'm truly sorry, luv. It's my responsibility to make sure there's food in our home, and I couldn't pass by such a grand kangaroo. It will go a long way toward feeding us. It's my duty to take care of you and one day our children too."

He gently squeezed Hannah's hand. "You've got to put this behind you."

"I know."

"There will be worse things to come, we can count on that. I wish I could protect you from all the disappointments and harshness, but it's not possible."

John's expression of devotion drove away Hannah's depression and anger. She loved him. "I'm sorry for behaving so wretchedly. I don't know what's come over me."

"It's all right. I say we enjoy our meal and each other."

Hannah took a bite of stew. John was a fine husband and honorable. He deserved to know the truth about her past. She should have told him before he'd married her.

How could I have withheld something so important? He deserves better. Tears pressed against the back of her eyes, and she fought to suppress them. She broke off a piece of bread. *I lied to him. He had a right to know and I was dishonest.*

Now it was worse than before. Clearly God was not going to bless them with children. It was her fault and John should be told.

She set her bread on the table and pushed aside her bowl. Did she have the courage to speak the truth? Her throat was dry and her stomach tumbled with apprehension. In a voice barely more than a whisper, she said, "There is something I must tell you."

Her heart beat so fast, Hannah could barely catch her breath. She tightly clasped trembling hands on the table in front of her.

"I didn't tell you everything about myself . . . about my past." She glanced at John, then back down at her hands. "I intended to tell you before we were married, but you wouldn't let me." Hannah knew she was shifting the blame to him. "No. That's not quite true. I wanted to tell you, but I was afraid." She looked into his hazel eyes. "When you shushed me the night I went to your cottage, it was easier to say nothing."

John looked puzzled and concerned. "What didn't you tell me? What's happened?" He knit his brows. "Tell me, luv. I want to help."

Hannah took a steadying breath. "John . . . there will be no children . . . not for us. And it's my fault."

"You can't know that. It's God's will to determine."

"Yes. That's true. And . . . and once he did bless me with a child." Hannah's nerves were so tightly strung that she felt that the muscles throughout her body might actually burst.

"When I lived in London after my mum died . . . I worked for a magistrate . . . a Mr. Walker. One night . . . he came to my room and he . . . he forced himself upon me."

John's expression became a mix of horror and confusion. He pushed against the table and straightened his arms. "What are you saying?"

"He raped me." The scene played through Hannah's mind. "I tried to fight him off. But I wasn't strong enough." She pressed a hand to her mouth. "I ran away. And for a while I lived on the streets. I looked for work, but no one would hire me. Finally I was so hungry that one day I stole a loaf of bread."

Hannah pressed her hands, palm down on the table. "I was arrested. And the man who raped me, Mr. Walker, was also the judge who sat over my hearing. He lied about it all, even said I'd stolen a silver chalice from his home. He sentenced me to transportation." Hannah tried to wet her lips, but there was no moisture in her mouth. "And then . . . then there was a child."

John's eyes had turned hot and hard.

Oh, Lord, please help him to forgive me and to still love me. Hannah knew she could lose him, but now that she'd begun, she must tell him all of it.

"While I was on the ship I learned about the child. I couldn't have a baby in that wretched place. I couldn't face the disgrace. I asked God to take it from me."

John stood and knocked his chair over backward. "Enough. I won't hear any more." He crossed his arms over his chest and turned his back to her.

Hannah knew she should stop. John had heard enough. But now that she'd started, she needed to finish—to be rid of it. "Please, John. Please hear me out." She was crying now. She stood and moved toward him.

He stepped away.

Hannah continued. "I knew it was wrong, but I prayed the baby would die. And it did. It was born too early. Lydia helped me, but she couldn't save the baby." Feeling the horror, tears ran in rivulets down Hannah's cheeks. "She took the baby out in a chamber pot."

John whirled around and faced Hannah. The amber in his eyes had gone cold.

Hannah could barely speak, but she continued. "I'm sorry. I know now the child was God's blessing and I refused it. He's punishing me. We won't have children. There'll never be any."

John glared at her, his eyes hot with revulsion and anger. "You lied to me. Why? How could you?"

"I was afraid. I just couldn't tell you."

102

He shoved his fingers through his hair. "Was it really a rape? Or did you entice this Mr. Walker?"

John might as well have plunged a knife into Hannah's heart, the pain was so agonizing. Suffocating pressure squeezed her chest. She struggled to breathe. "No. I never did. I pleaded with him to stop, but he wouldn't. I never tempted him. Never."

Desperate, Hannah moved to John and grasped his hands. "Please believe me. Please forgive me. I never wanted to deceive you."

"But you did." John ripped his hands out of hers. "How can I ever trust you again? You're my wife, the one I should believe in more than any other. But now . . . how can I . . . how can I believe anything you say?"

Hannah dropped her arms to her sides. "This is why I didn't tell you. I was afraid you'd hate me, that I would lose you."

John grabbed his hat and coat. He pressed the hat onto his head and pushed his arms into the coat sleeves. "And now you have." He opened the door and stood staring at Hannah as if she were some sort of apparition. Tears glistened and he shook his head. "How could you wish for the death of a child? Any child? You're not the person I thought you were." He stepped outside and slammed the door behind him.

Hot anger and hurt drove reason from John as he stormed toward the barn. Rage blinded him and blood pumped through his veins with a ferocity he'd never known. He saddled his horse, swung up onto its back, and charged into the darkness.

I thought you were special—above reproach. His first wife's laughing face flashed through his mind. This wasn't the first time a woman had betrayed him.

When he reached the road, he glanced back at the house. He could see Hannah silhouetted in the window. He knew she was remorseful and frightened, but he didn't care. He couldn't speak to her or even stay in the house with her. She'd lain with another man, her employer, and then had seen an innocent child as nothing more than an inconvenience.

Without care for his own safety, John urged his horse into a full gallop. He rode hard and didn't stop until the horse was in a lather and laboring to breathe. Finally he slowed and stopped. The moon was only a slice of light in a dark sky and cast its narrow beam across the glossy river. John dismounted and moved to the water's edge. He gazed into the dark depths, seeing only inky blackness and shadows.

How could she have deceived him? And what should he do now? How could he live with this? He considered casting himself into the river and allowing the water to sweep him and his sorrow away.

Finally, he moved to a tree that reached out over the river. He tied his horse and then sat with his back pressed against the trunk. For a very long while, he sat in the dim light of the moon, staring at nothing, his mind empty of everything except feelings of betrayal.

Gradually the blackness lifted and his mind carried him back to the scene with Hannah. What should he do now? Should he divorce her? And what then, if he did? The thought of living without her seemed unbearable. A life that did not include her seemed unimaginable. But some evils could not be undone. Things could never be the same between them.

He closed his eyes, seeing only a long, dark tunnel of gloom stretching out before him. If he returned, there would be no trust and no children. He'd always envisioned himself as a father. The idea of never fathering a child was beyond comprehension.

Hours passed with no sense of time. Gradually Hannah's face crept into John's consciousness, and he remembered *her* rather than her sin, her betrayal. She'd never want to hurt him. She was a gentle soul, toward everyone. And he'd never witnessed any haughtiness or coarseness in her.

John realized the truth. *The magistrate must have assaulted her. She'd never entice such behavior.* Shame over how he'd treated Hannah and the way he'd spoken to her pressed down on him.

He remembered how it had been when he'd courted Hannah and how she'd tried to avoid his advances. He'd been the one who sought after her. Even when she'd told him she couldn't love him, he'd pursued her.

Remorse filled him. *This is my fault too. She wanted to tell me. I wouldn't listen.*

His thoughts carried him to what had happened to Hannah, and how another man had defiled her, had laid his hands on her. He tightened his jaw and balled his hands into fists. On their wedding night he'd gone to Hannah believing she was pure.

He squeezed his eyes closed. "God, what am I to do? Tell me what to do."

His mind returned to the ship and the horrible conditions. No woman would want to bring a child into the world in such a place. *But it was more than that. She said something about her honor. When she'd wished for the death of the child, it hadn't been only about the baby; Hannah was afraid of dishonoring herself.*

John remained at the river until morning light touched the sky, and then he climbed back onto his horse and rode toward Sydney Town. It had been too long since he'd had a pint. He needed one now.

9

Hannah swept dirt into a dustpan, being careful not to miss even the tiniest speck. If she concentrated on her work, she wouldn't have to think. Carrying the pan to the yard, she tossed its contents and watched as a breeze carried away the dirt. If only it were that easy to cast away transgressions.

With a heavy breath, she turned and looked toward the road. She saw no one. Where had John gone? Would he return? Pain pierced her heart; she might never see him again. *How will I manage if he never comes back? And if he does, what will I say?*

She walked to the house and slowly climbed the steps. It had been two days since he'd left. *If he were going to get over being angry, he would have done it by now, wouldn't he? Where can he be?*

Hannah had considered going to the Athertons' to see if he was there but decided against it. She didn't want anyone to know that they'd fought and that he was gone. She sat on the top step and allowed her eyes to roam over the green grasses and then to the river. The earth smelled damp and the air was cool. "Where is he? Lord, have I lost him forever?" She covered her face with her hands and sobbed.

The creak of the barn door cut into the quiet. Hannah looked up to find Quincy staring at her. With a quick nod and wearing a cheerless expression, he strode toward his cottage, Jackson at his heels. Hannah swiped away her tears and hurried inside.

She shut the door and, fighting to keep her emotions under control, returned the broom and dustpan to their place beside the hearth. She could feel tears burning, and the agonizing ache inside would not relent. Holding back the anguish, she looked at the lifeless hearth. She ought to build a fire and make something to eat. John would be hungry when he returned.

Her grief suddenly overwhelming her, Hannah dropped to her knees and sobbed, "Lord, please do not allow this. Make it right. I beg you. I was wrong. All of this is my fault. I know John deserves better than me, but . . ." She fought to catch her breath as she imagined life without him. "I can't bear to lose him. Please bring him home."

For a long while Hannah remained on her knees, praying and beseeching God, seeking his forgiveness and asking that he mercifully restore her marriage. Weak from weeping, she finally stood. She poked the ash and then added tinder to the glowing coals. She went to the front porch to get wood and stopped there to watch the empty road. If only John would return.

Quincy walked out of the barn carrying a pail of milk. He headed toward the house. Using the corner of her apron, Hannah wiped away the remnant of her tears, turned to the stack of wood, and picked out a few pieces. She faced Quincy. "Good day," she said, her words sounding hollow.

Quincy held out the pail. "Patience needed milking and I figured ye might be needing some fresh."

"Thank you."

"I'll take it in for ye." Quincy hurried up the steps and opened the door, standing aside for Hannah.

Hannah remained just inside the doorway, watching while Quincy placed the milk on the counter. He turned as if to leave, then stopped and looked at Hannah. "Not to worry. He'll be back."

"I pray you're right."

Quincy removed his hat. "I could find him if ye like."

"Where do you think he's gone to?"

"Sydney Town, most likely."

Taking in a shuddering breath, Hannah couldn't keep from looking toward the roadway. She willed John to appear. "If you go, I want to go with you."

"Don't figure that's a good idea. Most likely he'd rather ye didn't." He spoke in a quiet, even tone. "If it was me, I'd be discomfited if me wife came looking for me." He smoothed back short-cropped hair and offered a kind gaze. "I'll find him for ye."

Hannah felt a flicker of hope. "It would do my heart good to know he's well."

"I'll do me best." Quincy returned his hat to his head. "I'll leave straightaway, then."

"Can you wait a moment? I'd like to write him a note. Please wait."

Quincy shrugged. "S'pose it'll do no harm. I'll get me horse ready and be back." He walked toward the barn.

Hannah closed the door, then took pen, ink, and paper down from a shelf. Sitting at the table, she opened the ink bottle and dipped in the pen. She held the pen above the paper, but couldn't think of what to say. *What will bring him back to me?*

She closed her eyes and whispered a prayer. "Father, give me the words. Tell me what John needs to hear so he can believe in me again. Please open his heart to me."

She put the pen to the paper. "My dearest John. I pray Quincy has found you well and safe. I've been worried to distraction and utterly desolate since you left.

"The fault for all that has happened rests upon my shoulders. I should have told you the truth long ago. You said you feel betrayed, and you should. It was wrong of me to keep such a ghastly secret, especially from you, the one I trust above all others. Please believe that if it were possible to go back and begin again, I would tell you.

"I beseech you to forgive me. I need you. I love you. I will always love you." Hannah stopped and stared at the paper. What more could she say? She signed it, "Always your loving wife, Hannah."

She blew on the paper to dry the ink and then reread what she'd written. Squeezing her eyes closed, she prayed, "Father, help him understand, help him to forgive me." She folded the letter in half and held it against her chest as she walked to the door. *Bring him back to me.*

When she opened the door, Quincy stood alongside his horse at the foot of the porch steps. He looked uncomfortable and glum. "I'm ready to go."

"Give him this." Hannah extended the note. "Make sure he gets it."

Quincy tucked the letter into his coat pocket. "Not to worry. I'll find him." He shoved his foot into the stirrup, pushed up, and settled into the saddle. "I locked Jackson in a stall inside the barn. Figured it best to leave him here with ye." With a quick tug on the reins, he turned the horse toward the road and trotted off. Hannah watched until she could no longer see him and then stepped back inside and closed the door. The house felt empty.

"I must speak to Lydia."

She added wood to the fire, then took down her cloak from its peg beside the door, pulled it about her shoulders, and hurried out of the house toward the barn. After making sure Jackson had water, Hannah saddled her mare, and without thought of the disagreeable stirrup stockings, she settled atop the horse and headed for the Athertons'.

When she approached the Atherton home, Hannah was reminded of her unconventional mode of travel by the stares she received. Perhaps the wagon would have been a better choice, but it would have taken too much time to harness the horse, and riding was faster. Under the circumstances she cared little what others thought.

She rode directly to Lydia's cabin, dismounted and tied the horse to the porch railing, then walked up the steps and knocked on the cottage door. No one answered. *She must be in the main house.*

Hannah headed toward the Atherton home. When she reached the back porch, she didn't bother to knock but stepped inside, striding through the porchway and into the kitchen. It smelled of baking.

Mrs. Goudy smiled at her. "Hannah! Grand to see you!" She set a pie on the broad kitchen counter. "What a pleasant surprise." She gave Hannah a hearty hug. "I wish you'd come to visit us more often."

The woman's kindness broke down Hannah's reserve, and

she could feel the sting of tears. "I'm glad to be here," she barely managed to say.

Mrs. Goudy held her at arm's length. "What is it, dear? What's the trouble?"

"I'm fine, truly. Just a bit emotional is all." Hannah couldn't tell Mrs. Goudy that John was gone. She'd want to know what could make him so angry that he'd leave.

"Is that all?" Mrs. Goudy eyed her with suspicion.

Deidre wandered into the kitchen and turned cold eyes on Hannah. She reminded Hannah of a cat gazing at some unsuspecting little bird.

"Why, Hannah, what are ye doing 'ere? It's not like ye to come all this way during the week." She glanced out the window. "And where's that handsome husband of yers? I was hoping to have a word with him."

There was something in her tone, something threatening that set Hannah's nerves on edge. "He's off on business," she said as nonchalantly as possible. "I thought it a fine time to visit friends."

"Oh." Deidre swept up a loose tendril of blonde hair and tucked it in place. "Well, if yer looking for Lydia, I saw her in the parlor a few moments ago." She smiled—it was not the warm smile of friendship but rather a cool and dismissive one. With that, she walked toward the pantry.

Mrs. Goudy returned to the stone oven and retrieved another pie. She glanced at Hannah. "You're sure you're all right?"

"Absolutely." Hannah edged toward the door leading to the dining room. "I'll just have a look to see what Lydia's up to." She tried to keep her tone light.

Hannah moved through the familiar dining room, crossed the stone entryway, and stepped into the parlor and onto its colorful rug. Lydia was cleaning a window and didn't notice her.

"Lydia."

Her friend turned about with an "Oh!" She pressed a hand to her throat. "You frightened me. I wasn't expecting anyone. I guess I was off in my own world." She smiled. "Grand to see ye. It's been too long since ye've come for a visit."

Hannah hugged her. She needed to talk, but not here. "Can you take a bit of time so we can chat?"

"Of course. Please, sit."

"Can we go to your cottage?"

"All right." Lydia's expression turned to concern. "What is it? Something's not right."

"I'll tell you, but not here."

"All right, then. I'll let Mrs. Goudy know where we've gone to in case she needs me." Lydia moved to Hannah and placed an arm protectively about her shoulders. "Come on. We'll talk."

The two friends sat across from each other at Lydia's small table. "Are ye thirsty?" she asked. "I can get us something to drink."

"I am. It was a bit of a ride here. A glass of water would suit me fine."

"Ye came by yerself?" Lydia moved to a counter and lifted a pitcher of water. She filled two glasses and carried them to the table, setting one in front of Hannah.

"Yes."

"And on horseback, I see."

"I did. I like to ride." Hannah sipped the water, uncertain just how to begin the conversation.

"So, what's brought ye all the way here in the middle of the week?"

Hannah set her glass on the table. She looked at it and not at Lydia. "John's gone."

"What do ye mean, gone?"

"We had a terrible fight and he left me."

"Oh." Lydia rested an arm over the back of her chair. "I thought ye had something dreadful to tell me." She offered a gentle smile. "He'll be back, most likely in time for dinner. Men don't like to miss a meal." She patted Hannah's hand. "Ye don't need to fret so. Every couple has their rows now and again."

"You don't understand. He left two days ago." Hannah ran a finger around the rim of her glass. "I told him about Mr. Walker and the baby."

Lydia took in a sharp breath. "My Lord. And he left, eh?"

"Yes. It was awful. Just as I'd feared. He was so angry. I've never seen him like that . . . never."

"I'm sure he'll see reason and be home soon."

"I don't think so. He accused me of enticing Mr. Walker. He believes it was my fault." Hannah could feel the stabbing pain of John's accusations.

"Truly not."

"He said he could never trust me again." Hannah's eyes brimmed with tears. She tugged a handkerchief out from beneath the cuff of her sleeve and dabbed at her eyes.

"Oh, he doesn't mean that. We all say things we don't mean when we're angry. I'm sure he'll get over it. He just needs a bit of time." Lydia laid a hand on Hannah's arm. "He'll come to his senses and realize the truth."

Hannah gently blew her nose. "I want to believe that, but when I told him that I'd prayed the baby would die, he became

113

enraged. He said no decent woman could want her own child dead." She pressed trembling fingers against her lips. "I'll never forget the look of revulsion in his eyes. He hates me." Heartache shot through her. "He'll never forgive me. Never."

Lydia moved around the table, knelt beside Hannah, and put her arms around her. "I'm sure that's not true. He's angry is all. John could never stop loving ye." She patted Hannah's back the way she might a child. "He'll be home, ye'll see. Yer love is stronger than this." She smiled and gently wiped tears from Hannah's cheeks. "I know it is."

"How can you know that?" Hannah was sure Lydia was wrong. Fear brought more tears. "I'm afraid. What if I've lost him?" She glanced at the window, hoping she might see him. Of course that was a silly notion. "Quincy thinks he may be in Sydney Town. He's on his way there now to see if he can find him."

Lydia returned to her seat. "He will, and he and John will come home. Ye'll see I'm right." She rested her arms on the table. "The two of ye will grow old together, I'm sure of it."

Hannah nodded. "That's what I always thought. But you didn't see how angry and how hurt he was. He felt utterly betrayed. You and Mrs. Atherton were right." She tried to keep her chin from quivering. "I should have told him the truth before we were married." She covered her face with her hands and massaged her forehead with her fingertips. "But I know that if I'd told him before, I would have lost him for sure. I may have lost him anyway."

"Try to be hopeful." Lydia's eyes teared. "We all must be."

Lydia rarely cried. Something must be terribly wrong to move her to tears. "What's happened? What is it? Something besides my problems is bothering you." Hannah dabbed at her

114

eyes and carefully tucked her handkerchief inside her cuff. "Here I've been talking about me and John, and you've troubles of your own."

"No. It's nothing."

"It is. Tell me."

Lydia tipped her glass slightly and gazed at the water inside, then looked at Hannah. "It's David. He's not come by to see me for some time. He's been here, but he's not talked with me. He did see Deidre. I'm certain he's tossed me over for her. And I can't blame him. She's beautiful."

"She's comely enough and soft-spoken, but no more educated and not nearly the person you are. I can't believe David would be interested in her. He has more insight than that. Deidre's devious. I don't trust her, not a bit."

"I don't either. Not anymore. At first she seemed quite nice. But I know better now." Lydia clasped her hands in front of her. "I'm worried about David. Deidre just wants a man who will take care of her. She doesn't love him."

"I'm so sorry, Lydia. David seems to be a levelheaded sort, but if he believes Deidre is better for him than you, then you're better off without him."

"I suppose." Lydia didn't sound convinced. She pushed away from the table and stood. "My troubles are nothing. Ye've much more to be concerned 'bout. But I'll wager that by the time ye return home, John will be there."

"I pray you're right."

"Will ye stay and have dinner with me? Mrs. Goudy's made a roast and fresh-baked pies."

"Sounds delicious, but I dare not stay. I want to get home before dark."

"I'm sure Perry can take you in one of the buggies. It's been a long while since we supped together."

Hannah was torn. On one hand, she hoped to find John at home, and on the other, she hated the thought of returning to an empty house. Time with friends would be a good distraction. "Do you think Catharine will mind?"

"Heavens, no. In fact, I'll wager that if I invite her to join us, she will."

"All right. I'll stay."

⁕

Hannah stood beside the buggy. "I've had a grand time," she told Mrs. Atherton.

"So pleased you came by. Say hello to John for me. And tell him to work a bit less. One needs to have some leisure now and again."

"I'll tell him." Hannah felt a twinge of guilt. Except for Lydia, she'd told everyone John had been unable to join her because of work.

Mrs. Atherton hugged Hannah. "Come again soon."

"I will."

Lydia grasped Hannah's hand. "I'll see you on Sunday, eh?"

"I'll be there."

Perry assisted Hannah into the buggy, then climbed in beside her. Her mare was tied to the back. He slapped the reins and the horse stepped out briskly. "It's going to be a fine evening. A bit chilly, but good for a drive through the countryside."

"It is. Thank you for seeing me home. I feel badly that you'll be returning after sundown."

"I'll light the lanterns and they'll help me find my way just fine." He turned his attention to the horse. "It's a pleasure to

116

be of help to a friend." He gave Hannah a sideways glance. "Lydia told me."

"What did she say?"

"Just that the two of ye had a row."

Hannah's anger flared. *Why would she say anything? She knows I wanted it kept secret.* She glanced at Perry. "We did argue." Hannah wasn't sure she wanted Perry to know anything more, but she knew he genuinely cared about her and John. He was a true friend. "The truth is . . . he left. And has been gone for two days."

"That's not like him. What got into him?"

"It was a very bad fight."

"Still, it seems a bit out of line." He tapped the horse with his whip. "He'll be back—probably there now."

"I hope so."

The ride home was pleasant. Perry talked about his work for Mr. Atherton and about his promising relationship with Gwen. Hannah was happy for him but couldn't help but think about Lydia. If only things would have worked out between her and Perry—that would have been best.

Darkness swept over a blazing red sky. Perry stopped and lit the lantern. "Hope there's enough oil to last 'til I get home," he said, climbing back into the buggy.

By the time they reached Hannah and John's house, a promise of moonlight brightened the horizon. A light was on in the house. Hannah's heart quickened. "John. He's home."

"See, I told ye."

Just as Perry pulled the buggy up in front of the porch, the house went dark. "Strange." He pulled the brake and secured the reins, then climbed down, turning to assist Hannah.

"Wait 'ere. Something's not right."

"There's no light in Quincy's cabin either," Hannah said. Jackson barked and whined from inside the barn. If John had returned, he'd certainly have let the dog out.

Perry lifted one of the lanterns and grabbed his musket.

Fear ignited inside Hannah. "What are you thinking? Who could it be except John?"

"If he were home, why'd he put out the light? And he's not come out to greet us." Perry headed toward the house.

"Please be careful," Hannah whispered, her heart hammering against her ribs.

10

Perry moved cautiously toward the front steps. The lantern in one hand and his musket clutched against his chest with the other, he glanced back at Hannah.

She offered what she hoped was a heartening smile but couldn't keep her eyes from the front door. Who could be in the house? Why would they put out the light? Hannah prayed, but all sorts of frightening possibilities flooded her mind.

What if some horrible man waited inside . . . waited to slay them? If that were true, Hannah couldn't allow Perry to face him alone. She searched about for something to use as a weapon. All she found was the driving whip. Hands shaking, she grabbed hold of it and followed Perry.

Holding the lantern higher, he turned to Hannah. "Stay back," he whispered.

"I left the pistol on the hearth," Hannah said softly. "What if the intruder has found it?"

"That's not for ye to worry 'bout." Perry glanced at the house. "I know what to do with this sort."

"I don't want you to go in alone. I want to help."

Perry glanced at the whip in her hands. "With that? Ye can't be serious." He grinned.

"It's better than nothing." She set a determined look on Perry. "I'm going with you."

"All right, then. But stay behind me." Perry stepped onto the small porch, and a board creaked beneath his feet. He stopped and listened. There was no sound from inside. He pressed his ear against the door and then took hold of the handle and quietly lifted it. When there still was no response from within, he pushed open the door. He held the lantern aloft and illuminated the room.

Hannah held her breath. Her body quaked with tension.

Without warning, something slammed down on Perry's arm from behind the door, knocking his musket out of his hands. The weapon, an iron poker, came down again, this time hitting the lantern and sending it to the floor. Oil spilled onto the boards and caught fire.

A man emerged and swung the rod again, slamming it into Perry's face.

A sickening crack resounded and Perry fell. He lay facedown, arms limp at his sides. A crimson pool puddled on the floor. Perry didn't move.

The man who hit Perry grabbed the cloth from the table and threw it over the small fire, stomping it out with his feet.

Hannah went to Perry, but before she could tend to him, the intruder grabbed her, pulling her against him and entrapping her in powerful arms. She screamed and tried to break free.

"Shut up!" He clamped a hand over her mouth.

Still screaming through the filthy palm, Hannah tried to wrench free. The man's hold only tightened.

"I said, shut up!" He smacked her across the side of the head.

Light exploded within Hannah's skull. Pain radiated into her

120

neck and shoulder. The room spun and she thought she might faint. She stopped struggling.

The man's hold remained tight. "I'll let ye free if ye promise not to run off."

Hannah managed to nod.

"Ye sit right 'ere and don't move." He pushed her into a chair and then let her loose.

"Stay put." Keeping an eye on Hannah, he moved to the hearth, took a partially burned stick from the glowing embers, and lit the lantern on the hearth. He carried it to the table and set it down.

It illuminated the room enough that Hannah could better see Perry. He remained motionless. She stared at him, trying to see if he was breathing. She couldn't tell. What if he was dead? She balled her hands into fists, hoping to control their trembling. Jackson barked ferociously from inside the barn. He knew there was trouble.

The lamplight brightened and Hannah was able to get a good look at her assailant. He was young, unshaven, and his long hair hadn't seen a washing in many weeks. His clothes were ragged and filthy. *Most likely an escaped prisoner.*

He pointed the musket directly at her, nodded toward Perry, and said, "Tie him."

"But he's hurt. He needs help."

"Tie him." The man's voice sounded raspy.

Hannah took a piece of rope hanging from a hook on the back wall and moved toward Perry. He was so still. *Lord, please don't let him die.* She knelt beside him and laid a hand on his back. It rose beneath her palm. He was still alive!

"Tie his hands behind him."

"He needs a surgeon."

"Do it. Now!"

I'm sorry, Perry. Hannah reached across his body and lifted one arm, then the other, and as gently as she could, secured his wrists with the rope. She left the knot loose.

The intruder poked her with the toe of his boot. "Ye think me an idiot?"

Unable to keep from trembling, she glanced up at him.

"Tighten it."

Hannah took in a quaking breath. "He's injured and unconscious. He'll cause you no harm."

The man grabbed a handful of Hannah's hair and wrenched her to her feet. Holding her face close to his, he growled, "Ye talk back to me and ye'll end up like yer man, 'ere."

His breath smelled like rotting fish, and Hannah felt bile rise in her throat. She swallowed hard. Her scalp burned. "All right. I'll do it."

He let her go and Hannah forced herself not to rub her throbbing scalp. She retied Perry's hands, then stood and faced the convict. "What do you want? I've nothing of value, but take what you like."

He glanced at the empty hearth. "I'm hungry. What 'ave ye got?"

Hannah was glad she'd not cooked anything. This man deserved nothing hot in his belly. "I've some bread and cheese. And milk."

"Get it, then."

Hannah sliced pieces of bread, set them on a plate, and then added cheese. The man stared at the food, his eyes lit with hunger. He was thin, nearly to the point of starvation. She set the plate on the table and the intruder sat down, keeping the musket in one hand. Hannah filled a mug with milk and placed

122

it in front of him. He stuffed bread and cheese into his mouth and chewed, keeping an eye on Hannah. His mouth full, he gulped down milk.

Hannah picked up the last of the bread and wrapped it in a towel.

"Don't do that. I'll want all of it. The cheese too."

Placing the food on the table, she backed away. Her eyes went to Perry. Was he still alive? For a moment, she saw herself telling Gwen and Lydia about his death. *No! None of those thoughts,* she told herself.

The man continued to stuff himself and finished off the milk. "Ye got something to drink besides this? I could do with a pint."

"No. We've nothing except milk and water."

"I'll take water, then."

Hannah quickly filled a mug from a pitcher and gave it to him. Jackson continued his barking.

"Sit there." He nodded at a chair near the hearth. When Hannah was seated, he studied Perry for a moment and then returned to eating. Finally, his appetite satiated, he slumped back in his chair and belched. "Never did get enough to eat at the gaol."

Hannah wished he would leave. What more could he want? She gazed at Perry. He looked ashen. How long could he live without help? She stood and took a step toward him.

"Sit!"

"Please. My friend needs a doctor. He'll die—"

"Sit now!" His voice boomed and Hannah had no option but to obey. Glaring at her, the intruder stood and shoved the remaining food into his shirt and pants pockets. His gaze moved about the room, stopping when he saw the pistol on the mantel. He strode across the room, grabbed it, and shoved it into his belt. "Ye have powder?"

"Yes. There." Hannah pointed at a shelf in the kitchen.

"Get it."

Hannah moved swiftly. The sooner he left, the sooner she could get help for Perry. She handed him the pouch of black powder.

He grabbed it and looped the strap of the bag through his belt. "What else ye 'ave to eat?"

"I've more bread and we've some apples."

She heard something outside and glanced at the door. The escapee heard it too and moved to the window. Careful not to expose himself to anyone who might be outside, he peered out. "Ye expecting anyone?"

"No. No one." She stared at the door. *Lord, please don't let John step into this.*

A sound like creaking boards came again. The convict turned and grinned at her. "Nothing but the horse pulling against the buggy." He returned to the table. "Get a bag. And that bread."

Hannah took the other loaf of bread out of the cupboard and held it against her abdomen. "The bags are in the barn."

"All right, then. We'll go get them and those apples." He moved toward the door. "Bring the lantern."

Hannah did as she was told.

He motioned her toward the door and then followed her out. Hannah's mind went through escape scenarios. Perhaps she could hide in the field. He'd have a time finding her. She could make her way to the Connors'. They'd help her.

But even as she considered fleeing, she knew he'd catch her. And what about poor Perry? Hannah fought a tide of tears.

When she stepped inside the barn, her thoughts turned to defense. If she could find a weapon, maybe she could catch him unawares. She glanced at a pitchfork leaning against the wall.

"Try it. See where it gets ye." The man's lips lifted in an ugly grin. "Using a pitchfork against a musket—how do ye think ye'll do, eh?" He laughed.

Hannah didn't respond. She lifted a cloth bag out of a wooden box.

"You have a fruit cellar?"

"No. We've only just built this place. The apples are in a bin . . . here." She moved toward the north wall.

The intruder's eyes shot about the barn. Jackson leaped against the stable gate, growling and yapping. "Shut up! Or I'll shut ye up!"

"Jackson, hush," Hannah ordered. The dog quieted.

"What else ye 'ave?"

"We've carrots and potatoes."

"I'll have some of them too." He nodded toward the river. "What's in the springhouse?"

Hannah set apples in the bag. "Milk, butter, and cheese."

"All right. Hurry up."

Hannah added carrots and potatoes to the sack and tried to hand it to him.

"You hold it. Head for the springhouse."

The lantern light cut through the darkness as Hannah led the way down the drive. The man followed. She wondered what he'd do when he had what he wanted. *Lord, please make him leave. Don't let him hurt me or poor Perry any further.*

Once inside the springhouse, the escapee wanted only cheese. He ordered her to add some to his stash. Hannah placed three balls in the bag.

"All right. Back to the house."

"What more can you want? I've nothing more to give you. Please go. Leave me to care for my friend."

The man grabbed Hannah's wrist and twisted her arm back. "Maybe I'm not leaving, eh? Maybe I'll take ye with me."

Hannah's throat constricted, threatening to cut off her air. *God, no. Save me. Save Perry.* Although feeling panic, Hannah somehow found calm and countered with, "If you take me, I'll only slow you down. Plus you'd attract attention to yourself. And my husband will hunt you down."

A shrewd look passed over the man's face. "If that man on the floor back there isn't yer husband, then where is yer husband, eh?" He smiled.

"He's on his way home this minute. He'll be here soon. I implore you, let me be. It will go hard on you if you're found out."

A look of cunning crossed the man's face. "He's not coming, is he? As far as I know, he may not even exist." He smiled. "All I need is one night. Just one." His tone sounded almost tender. He pulled her close and pressed his face against her hair, breathing deeply. "Ye smell of soap and lavender." Abruptly he shoved her away from him. "Back to the house."

Flashes of memory taunted Hannah as she moved on. Pictures of Judge Walker shouted at her from the past. What if this man raped her too? *Lord, I couldn't bear it.*

When Hannah stepped into the house, a wave of relief swept through her. Perry was sitting up. His hands were still tied behind his back, and blood dribbled from a cut beneath one eye and the bridge of his nose. She hurried to him. "Thank goodness. You're all right."

"So, ye've come to, eh?" The man jeered. "Seems I put ye to

sleep right well, though." He laughed. "Not so bright of ye to poke yer head in like that."

Perry peered at him through blackened eyes. "Ye've managed to lay me flat and ye've got what ye came for." His eyes settled on the bag. "Nothing more for ye here."

The intruder looked at Hannah. "I want ye to put some of that flowery soap of yers in the bag."

Hannah stared at him. It seemed an odd request.

"Get it."

It mattered little why he wanted it, if only he took it and left. She grabbed some of the precious soap, tied it in paper, and added it to the other items. He watched her closely.

Without warning, Perry leapt from the floor and grabbed the musket. The two men wrestled over the weapon, knowing that the one who possessed the musket held sway over the other. There was nothing Hannah could do but watch. Suddenly, a loud blast reverberated through the house and Perry fell backward against the wall. Blood quickly soaked his shirt.

"My Lord!" Hannah screamed. "You've killed him!" She hurried to her friend. Pressing a hand against his wound, she glared at the intruder. "You'll hang for this!"

Wearing a smirk, he said, "I'll not hang, for this or anything else." He grabbed the bag of goods and headed for the door. Flinging it wide, he stepped outside and disappeared into the darkness. Hannah heard the galloping steps of her mare as the prisoner escaped.

She turned her attention to Perry. "Are you all right? Are you with me?"

Perry managed to nod.

Hannah ripped open his shirt. A tattered wound marked his side. *Oh Lord, what am I to do?*

She grabbed a cloth from a kitchen shelf and pressed it against the injury. "Push your arm down against this. It will slow the bleeding." Hannah knew she needed to get Perry to a physician. "Can you walk?"

He opened one eye and then the other. "I'll try," he gasped.

"You need the surgeon." Hannah put her shoulder under his arm and pushed while he struggled to find his feet. "Lean on me. I'll take you to Dr. Gelson."

With Perry draped over her, Hannah made her way to the buggy and then helped him struggle onto the seat. He sat hunched over and fighting for breath.

"Thank the Lord he didn't take the buggy," Hannah said, climbing in beside Perry.

"Too easy to . . . find him . . . if . . . he's in the . . . buggy."

Hannah rested a hand on Perry's shoulder. "Lean on me."

With a nod, he rested against Hannah. She released the brake, grabbed the tracings, and turned the horse toward the road. With a lash of the reins, the animal moved at a fast trot. Hannah was thankful for a risen moon, for it made it easier to see. She glanced at Perry. "How did you free yourself?"

"Ye don't know how to tie a decent knot." He gasped as pain cut through him.

"I'm terrible at it, but I did try to leave it as loose as I could. I was hoping you'd get free."

When Hannah reached David Gelson's office, she scrambled down from the buggy and ran to his door. Pounding on it, she cried, "Doctor! Doctor Gelson! We need help!"

A moment later David appeared, looking disheveled, but alert. "Hannah? What's happened?"

"It's Perry. He's been shot."

Carrying a lantern, David hurried to the buggy and gave Perry a quick look.

"Is he going to be all right?"

"I can't tell for sure, at least not until I examine him further." He handed the lantern to Hannah and then hefted Perry out of the buggy. Supporting him, he slowly made his way into the office. Once inside, he carefully laid Perry on an examining table and checked his injuries. "Looks like he took a pretty bad beating."

"He did."

"What happened?" He probed the wound and Perry groaned.

"An escaped convict was at my house. He attacked us."

"Where's John?"

The reality of John's absence swept over Hannah, and she suddenly felt utterly alone. "He's in Sydney Town," she said as casually as she could.

Dr. Gelson nodded. "The ball's lodged somewhere in his side. I'll have to remove it." He looked at Hannah. "I could use assistance."

"I can do it."

"Good." David turned to Perry. "I'll have to go in after the slug. And it's going to hurt."

"Do what ye have to." He met the doctor's eyes bravely. "This isn't much. Grew up on the streets of London and seen a lot worse."

"All right, then." David measured powder into a glass of water, stirred the mixture, and then lifted Perry and had him drink it. "This will help."

Perry grimaced. "Tastes vile."

David lowered him back to the table. "That it does." He walked to a cabinet, took out surgical instruments, and set them on a stand beside the table. He tied on an apron and gave one to Hannah. "You'll need this."

Hannah held up the apron, fear taking hold. She'd never helped with anything this bad, but Perry needed her. She put it on.

"No matter how I holler, pay me no mind," Perry said, his speech slurred.

"I promise," David said with a teasing lilt to his voice. He swabbed the area to be worked on.

Perry grabbed the doctor's arm. "Thank ye," he rasped.

"You're welcome." David rolled Perry onto his side. "But you might feel differently in a few moments."

11

The driver pulled the team to a stop in front of Hannah's home, then climbed down and opened the carriage door. Mr. Atherton leaned forward on his seat. "Hannah, I wish you'd reconsider and stay at our place until John returns."

"I'm fine, truly," she lied. After what had happened, all Hannah wanted was to stay with the Athertons. But she couldn't bear the thought of John returning and her not being here.

Mr. Atherton stepped from the carriage and turned to assist her. Taking his hand, she said, "He'll most likely be back this afternoon." She managed a smile. "Please don't worry about me."

Jackson's yapping came from inside the barn. "Oh dear! Poor Jackson. I forgot he was locked up."

"I'll see to him."

"Thank you."

"Well, I'll have a look about while I'm here." He raised one eyebrow. "That is, if you don't mind."

"Of course not. Thank you." Hannah moved up the walk toward the house. Memories of the previous evening's events singed her thoughts, taking her breath from her.

"I'll go in first." Mr. Atherton moved past Hannah and onto

the porch. He opened the door and stepped inside just as Perry had done.

Hannah felt a flash of alarm and almost called out to him. She stopped and waited, keeping her hands clasped tightly and pressed against her abdomen.

Mr. Atherton returned to the porch. "I think it best that you not stay. There's quite a mess . . ."

"Perry's blood," Hannah stated flatly. "I know."

"Let me send someone to clean it for you."

"No. I can do it." Remembering Perry's surgery, a flush of pleasure went through Hannah. She'd been a competent assistant to Dr. Gelson. "I'm not afraid of a bit of blood," she said.

Mr. Atherton shrugged and stood aside for her. "You're a stubborn one, Hannah Bradshaw."

"I suppose I am, now and again." She smiled and stepped inside. Her eyes went to the scorched floor and bloodstains, and the frightening experience rushed back at her. She suddenly felt light-headed and overly warm. She pressed a hand against the wall to steady herself.

"Hannah? You all right?"

"Yes. Fine. Just give me a moment."

"You're white as a ghost."

After taking a breath in through her nose and slowly breathing out through her mouth, she felt steadier. "I'm fine."

William Atherton moved to the bedroom door and glanced inside. "No one here." He walked to the flight of stairs. "I'll have a look in the loft." He carried his tall frame with ease as he climbed the steps. He disappeared, and she heard his footfalls overhead. A few moments later, he stood at the top of the stairs and then headed back down. "It appears you're quite alone."

His last words echoed in Hannah's mind. *Alone. Yes, I'm alone.*

Mr. Atherton took the final step. "It would seem Perry put a scare into that mongrel. I daresay, he'll not set foot on this property again." He grinned, but his expression quickly turned sober. "I can understand how it might be difficult for you to be here. You don't need to be brave, Hannah. And it would give Mrs. Atherton ease to know you're safe with us."

Hannah wished she could go with him. The thought of spending a night alone in the house sent a shiver through her, but John was more important than her fears. She must stay in case he returned.

"Thank you, but I want to be here when John gets home." Hannah felt a flicker of shame. She'd still not told anyone, except Lydia, what had really happened.

"All right, then." Mr. Atherton moved to the door.

A distressed moo came from the direction of the barn. "Oh, poor Patience. She must be miserable by now."

"After I have a look around the property and check the barn, I'll take care of her and leave the milk in the springhouse." He tipped his hat. "After that, I'll be on my way."

"Thank you. I can't find words to express my gratitude."

Mr. Atherton stepped onto the porch.

Hannah stood in the doorway. "Mr. Atherton . . . it's a comfort to know Perry's being well taken care of."

"I doubt Gwen will take her eyes off of him, at least until he's back to himself." Mr. Atherton grinned. "He'll mend just fine." He walked down the steps. "Good day."

Hannah closed the door and turned to face the empty house and its lingering memories. The room felt cold. "I'd best get a fire going before I do anything else."

Using the same poker the convict had used against Perry, she stirred the ashes, hoping to find hot coals. She didn't relish the idea of starting a new fire with flint and straw. However, the fire was completely dead.

She took down the flint and set to work. It wasn't long before smoke and finally a small flame flickered. She quickly added more straw and blew on it as she added slivers of wood and then small pieces of acacia. Hannah fed the fire with bits of kindling, and when it crackled with vigor, she added small pieces of wood and then logs. Soon it snapped and popped, putting off heat that would drive the chill from the house.

She heard Mr. Atherton's carriage pull away and went to the window. As she watched it disappear from sight, isolation seemed to envelop the property and Hannah. Visions of a bloodied Perry and of the dreadful intruder trampled through her mind, and she pushed down rising fear.

"That's enough," she scolded herself. "I've other things to think about."

She removed her cloak, hung it on the rack beside the door, and tied on an apron. Set on erasing all evidence of the intruder, she first picked up the broken shards of glass and disposed of the lantern and wiped away oil remnants. The blackened wood could be sanded clean. Next she took the plate and mug the intruder had used and set them in the sink. She'd wash them later. After wiping the table, she turned to the bloodstained floor. It would take soap and a good scrubbing.

Her thoughts went to Perry. He'd been brave. Even while undergoing surgery, he'd not cried out. And David Gelson had shown himself to be a competent surgeon. As it turned out, he was also kind and truly concerned about his patients, even Perry. He was a gift to the community of Parramatta and

Hannah could find no fault in him. *If only he could see Lydia for who she is. Lord, open his eyes.*

Dragging herself back to the present, Hannah rested her hands on her hips and studied the stain. "It won't disappear on its own." She moved to the door and stepped onto the porch. A brisk wind, carrying the pungent smell of eucalyptus, swirled up dirt and leaves. Hannah couldn't keep from looking down the road. Taking a deep breath, she closed her eyes. *Lord, please bring John home to me.*

Jackson trotted out of the barn and bounded toward her. With a laugh, Hannah patted his back and scratched him behind the ears. "Oh, Jackson, it's good to see you."

He licked her face and wiggled from front to back, and finally assured she was well, he moved off, his nose to the ground.

A creak came from the direction of the barn, and Hannah's heart quickened. Had Mr. Atherton checked thoroughly? What if the convict was hiding inside? *Stop it. He's gone.*

Unable to eliminate her fear completely, Hannah went to her bedroom and opened a drawer in the armoire and took out a pistol and leather pouch with gunpowder. She pushed the gun inside her waistband and dropped the pouch into her apron pocket before heading for the front door.

Picking up two wooden buckets, she walked toward the river. Aside from the sporadic bursts of wind, the countryside seemed peaceful enough. It was quiet except for the occasional birdcall. Hannah usually enjoyed the serenity of the countryside, but today it was unsettling, and she found herself longing for the noise and bustle of London. She'd not thought of the city in a long while.

Her old life reached for her. She and her mother had lived simply, the two taking up little space in their small cottage.

135

While working on gowns for the prosperous, they'd sip tea and chat. Sometimes in the evenings they would read stories or study the Scriptures. An ache for those days and for her mother swelled inside Hannah.

Oh Mum, I miss you so.

Caroline had been a woman of faith, always steadfast and living what she believed. Hannah needed her steadiness now. What would she do if left here alone? She couldn't care for the farm on her own. She'd be forced to return to work as a domestic. Although the Athertons would kindly take her back, they had no need of another housemaid, and Hannah wasn't about to accept their charity. They'd already done so much.

Most likely she'd have to leave Parramatta and seek employment in Sydney Town. It would be difficult finding work with so many prisoners available to fulfill the needs of residents. *I could end up living on the streets just as I did in London.* The possibility hit Hannah with a sickening thud.

Tears burned her eyes. Wiping them away, she set down a bucket and looked up at dark, swirling clouds. They were indistinct and blurred, just like her life. Nothing was certain. Shivering, she picked up the bucket and hurried on her way.

The sound of a rider carried up from the road, and fear shot through Hannah. What if it was the escaped convict? She dropped the buckets, grabbed the pistol out of her waistband, and crouched low to the ground. Blood pounded in her head.

With a bark, Jackson dashed down the drive and disappeared. "Jackson! Jackson, come back here!" The dog didn't return.

You're getting upset over nothing. People travel the road all the time. Most likely it's a neighbor. Hands quaking, Hannah pulled the striker back halfway and added a small amount of gunpowder. Pushing the bag of powder into her apron pocket, she looked down the road, gripping the gun in both hands. What should she do if it was him? She'd never shot anyone before. Could she?

The horse's footfalls came nearer. It sounded like more than one rider. *Don't let it be him, Lord.* The gun shook in Hannah's trembling hands. Trying to quiet her breathing, she waited.

And then a man came into view.

"John!" Still holding the pistol, she watched him ride closer and then turn up the drive. Quincy followed close behind him.

Doubts replaced Hannah's initial joy. What would she say to him? What if he hadn't forgiven her and was still angry? What if he'd returned simply to gather his things?

John's expression was solemn.

Hannah stood, nerves prickling along her arms.

He rode toward Hannah and stopped a few paces in front of her. He didn't say anything right away, then asked, "Why do you have the pistol?"

She looked at the gun in her hands. "Oh. I . . . I forgot." She gently released the striker and dropped her arm. In those few moments, her mind carried her to a hurting place. Why hadn't he asked after her welfare? He'd not even said hello, had given no explanation or apology. And if he hadn't left her alone . . . Resentment replaced Hannah's relief. She squared her jaw. "A woman alone has need of caution."

John didn't reply, but Hannah could see that her tone had offended him. She didn't care. He'd been gone three days with no thought of her. "I'm on my way to get water." Without saying more, she tucked the pistol into her waistband, picked up the buckets, and walked toward the river. She barely glanced at Quincy.

Silence swelled behind her. She knew John and Quincy were watching. She heard the horses move away, but she kept walking, fighting tears every step.

❦

With both buckets nearly full and water sloshing over the sides, she made her way toward the house. There was no sign of the men. *No doubt they're in the barn.* She stepped onto the porch and set one bucket down. Grabbing a bristle brush and soap from a shelf, she dropped them in the bucket, picked it up, and walked inside. *I won't say a word,* she vowed, pouring water for dishes into a four-legged pot in the hearth. Next she went to work cleaning the stained floor.

When John walked in, Hannah was on her hands and knees scrubbing the planked flooring. He set his musket in its place over the mantel and then removed his coat and hat.

Hannah didn't look at him. She pressed down harder with the brush and scoured ferociously. Her shoulders ached. The soapy water in the bucket was tinged red, and the floor had a pink cast.

"What sort of spill is that?"

"It's Perry's blood." Hannah kept working.

"His blood? What happened? Is he all right?"

Hannah stopped and sat back on her heels. She fixed John with an angry stare. "He'll live. But he's suffered dearly."

"Why was he bleeding in our house?"

There'd already been so much thought and so much talk about what had happened that Hannah would have preferred saying nothing more, but there was no way around it. "I was in

138

need of a friend yesterday, so I went to see Lydia. She invited me to stay for dinner, which I did gladly. When it was time to return home, it was late, so Perry accompanied me."

The fear was fresh, forcing Hannah to stop. She let her wet hands rest in her lap. "It was dreadful. An escaped prisoner was in our house. I think he may have watched me go and knew I was alone." Hannah was angry and wanted to hurt John, to make him sorry that he'd left her.

His face ashen, he stared at her. "Are you all right?"

Hannah nodded.

"What did he want?"

"It seems he was looking for food. At least that's all he demanded." Hannah's mind carried her back to the darkness in the house when she and Perry had arrived. She could feel the terror.

"When Perry stopped the buggy in front of the house, a light suddenly went out. Poor Perry went ahead of me to have a look. The moment he stepped through the door, the intruder struck him with the fire poker. Perry was rendered unconscious."

"Did he hurt you? Did he touch you?"

Offense burned through Hannah like a fire out of control. "Is that all you can think about? Did he touch me? Do you think I enticed him?"

John winced. "Of course not. It's just that I can't abide the thought of you being injured in any way."

"I wasn't hurt," Hannah stated flatly, her conscience pricking her. She was purposely being unkind. "The man wanted food. I fed him.

"When Perry came to, he thought I was in jeopardy and tried to wrest the musket from the man. He was quite brave, but during the skirmish he was shot."

Pale and clearly shaken, John sat in a chair. "I'm sorry. I should have been here."

"Yes. You should have been."

Silence pervaded the room. And with it, Hannah's outrage slipped away. She could see John's anguish. She was adding to his burden. "It is I who am sorry. You had a right to be angry with me."

John's amber eyes looked tortured. "Angry, yes. But I shouldn't have left you alone."

Hannah wiped her hands on her apron and moved to her husband. She knelt in front of him. "I don't blame you." She rested a hand over his. "Can you forgive me?"

"It is I who must ask your forgiveness. I behaved outrageously. I was thinking only of myself." He shook his head. "To have accused you as I did. Even the thought of it shames me."

Hannah gazed into his eyes. "There have been times that even I wondered if I shared fault in the attack. I've tried to remember the days before and have asked myself if I did anything to provoke Mr. Walker's advances." She wiped at a stray tear.

John cupped Hannah's cheek in his hand. "Of course you didn't. You could never do such a thing. I know that. I knew it three days ago. But selfishness took hold of my mind. All I could think of was my pride. I'm truly sorry."

Hannah rested her cheek against his hand and kissed his palm. "I should have told you. Mrs. Atherton and Lydia both advised me to do so. But I was afraid. Afraid that you'd hate me and that I'd lose you." She looked up at him. "I've thought and thought and I know I didn't tempt Mr. Walker. In all my considering I can't find even one instance."

"I know, luv." John's expression was tender. "I feel deep disgrace and regret at having added to your agony."

Hannah offered a smile of encouragement. "I forgive you." She steeled herself, knowing they must still discuss the child's death. She straightened her spine but kept hold of his hand. "And what of the baby?"

"I've not forgotten what life was like on that ship. The idea of birthing a child on board is more than any person could bear. I understand your desire to spare an infant the torture of such an existence." His eyes shimmered with tears. "Instead of facing the atrociousness of a prison, it went straight to heaven."

"True, but she should have known the warmth and love of her mother. Instead she tasted an early death. My heart was not noble." Hannah took in a quick breath. "I could think only of myself. I wanted her to die because the disgrace of being a convict was already heavy upon me, and I couldn't abide the shame."

Hannah felt the dishonor as if it had just occurred. "I didn't trust God to care for me and the baby. I was faithless. I am faithless even still."

"You're not." John stood and pulled Hannah to her feet. "All the agony you've carried." He drew her to him. "I should be comforting you, and instead I've added to your hurt."

Hannah could scarcely believe John's change of heart. To be loved so was beyond comprehension. She wrapped her arms about his waist and held him tightly.

For a long while John and Hannah stood like that, finding comfort in each other. Finally, he stepped back and smiled down at her. "I missed you. Every moment I was away, I wanted to return."

"Then why were you gone so long?"

He closed his eyes for a moment. "I was furious the night you told me—self-righteous and pompous." He shook his head.

"I spent the night along the river. The morning offered me no wisdom, so I rode to Sydney Town." He glanced at the ceiling and took a slow breath. "I went to a pub and started downing tankards of rum. Even before my mind cleared the next day, I knew I'd been wrong. But before I could come back to you, I needed God's wisdom.

"I walked the streets and along the bay. In the quiet, God helped me see my selfishness and reminded me of your righteousness."

"My righteousness?"

"We've talked about it. God has forgiven you, and it's as if you have no sin." He looked down at his hands. "For a time, I forgot that."

Hannah didn't know how to respond.

John kissed her. "Every day I thank the Lord for you. And I thank him even more now because he protected you while I was gone. The man . . . what became of him?"

"I don't know. He shot Perry, took my horse, and fled. I imagine he's far from here."

"I'll report the episode to the constable."

"Mr. Atherton already has. He and some of his men have searched for the convict, but he's not been found."

"And Perry? How is he?"

"Gwen is caring for him. After the shooting, I took him to Dr. Gelson's office. He saved Perry's life. He's a fine surgeon."

"Thank the Lord for that."

Hannah smiled. "You would have been proud of Perry. He was quite brave. He nearly wrestled the musket away from that man. If not for its discharging, I'm sure Perry would have overpowered him."

"Perry has always been spirited. I owe him dearly. If not for him . . ." His words faded and he looked intensely at Hannah. "I couldn't bear it if anything happened to you." He gripped her upper arms. "I'll never leave you like that again. And after this, when we quarrel, we'll find a better way to work it out, eh?"

Hannah nodded, but inside her stomach was still in knots. She wanted to remain in the quiet pool of love, but there was more to be discussed.

"John, you know that I shan't have children. God is disciplining me, I'm certain of it. He'll not bless me with a child."

John enfolded Hannah in his arms and held her a moment before speaking. "If God sees fit to bless us with a family, then I shall rejoice. And if he doesn't, there's nothing can be done about it." He caressed Hannah's hair. "I'd rather live with you and without children than spend my life with any other." He stepped back and placed a finger under her chin, tipping up her face so she looked at him. "I also know that God loves you and he blesses those he loves. We'll have a family, in his time."

12

Hands folded in her lap, Hannah pressed her back against the wagon's seat. She gazed at green hillsides lying warm beneath the morning sun. Soft, round clouds rested against a blue sky, and a breeze rustled short grasses.

The ugliness that had taken place two weeks previously was far from her thoughts. "I like August. It may well be my favorite month. It's not so hot as to cause discomfort and neither is it cold."

"We might have some cool weather yet," John said, lifting the reins and clicking his tongue. "I was lucky to get this mare at such a reasonable price. Fine thing, coming on that sale like I did."

"She seems to be a good horse."

"Not as fine as your mare, but she'll do." He gazed at the river.

"It's a perfect day for a picnic. I'm glad we've planned one for after services. I do hope Lydia and the Athertons will join us."

"They may have other plans." Transferring the reins into one hand, John put an arm around Hannah and squeezed gently. "I wouldn't mind too much if it were just you and me."

Hannah leaned against him, thinking she'd never been quite so happy as she was at this moment. She languished in the goodness of life.

They moved through the hamlet of Parramatta, rolling past the general store and the smithy's. Dr. Gelson's office had a sign in the window saying that if an emergency arose, he could be found at the church.

"I think it's a pity David's no longer seeing Lydia. She'd make him a splendid wife."

"I agree she'd make a good wife, but perhaps not for David."

"She'd be much better for him than Deidre. I don't understand why he's interested in her."

"She's a handsome woman."

"And Lydia's not?"

"Well, she has her own beauty."

Hannah knew the difference. Lydia was handsome, in a healthy, wholesome way, and Deidre was stunningly beautiful. "That may be true," Hannah said, "but external beauty means nothing if the inside is ugly."

"You've said those kinds of things before about Deidre. Why do you think she's ugly inside? She's never done anything hostile against you . . . has she?"

"No. I'm not certain why I feel so strongly about her, except that she's been somewhat intolerant toward me. And although she and Lydia were supposed to be friends, she still went after Dr. Gelson. That's a betrayal. I believe she's two-faced, to the extreme."

"You're being a bit harsh, don't you think? Perhaps it was Dr. Gelson who did the going after, as you say."

"I suppose it's possible. But I don't trust her."

"Have you just cause?"

Hannah thought over John's question. Had Deidre actually ever done anything outlandish or deceitful? Hannah had to answer no, but every time the woman sauntered up to John and batted her eyelashes at him, Hannah bristled.

"I simply know I'm right. I don't have an explanation." A breeze caught at Hannah's bonnet, and she pressed a hand on it to hold it in place. "But in light of God's commandment to love one another, I'll do my best to be kind."

"She's probably not a bad sort." John slapped the reins to hurry the horses along.

The church grounds were congested with buggies, wagons, and carriages. John pulled his wagon up alongside one of the Athertons', the one used by the servants. He stepped out, tethered the horses, and gave Hannah a hand down. "Looks like most of the district is here this morning."

"That's what fine weather will do; it brings people out." Hannah closed her eyes and tilted her face into the sunlight. "It feels good to be outdoors." She looped her arm through John's and they walked toward the church. Her step was light. She always looked forward to Sunday services. It was a time to see her friends and to learn of local news. Plus Reverend Taylor always had something worthwhile to share.

The reverend stood at the top of the steps. As John and Hannah approached him, he reached out a hand to John. "Grand morning, don't you think?" He clasped John's hand.

"That it is. Hannah and I thought a picnic would be fitting for such a fine day."

"I quite agree." The reverend smiled at Hannah.

"Would you care to join us?" she asked.

"I'd love to, but I've already accepted an invitation from the Parnells." He smiled. "It promises to be a lively time. Lottie is always full of questions and stories. Adorable child, that one."

"She is." Hannah smiled and nodded, while inside she felt the longing to mother the little girl. Even after all this time, it still felt as if Lottie belonged with her. Hannah knew better. The Parnells were admirable parents, and Lottie was blessed to be part of their family. It had been an act of God that put the three of them together. And it was reprehensible of her to want anything else for the child or for Charles and Grace. *Forgive me, Lord, for my self-interest.*

John held Hannah's elbow and steered her indoors. Hannah looked about for Lydia. She was seated midway, beside Mrs. Goudy. Gwen and Perry shared the same pew. Perry looked much better than the last time Hannah had seen him.

Hannah leaned in close to John. "Can we sit with Lydia?" she whispered.

"Of course." He moved up the center aisle.

Deidre stood along an outside wall. Her eyes followed John, then moved to Hannah. Her expression was haughty. Remembering that she'd decided to try to be friendly, Hannah smiled. Deidre simply stared back at her.

"Hannah. Grand to see ye." Lydia moved to the aisle and pulled Hannah into her embrace.

Hannah kept her hands on Lydia's arms as she stepped back. "You look well," she said, but her mind remained with Deidre. She'd seen something in the woman's eyes, something that frightened her. She tried to focus on Lydia. "What is it that's different? Oh, your hat. Is it new?"

Lydia touched the brim of the deep blue bonnet. "It is. Thought it was time I replaced my old one."

147

"I love the flowers," Hannah said of the small rosettes that rimmed the cap.

John moved down the row toward Perry. "You're looking fit. Just a bit black around the eyes." He grinned.

Holding one arm tucked next to his side, Perry stood slowly. He seemed a bit shaky. "I'm better. Thanks to David Gelson. He's a fine surgeon." He tossed a glance at the doctor. "Can't hate him any longer, eh?"

"Should say not." John rested a hand on Perry's shoulder.

"Must say, I can't understand his taste in women, though."

John glanced at David who chatted with Deidre. He escorted her to a seat near the front. "They make a fine-looking couple."

"Lydia's a better match for him. I'd think he would see that. I can't figure out how he could throw her over for Deidre."

Lydia turned to Perry. "I'd prefer that ye not speak as if I'm not here."

In his usual slapdash way, Perry had spoken out of turn. Hannah smiled. At one time, she'd thought him coarse and even thoughtless, but she knew better now. Perry could sometimes be abrasive, but he had a good heart.

"Speaking me mind is all," he said.

The reverend walked to the front of the church. Those standing took their seats and quieted.

John grasped Hannah's hand and held it against his abdomen. Hannah could feel his strength. With him, she was safe and protected. She wondered at God's goodness. Although she didn't deserve a fine man like John Bradshaw, God had given him to her. *It's God's love*, she thought, unable to restrain a smile.

Music filled the small sanctuary and voices merged as parishioners sang the hymn "Lo He Comes with Clouds Descending." As always, the music lifted Hannah's heart and carried her closer to God. At this moment, she could believe almost anything, even that she and John might one day have a child. Perhaps God *would* choose to bless them in that way. She rested a hand on her stomach, thinking about how it would feel to actually experience such a gift.

Reverend Taylor concluded the service with prayer, and Hannah turned to Lydia. "Would you like to join John and me for a picnic? I made a lunch. There's plenty."

"My stomach has been grumbling for the past half hour. A picnic sounds perfect."

Hannah looked at Mrs. Goudy. "Can you join us?"

"I'd like that."

"Perry and Gwen?"

Gwen knit her brows. "Sounds grand, but I think Perry's already done too much today. The doctor said he's to be careful and not overtax himself."

Perry's expression was apologetic. "I am a bit done in."

"Not long until you're right as rain," Mrs. Goudy said.

"I'm counting on it."

"We'll have you and Gwen over for dinner soon."

John moved toward the aisleway. "Hannah, are you ready?"

"I was hoping to have a word with Lottie and Mrs. Atherton."

"I'll see to the horses," he said and headed toward the church doors.

John took a handful of grain from a bucket in the back of the wagon and gave some to each horse. While the animals munched, he leaned against the rim of a wheel and watched as parishioners chatted and said their good-byes, then went on their way.

Deidre stepped out of the church. She looked as if she was searching for someone. When she saw John, she waved and walked toward him.

"Good day," John said, wondering why Hannah had such a dislike for the woman. She seemed pleasant enough.

"Good day, John." Her tone was clear and sweet. "Fine sermon, eh?"

"Indeed. Quite uplifting. The Word of the Lord sometimes pierces my heart. Today the reverend left me with much to consider. Living one's life for the Lord is a lofty topic."

"That it is." Deidre swept up hair from her neck while offering John a coy look.

He felt slightly discomfited. "I see that you and David Gelson have become friends."

"We have at that." A smile played at Deidre's lips as if she were holding back a secret pleasure. An uncomfortable silence settled between them.

John looked to the church, wishing Hannah would hurry. "Have you any special plans for the afternoon?"

"No. Not really. I'll have a bit of lunch and then take up some mending that needs doing. And perhaps David will join me for dinner." She moved to one of the horses and ran a hand down the front of its face. "I've a bit of a dilemma, however. Perhaps you can be of some help."

"I'll try."

"I've recently learned something disturbing . . . about someone who attends this church. And it's a matter for prayer."

150

"Prayer is always a good thing." John patted the horse's neck. "And in what way can I be of help?"

Deidre moved around the horse until she stood close to John. "You know the person I'm speaking of." She let the sentence hang in the air a moment, then continued. "It's your wife."

"Hannah? What about her?" John puzzled over the comment. "Oh. You must mean the intruder. He's not been found. But you needn't worry. Hannah's doing quite well and so is Perry. I'll tell Hannah of your concern. She'd be glad to know of it."

"Yes, I heard about that. It's quite a shock to know that prisoners are running loose and might accost you in your own home."

"I doubt that you've anything to concern yourself with. It's a rare occurrence."

Deidre studied John, a strange expression on her face. "There's something else I wanted to speak with you about. I heard that once there was a . . . child . . . one that Hannah bore while on the prison ship."

At first, Deidre's words made no sense, but when the statement finally penetrated John's mind, he felt as if the wind had been knocked out of him. He managed to keep his voice controlled as he asked, "What are you talking about?"

"I was told she had a . . . a friendship with a well-regarded gentleman in London. And that the affair ended in quite a loathsome way. When she was thrown out of his house, she took some of the gentleman's belongings and was actually carrying his child."

Rage reared up in John. How dare this woman speak of Hannah's troubles and in such a perverse way.

She offered a sly smile, still holding John's eyes with hers. "I also know that she wanted that innocent little one dead."

John was so furious he didn't know what to say. If he acted as if he knew what she was talking about, he'd give away Hannah's past. Yet Deidre obviously already knew the truth—her version of it.

She moved past John and placed a hand on the mare's back. "I've been quite distressed since hearing this news. What a burden it must have been for Hannah . . . and for you, to carry such a secret. The dishonor must be stifling." Her tone kindly, she added, "Ever since I heard, I've been carrying you and Hannah to the Lord in my prayers."

"I'm sure you have," John replied in a derogatory tone. "I don't know how you came upon such a story."

"Indeed, it's no story, but truth." She stepped closer, and resting a hand against her throat, she looked at John from beneath lowered lids. "Such a tale could ruin someone like Hannah. How devastating it would be if it were to get around."

Suddenly John knew Deidre's intentions. He stepped back and moved to the wagon. "If you'll excuse me, I've an engagement."

Deidre followed him. "If you'll spare me a few minutes more." Her muddy green eyes locked with his. "From time to time I find myself a bit short on cash and goods. As you know, it's difficult for a woman on her own."

"Is it?" John fought to control his fury. He met her cool gaze with a heated one of his own. "Perhaps you can explain it to me."

"There are only so many hours one can work, and I've no husband to help me. I thought perchance if I were to be blessed with two good ewes I'd have enough wool for necessities. And my larder is a bit low. A hog would go a long way toward fending off hunger."

"Why is it that you come to me with these needs? I've barely enough to feed Hannah and myself."

Deidre's gaze moved to Hannah who had stepped out of the church and was followed by Lottie and Mrs. Atherton. "She's quite comely and seems genteel. What a shame it would be if word were to get out that she'd been sullied and then destroyed her own child."

"You have it wrong. What you're saying is not true!"

"Oh? Isn't it?" She turned her attention back to John. "All I'd need would be two sheep and one hog. I daresay, that's not so much to ask."

John clamped his jaw tight. "Your threats will have no influence over me."

Deidre turned toward the church. "Well then, I shall be forced to speak with the elders about this matter. How can they be of assistance to those in their flock if they've no knowledge of the need?" She daintily lifted her skirts and took a step toward the church. "I'm sure they'll be glad to know there's a call for spiritual guidance amongst the congregation." She smiled demurely.

John's outrage flamed, but what was he to do? He couldn't allow Hannah to be shamed in such a way. She was respected in this community. If word got out, she would be ruined . . . and so would he.

He railed against capitulation, but what other choice did he have? "All right, then. I'll see to it that you get your ewes and a sow."

"How kind of ye. Thank ye for yer generosity." Deidre took a step toward the church and then stopped and looked back at John. "Oh, can ye tell me when I can expect them?"

"Next week is the earliest I can get by your place."

"I'll have need before that. I think two days hence would be soon enough."

John sucked in a breath. "All right." He glared at the ground. "Tomorrow. I'll bring them tomorrow."

"Good." Deidre sauntered off toward David, who waited for her at his buggy. John's outrage billowed. *How dare she!* If he could have, John would have followed her and pummeled the woman, but of course that was impossible and would serve no good purpose.

Hannah walked toward John. "What did Deidre want?"

"Nothing. We were just chatting."

"Something's wrong. I can see it. What is it?"

"Everything's fine."

Hannah studied him. "I don't believe you."

"What could be wrong on such a fine day?" John tried to make his voice light.

Hannah stared at him and finally said, "All right, then. I suppose you'll tell me when you're ready." She watched David Gelson's buggy pull away, then turned back to John. "Lydia and Mrs. Goudy said they'd be pleased to join us for a picnic. Where do you think we should go?"

"I've changed my mind. We'll do it another time."

"But I thought we decided."

"Not today." John lifted and smoothed the traces that ran over the horses' backs. "We should go."

"What's happened?"

"Nothing. I'm just not feeling well."

"But you said everything is fine."

"It is, but I'm feeling a bit under the weather."

"What did Deidre say?"

"Nothing. Now, let's go."

Hannah looked wounded and John felt badly, but he couldn't bring himself to socialize—not after what had just happened. And he wasn't about to tell Hannah the truth.

Her shoulders drooped. "All right. But I'll have to offer my apologies to Lydia and Mrs. Goudy."

John watched Hannah walk away. She deserved none of this. She already had so much to bear. *Lord, why would you allow such a thing?* Gelson's buggy moved toward the road and Deidre's laughter carried across the grounds.

John clenched his jaw, his ire deepening. Hannah had been right about Deidre. *I'll do as she asked, but that will be the end of it,* John told himself. But he knew differently. This was only the beginning.

13

Hannah peered out the carriage window, excited about a day in Sydney Town with her friends. The coach shuddered as it dropped into a hole, and then jolted forward as it found its way out. She could smell the distinctive aroma that came only from the ocean—salt and sea life. Rather than rekindling ugly memories, it revived her. Once she'd thought the months aboard a prison ship had ruined her love of the sea and that she'd never tolerate the pungent ocean aroma. Thankfully, she'd been wrong.

Gazing at the aqua bay, she smiled. How good to be here. It had been too long. With the roads in such dreadful condition, she rarely visited. But today was to be a treat, a special time just for the ladies—her, Lydia, and Gwen.

"I daresay, Sydney Town's becoming a proper city," Lydia said, leaning over Hannah for a better look. "It's quite grown up."

"I love it here!" Gwen sat across from Hannah and Lydia and gazed out the window beside her. "It was good of the Athertons to let us use the carriage. It's much more comfortable than a wagon." She leaned an elbow on the window ledge. "It would be grand to have our lunch at a café. When I lived in London, I'd sometimes see the well-to-do in a fancy café. They'd be sitting at tables with linen tablecloths and flowers in the center, drinking from elegant goblets. I always thought one day I'd like to do that."

"I doubt Sydney Town has anything so grand as that, but I'm sure we can find one with good food." Hannah smiled at her two comrades. "Thank you for inviting me. It's been far too long since I've had such an outing."

"We thought it time you got away from that farm of yours and had a bit of merriment." Lydia grinned. "And I agree that lunch together would be fun."

Her eyes wide with anticipation, Gwen adjusted her bonnet. "I've so much to do. I'm not sure just what should come first." She pulled her cloak more tightly about her shoulders. "It's a shame the weather's turned cold. This would be so much more pleasant if it were warm."

"It is chilly." Hannah rested gloved hands on a coverlet draped over her knees. "I'm glad I thought to bring my lap blanket."

"I daresay, it's utterly cold, but then August can be that way." Lydia glanced at heavy clouds. "Perhaps there'll be a rain shower or two. Mrs. Atherton is hoping so. She said it's been too dry this winter."

Gwen leaned her head against the edge of the window and gazed out. "I do miss the snow. It seemed to make the world brighter and cleaner."

"Cleaner . . . until the horses and carriages started mucking things up. Then it was an utter mess." Lydia made a face that showed her distaste.

"Well, I don't miss the bitter cold at all," Hannah said. "There were too many days that no matter how much coal we fed the stove, the house never felt warm."

"I know all that, but when the snow first fell all soft and pure, the world would seem hushed and peaceful. I loved that." Gwen's expression was dreamy. "And summer was never impossibly hot, nor were there masses of feasting flies."

"No, just an incredible stink. And I rather like the heat and rain we get here," Lydia said.

With a secretive smile on her lips, Gwen clasped her hands in her lap. "Course this summer might be special."

"How so?" Lydia asked.

Gwen didn't answer, but the smile remained on her lips.

"You've a secret. What is it?" Hannah leaned toward her.

"Out with it. Tell us," Lydia teased.

With her hands clasped loosely, Gwen stretched her arms out in front of her. "I'm certain Perry's going to ask me to marry him." Her eyes danced with pleasure. "And I think summer is the best time for a wedding, don't ye?"

Lydia looked stunned for a moment.

Concern touched Gwen's eyes. "Ye don't mind, do ye? I know that once the two of ye—"

"No. I don't mind. I'm just surprised. I'm thrilled for ye. Don't worry 'bout Perry and me. We were only friends, nothing more. I think the two of ye are perfect for each other." Lydia reached across the space between herself and Gwen and grasped the young woman's hand. "He's lucky to have ye."

"I'm the lucky one. He's a fine man and sometimes treats me as if I'm royalty or something. And he doesn't mind at all 'bout me past, me being in gaol and all that has happened."

Nothing was said, but all three knew the atrocities committed against women prisoners. Every woman dreaded the possibility of what could happen and remembered the terror of night aboard a prison ship.

"I should think not," Hannah said. "He was a prisoner himself and a street rat before that."

"I'd not call him a street rat," Gwen said defensively. "He lived on the streets, but only because he had no other choice. And although I'm sure he wasn't beyond reproach, he never gave in to the temptations of thievery and some of the other violence. He remained an upstanding citizen, respectable."

Either Gwen was unwilling to look at the truth or Perry hadn't been forthcoming with her. Hannah knew the full story. Perry had never been as bad a scoundrel as some, but he'd done what was necessary to survive. She said nothing, not wanting to endanger the joyful glow on Gwen's face. How good to see her in love. "Perry's a fine man, no matter his past," she said. "And he'll make a good husband."

The coach jolted to a stop. The driver stepped down from his perch, opened the door, and gave the ladies a hand out. "I'll take the coach 'round to the stables and give the horses some feed and water. I'll be back for ye in three hours' time. Will that suit ye?"

Lydia glanced at the others. "That's fine with me. I'm sure I will have completed my errands."

"I'll be ready," Gwen said.

"Me too." A gust of wind swept cold, damp air up off the bay, and Hannah pulled her cloak closed at the neck.

The driver nodded and climbed back onto the coach seat. With a slap of the reins, he moved the team down the street.

"I've some things to get for Mrs. Atherton and for Dalton," Lydia said. "The mercantile ought to carry most of what I need."

Hannah wished she could do some just-for-fun shopping, but funds were limited. John's shirts were in bad condition, and she dare not wait longer to make him new ones. "I'm in need of broadcloth, so I'll join you."

Gwen held up a satchel. "My boots are so badly worn I can't put off repairs. I'll take them to the cobbler. Then I'm going to stop in at the millinery shop." She smiled at Lydia. "I love your new hat, and you've inspired me to get something new for church and special occasions."

Lydia smiled. "Good for you." She opened a small purse and fished out a few coins. "Shall we eat at the café across from the mercantile? I managed to save some coppers out of my pay."

Hannah mentally calculated the money she had and decided lunch was a manageable luxury. "I'd like to."

"I've barely enough, but I wouldn't pass it up," Gwen said. "As long as the cobbler's prices are unchanged." She grinned. "We'll be like proper ladies."

"Of course. We are proper ladies," Lydia said in a snobbish tone. She laughed and then went silent. The green in her eyes darkened as they settled on something across the street.

It was David. He hadn't seen them and walked briskly down the opposite side of the street.

"I am a lady, even if he doesn't see me that way," Lydia said tersely. She watched him until he stepped into the apothecary. Abruptly, she turned to Hannah. "We best be off if we're to be ready for the coach when it returns."

"I'll meet ye at the café in one hour, then?" Gwen asked.

"An hour." Feeling badly for Lydia, Hannah put an arm about her friend's waist and watched Gwen walk toward the cobbler's shop.

"Do ye think she and Perry will actually get married?" Lydia asked.

"I doubt she'd say so if she didn't believe it." Hannah gave her friend a squeeze. "They're a good match. She's fun-loving enough for Perry, but levelheaded too, so she'll make a good wife."

Lydia turned and walked toward the mercantile, the lightness gone from her step. She didn't even give the apothecary shop a glance.

When Hannah stepped into the store, a tantalizing jumble of smells greeted her—tobacco, peppermint, a mix of spices, and even baked goods. They'd recently started selling pastries and breads.

She wandered toward a shelf with a neatly displayed set of dainty cups and saucers. She picked up one of the cups, thinking how nice it would be to serve company in something so delicate.

"Nice, eh?" Lydia examined the matching saucer. "They're not much use to the likes of us." She returned it to the display shelf. "I don't even have me own house. Probably never will." She smoothed her skirt. "I'm not complaining, though. I've come a long way from the hold of the transport ship. I'm grateful for it."

The reminder kicked Hannah back to reality. "We have a lot to be thankful for." As she set the cup back on the shelf, the desire to own it no longer tugged at her. She moved toward the back of the store where the fabrics were kept.

She walked between two aisles of cloth, occasionally touching a piece of fabric and even smoothing it between her fingers. The lingering smell of dyes and the look and feel of the material carried her back to London and to her mother's shop. Tender memories enveloped her.

As she moved toward the heavier, less-refined material, a bolt of red taffeta seemed to reach out to her from the shelf. She couldn't pass it by. Picking up the fabric, she held it against her, remembering how once, for a young woman's coming-out, she and her mother had created a gown from a nearly identical piece.

"Can I be of help?"

The voice cut into Hannah's reverie. "I'm sorry, what did you say?"

A tall, broad-shouldered woman smiled. "Just thought I might be of help." Her eyes fell to the taffeta. "Lovely, isn't it."

"Yes. It is." Embarrassed, Hannah returned it to the shelf and moved on to the broadcloth. "I was thinking about this. Five yards should do."

"Of course." The woman stepped past Hannah and picked up a bolt of the broadcloth. "This is a lovely shade of blue."

"It is. It will do nicely. Thank you."

Hannah glanced back at the finer fabrics. Perhaps by summer she'd have enough money to purchase some for a new dress.

<hr />

Lydia had gone on to the millinery shop, hoping to help Gwen pick out a hat. She'd promised to meet Hannah at the café. Her arms laden with fabric, buttons, and thread, Hannah walked toward the eatery. She was half a block away when she saw her friends. Two sailors stood alongside them. It appeared they were blocking their way.

"Come on now," one of the men said. "Just a bit of fun is all we're asking for. I know ye could do with a quid or two, eh?" He offered a sickly grin and reached into his pocket.

"Let us pass," Lydia said boldly.

The other man stepped in front of her. "Ye know ye want to. Just say yes. We've had our share of convict lydies and we've shown 'em a good time. And ye look like ye could do with some fun."

Fear imprinted on her face, Gwen clasped a package to her chest and huddled close to Lydia.

"We've no intention of joining ye for a 'good time.' You've annoyed me long enough." Lydia tried to push past the man.

He grabbed her arm. "Ye think yer too fancy for the likes of me, eh? Don't fool yerself. Yer riffraff and no better than anyone else. And ye'll come along with me."

Without thought for herself, Hannah hurried to her friends' defense. "Stop it! Stop it this minute!" She tried to step between the man and Lydia, but he was having none of it. Not to be put off, Hannah demanded in her most authoritarian voice, "Release her!"

The man settled small, gray eyes on Hannah. "Or ye'll do what?" He sneered and then sniggered as he glanced at his friend and then turned back to Hannah.

The other man stepped up. "Eh, Patrick, what d'ye think?" He allowed his eyes to roam over Hannah.

His look made Hannah feel violated. She forced herself to meet his gaze and not back down.

"She'd make a fine treat, eh." He pressed in close to Hannah.

She stepped back, unable to stand the stink of him. "Don't touch me or I'll scream."

"Ye'll scream?" He feigned fear. "Scream away, then." He glanced up and down the street. "Hmm, seems there's no help for convicts these days." The ugly smile returned. "Have ye forgotten yer duty . . . to serve hardworking sailors like us?"

163

Patrick tightened his hold on Lydia and dragged her toward a hotel doorway. "We'll be done and out in no time. And ye'll be richer for it."

The other sailor looked from Gwen to Hannah. "If ye give us any trouble, ye'll not get paid."

Hannah's stomach roiled, but his comments only made her angrier. "We're not convicts. My husband and I own an estate not far from here, and these ladies work for me."

With a knowing expression, the man studied Hannah. He lifted his eyebrows in an exaggerated way. "Ye expect me to believe that?" He laughed. "I suppose that's why yer dressed in such finery, eh?" He lunged at Hannah and grabbed her wrist. Her parcels fell to the walkway.

Hannah was about to scream when a hand clapped hold of the sailor's arm and wrenched him away. David Gelson thrust him backward, slamming him against the wall of a building. The air left the sailor's lungs in a loud wheeze. He slumped to the ground, gasping. David turned to the one holding Lydia. "Unhand her!"

Patrick glared at David. He didn't free her, but instead yanked her closer. "And who do ye think ye are?"

David pulled a pistol out of his belt and leveled it at the man. "A man with a gun," he stated disdainfully. "Now, release her." He fixed Patrick with a lethal stare.

The one on the ground tried to push himself up, but without thinking Hannah smashed the heel of her shoe into his face. He hollered and covered his face with his hands. Blood dribbled through his fingers and down his chin. Although shocked at what she'd done, Hannah liked the sensation of power, especially over such a loathsome person.

The scoundrel holding Lydia glanced at his friend, then

looked back at David, his eyes fixed on the pistol. "Ye'd kill a man over a tart?"

"She's no tart, but yes, I would." David's voice was deadly calm.

Patrick studied him, then took a step back and at the same time let go of Lydia's wrist. "We meant no harm. Figured they'd be happy to earn a few extra guineas; they're nothing but strumpets anyway." He tossed Lydia a scornful look. "But not worth the trouble. We'll be on our way." He moved to his friend and hauled him up from the ground. With another nervous glance at the pistol, the two moved away, disappearing around the first corner.

When they were out of sight, David pushed the pistol into his holster and turned to the women. "You ladies all right?" His eyes went to Lydia.

"We're unharmed." Lydia tidied her hair and smoothed her skirt. "Thank ye for the help."

"Yes, thank ye kindly." Gwen retied her bonnet. "Vile men like them oughtn't be allowed on the streets." She glanced down the road. "If not for you, I don't know what would have become of us."

"Thank you, David," Hannah said. "It seems there's nothing you can't do. If you'd not come along when you did . . ."

He smiled and a dimple appeared in his right cheek. "Glad I could be of assistance." He tugged at his waistcoat and smoothed his jacket. "And what brings you ladies into town?"

"We've errands to do for the Athertons," Lydia said, her voice sounding slightly ragged.

"And I'm here at Lydia and Gwen's invitation," Hannah said. She bent to retrieve her purchases.

"Allow me." David quickly gathered up the packages and sundry items and handed them to Hannah.

"Thank you." Hannah held the parcels against her chest. "We were about to go to lunch, would you care to join us?"

David glanced at Lydia, then looked at Hannah. "There's nothing I'd rather do, but I've a patient to see." He leveled a meaningful gaze on Lydia. "Perhaps another time?"

"Are ye speaking to me or to all of us?" Lydia challenged.

He smiled and the dimple reappeared. He glanced at each of the women. "I'd enjoy the company of any one of you." His eyes moved to Lydia. "But I'd especially like to spend a bit of time with you."

She folded her arms over her chest. "And what about Deidre? I doubt she'd approve of our spending time together. I thought the two of ye were a pair."

"Deidre has no say about whom I see or when. And just so you know, she and I are nothing more than acquaintances."

Arms still folded, Lydia didn't reply, but she held his gaze.

"Perhaps I could call on you at the Athertons'?"

"And why would ye do that? I'm not the kind of woman ye'd want to be seen with. I'm not at all genteel and I can promise ye I never will be."

"You're genteel enough for me."

"That's not what ye used to think. Why the change of heart?"

David glanced at Hannah and Gwen, looking a bit discomfited. His eyes meeting Lydia's, he said, "I've come to see I was wrong. I'm sorry." He reached for her hand. "Please, may I call on you?"

Lydia's gaze shifted to their two hands, then back to David's blue eyes. "If ye've a mind to call, then come 'round. I'll most likely be there."

166

David lifted Lydia's hand to his lips and pressed a gentle kiss against the back of her fingers. He released her hand and, with a nod to all the ladies, turned and walked away.

"My goodness." Gwen giggled. "He's smitten."

"He's not. I don't trust him," Lydia said. "I'm not the kind of woman for him." She glanced down at herself. "Look at me. I'm plain and broad in the hips. My mouth gets the better of me, my manners are not genteel, and I've no fancy clothing. He's used to another type of woman."

"Lydia." Hannah's tone was sharp. "Obviously he's searched his heart and come to a different conclusion. He's clearly taken with you." She jostled her packages, nearly dropping one. "Don't be so stubborn. And of course you're not at all plain. You've lovely green eyes and auburn hair. And broad hips are good for birthing babies." She smiled. "I'd say you're just what he wants."

14

"Did ye hear 'bout Charles Davies?" Perry asked John, following him out of the Atherton tool shop.

"What about him?"

"Got himself killed yesterday."

"What happened?"

"Guess he and his boy were fishin' along the river, and he had some kind of fit or something and fell in. The lad tried to save him, but . . . he couldn't do anything to help."

"Good Lord." John shook his head. "Davies was a good man, a fine bricklayer."

"He was indeed. The work he did 'ere was always first-rate."

John blew out a breath. "What about his boy? He lost his mother as well, didn't he?"

"Right. And a sister too. He's alone now."

"Poor lad. No other family?"

"Not that I ever heard of."

John was quiet. What could be said about someone newly orphaned? An image of his own father, showing him how to secure a worm on a hook, flickered through his mind. He couldn't imagine having to grow up without him. "What's to become of the boy?"

Perry shrugged. "Heard he was stayin' with the Roberts family. Not doin' so well, though. Won't speak a word."

"Can't say that I blame him. Thomas is his name, right?"

"Yeah."

"How old is he?"

"Ten, I'd guess."

Heaviness of heart settled over John. "It's a shame."

"Figure the Lord will look after him."

John nodded. "Well, I better be on my way." He moved to his horse, untied the reins from the hitching post, and swung up into the saddle. "Hannah's waiting for me. If I don't get home soon, she'll start worrying."

"Right then, have a good day."

John rested his hands on the saddle horn. "By the way, the shop's looking splendid. You're doing a fine job."

"I wouldn't even be 'ere without ye. Yer the one put Mr. Atherton on to me." Perry lifted his hat slightly before resetting it on his head. "So, I thank ye." He smiled. "I like the work. And I'm a pretty good hand at toolmaking. Who would 'ave figured, eh?" He grinned.

"I knew you'd do well." John lifted the reins.

"Another thing, before ye go—I was wondering what ye think of me getting married?"

John raised his eyebrows. He'd been waiting for Perry to say something about Gwen. "I guess that would depend on who you're thinking of marrying."

"Gwen, of course. She's a fine gal. What do ye think, eh?"

"The two of you seem right for each other. I think it's a good idea." The horse restlessly moved from one foot to the other.

169

"What about Lydia? Do you still have feelings for her? I'd hate to see you marry Gwen when you're smitten with Lydia."

Perry scratched the back of his head, pushing his hat forward. "Don't know that I'll ever be over her completely. But I know we're not good for each other, not that way anyways. I've a good friend in her, though." He looked toward the main house. "And Gwen, well, she's a good lady. I love her. And I think she loves me."

"If you love her, that's all that matters." John smiled.

With a nod, Perry took a step toward the shop. "So, ye'll be back next week, then?"

"Sunday. Hannah and some of the ladies have planned to get together after services." A gust of wind caught at John's hat. He grabbed hold of it and glanced at dark clouds rolling across the sky. "Looks like foul weather. Better get home before it hits. I've a batch of new lambs that'll need sheltering. They seem almost eager to die in their first weeks—doesn't take much to put them down."

"I heard ye had some new ones." Perry shook his head. "Can't see ye caring for lambs."

"It's hard work. Maybe you ought to try it."

"Not for me. I'll see ye Sunday." Perry sauntered toward the shop.

John rode away, trotting toward the road. His thoughts immediately went to Charles Davies and his son, Thomas. Thank the Lord there's someone to care for the lad.

Deidre strolled across the grounds and stepped into the roadway. Wearing a friendly expression, she planted her hands on her hips and waited for him.

She's the last person I want to see. John pulled back on the reins and slowed his horse, then stopped alongside Deidre.

"Good day." Her eyes held John's. "I was hoping to have a word with ye."

"Oh? What about?" John knew exactly what about.

"Life can be dreadful, especially for a woman living on her own. It's a lonely, harsh existence. I've nearly no supplies at all. I won't make it to summer."

John's anger boiled and he gripped the reins more tightly.

"I was wondering if ye could see yer way to sending me another hog and getting some staples for my larder."

"I already gave you more than I had to give, and it's only been a couple of weeks since. If you're running short, then I'd say you ought to guard your goods more carefully."

Her butter-soft tone gone, Deidre asked, "Are you suggesting that I'm careless and wasteful?"

"Make of it what you like."

She folded her arms over her chest. "No matter. I shan't make it without help. And you're the one God's called to come to my aid."

"He's not called me to do anything for you." John looked down the road. He wanted to charge past the malicious strumpet and get home to Hannah. "I've done all I can."

"No ye haven't." Deidre's eyes narrowed. "Ye'll do more."

John squared his jaw and glared down at her. "I won't. I'll do nothing."

She sighed in an exaggerated way. "Ye will. Ye've no choice." She smiled malevolently.

John could stand no more. He leaned forward and tried to ride past. She moved quickly to block his way and grabbed hold of the reins. Startled, the horse pulled against the restraint, dancing and tossing his head.

She held tight. Deidre was sturdier than she looked. "I'll expect flour and cornmeal, some turnips, molasses, and another hog. And I'll be needing cash for fabric."

"What in the world will ye do with another hog?"

Deidre looked at him with a wicked grin. "I've been awfully hungry of late."

"You sold it!" John exploded. "I can't do more. You'll have to look elsewhere for your help."

Deidre smiled and acted as if she'd not heard him. She stepped back a pace and lifted her skirt just enough to reveal the toe of one shoe. "I'll be making a trip to the cobbler's. My shoes are in deplorable condition as ye can see."

"I don't care a whit about your shoes. Let loose of the reins."

Deidre's expression turned hard. John felt as if he were facing off with a deadly viper. *She'd murder if it suited her.*

"You'll do as I say or I'll go to Reverend Taylor."

"You've chosen the wrong man for your extortion. You'd be better off finding someone who had something to give."

"But this is much more fun." Deidre chuckled.

John knew he was trapped. What could he say that would make a difference? "How am I to give you what you're asking for without being found out? Hannah will notice that goods are missing. I already lied about the ewes and the hog."

"Did ye come up with a good story?"

John glared at her. He wasn't about to tell her anything. But he remembered the guilt he'd felt when he'd told Hannah the ewes had wandered off and that he'd sold the hog. He wasn't accustomed to lying.

"What ye say to yer wife is yer problem. It doesn't bother me in the least if she knows. Why do ye care?" She turned away and started back to the house. Glancing over her shoulder, she said, "I shan't be working tomorrow. I'll expect ye."

John felt like a rat caught in a trap. While he watched her walk away, her question, "Why do ye care?" rang through his mind.

Of course I can't tell Hannah. She already has enough to worry about. What good will it do if I tell her? John knew there was more to it. Deidre made him feel small. She had power over him. It was his duty to look after and to protect Hannah, and he was failing her.

There was a truth John didn't want to look at—something he could scarcely consider. The secret Deidre held was ugly. Just that she knew was frightening. How was it that she had knowledge of Hannah's past? A past John wanted to forget, to pretend had never happened. If Hannah were to stand with him against Deidre, her past couldn't be forgotten—instead it became part of the present.

His jaw set, John scanned the Atherton grounds and seemed almost unaware of Hannah. He offered her a hand down from the wagon, then reached into the back and lifted out a picnic basket. "Where would you like it?"

"Because the weather's so nice, Catharine thought it best to eat on the veranda." She glanced up at a cloudless sky, then back at John. He'd not been himself. He was quieter than usual and seemed tense. "John, is everything all right?"

"Yes. Of course."

"You're sure?"

"What could be wrong?"

"That's what I'm wondering. You don't seem yourself."

"Everything's fine. I've a bit of a headache is all."

"All right, then. I'll find Lydia." Still certain something was troubling John, Hannah strolled toward Lydia's cabin. The door opened before Hannah had a chance to knock.

Wearing a broad smile, Lydia grasped Hannah's hands. "This will be great fun. David is joining us." She stepped onto the porch. "Do I look all right?" She made a small turn.

"Yes. Lovely."

"I mean, is my hair in place and—"

"You look beautiful. And David will think so too."

"I know I shouldn't worry. But it hasn't been that long since we started seeing each other again."

"I doubt you have anything to fret about."

Lydia looped her arm through Hannah's. "I hope yer right." The two set off toward the main house. "It's grand that the Athertons have included me. After all, I'm a domestic and a convict."

"They're truly gracious people."

"I daresay, there are some who would take offense if they knew."

Hannah felt her stomach rumble. "I'm starved. John stayed after church to speak to the reverend. He's making some tools for the church that will be kept on the premises."

"That's a fine idea." Lydia's stomach growled loudly and she exclaimed, "I'm so hungry I could eat an entire cow."

When the two friends climbed the veranda steps, Catharine Atherton greeted Hannah with a hug. "You're looking lovely, dear. I wish you'd visit more often."

"I'd like to, but there's always so much to be done at home." She moved onto the veranda and smiled at William Atherton who sat in a slat-backed chair. "Thank you for inviting us."

William stood. "We're glad to have you." After Hannah and Lydia found seats, he sat down.

174

"It's not too chilly, is it?" Catharine asked, taking the chair beside her husband.

"No. It's perfect," Hannah said.

William slung his right leg over the left. "Heard summer's expected early this year. Supposed to be hotter than usual too."

"I could do with some warm weather," John said, leaning against the railing. He kept looking about, as if searching or waiting for someone.

Hannah felt a queasiness in the pit of her stomach. Something was wrong. She could feel it.

"Is everything all right, John?" Catharine asked.

"Fine. Everything's fine," he said, sitting beside Hannah.

"Good. You seem a bit unsettled."

"Do I?" He leaned back and clasped his hands on his stomach. The pose looked relaxed, but he tightened and then loosened his grip several times while tapping the heels of his boots against the wooden floor of the porch.

When Mrs. Goudy served tea, Hannah thought she also seemed on edge and actually acted unfriendly toward John. She'd never been a callous person, so when she passed John by the first time while serving the tea, Hannah was sure it had simply been an oversight, but then she also ignored him when she distributed biscuits. Mrs. Atherton had to remind her to serve John. Mrs. Goudy did so but wasn't at all friendly when she offered him the sweet.

It was so unlike her that Hannah excused herself and sought out the cook. She stepped into the kitchen. "Mrs. Goudy, you seem a bit out of sorts. Is there something troubling you?"

"No, dear. I'm right as rain." She poured water into a crystal pitcher.

175

"You didn't mean to skip over my husband when you were serving, then?"

Mrs. Goudy didn't look at Hannah. And she didn't answer the question.

"There *is* something wrong. What is it?"

"Nothing. I'm sure your friends are missing you—"

"Have I done something to offend you? Or has John?"

"No. Of course not." She picked up the pitcher. "I'd best get back to work. And Dalton is expecting me. The Athertons have guests coming next week, and we need to work out a proper schedule and a menu."

Deciding to ignore Mrs. Goudy's unusual mood, Hannah took a step toward the dining room, but something inside told her it was more than Mrs. Goudy's bad mood. She turned back to face the woman. "Please tell me what's wrong. Perhaps I can be of some help."

The woman's blue eyes rested on Hannah. "It would be best if you let this go."

"But if I've done something."

"No. You haven't."

"What is it, then?"

Mrs. Goudy set down the pitcher. "I don't want you hurt, dear."

Alarm thumped through Hannah. "Whatever do you mean?"

"I'm not one to carry tales . . ." She compressed her lips. "But I also don't believe it's right to stand by idly while someone I care about is being ill treated."

"You're frightening me. What is it that has you so concerned?"

Mrs. Goudy glanced toward the veranda and then back at

Hannah. "There's no way 'round it, except to come out with it." Her eyes filled with tears. "I've seen John with Deidre O'Neil on more than one occasion. And I've heard tell he's been seen at her cottage as well . . . with gifts."

Shock and disbelief swept through Hannah. "What do you mean, he's been seen with her?"

"Just that. They've been alone together, and he's visited her cottage, always taking her things."

"Are you implying . . . that my husband has been unfaithful?" Trembling, Hannah's fingers played over her collar.

"I only know what I've seen and heard. And I know Deidre. She's out for men, especially those who might be of . . . benefit to her. I must admit I find the idea unbelievable. John's always seemed a gentleman, but the wiles of a woman have been known to bring down even the best man."

Hannah whirled around so her back was to Mrs. Goudy. Hurt and outrage boiled through her. She pressed a closed fist to her mouth. *How could he? John would never* . . . But even while Hannah tried to comfort herself with how noble John had always been, she also knew he was just a man. And recently, he hadn't been acting like himself.

"I'm sorry, dear," Mrs. Goudy said and hurried out of the room.

Feeling as if her feet were glued to the floor, Hannah stood in the kitchen, unable to comprehend the possibility that John had been unfaithful. *What should I do? How can I go out there and face him? Face them? They probably all know.*

"Hannah?" John called.

The sound of the door closing carried from the front of the house. His steps echoed across the vestibule and the wood floor in the dining room.

"Ah, there you are. I was wondering . . ." He stopped and stared at Hannah. "What is it? What's happened?"

Hannah glowered at him. "How could you?"

"How could I what?"

"You know what I'm talking about."

"I don't." He moved to Hannah, but she pulled away.

"I trusted you." She looked at John through a blur of tears. "And with Deidre? Why Deidre?"

"What do you mean?"

"I know. Mrs. Goudy told me. She saw you and . . . and her. Others have seen you too."

"What do you mean?"

"You've been seeing that woman! Stop acting innocent!"

John looked stricken. Hannah had hoped he'd deny the charges, explain that it was all just a misunderstanding. Instead he turned pale and said nothing.

"So. It's true, then." Hannah thought she might be sick.

"No. It's not what you're thinking. I was there, but I'm not interested in Deidre O'Neil, not like that. I could never be."

"Then what have you been doing at her house? And why have you been giving her gifts? And all without telling me."

John stared at the floor for a long while. When he finally looked at Hannah, his amber eyes were bleak. "I know it looks bad, but I've done nothing wrong." He hesitated, then added, "Except that I've kept something from you."

"You admit it, then."

His eyes bore into hers. "Of course not. I'd not lay a hand on Deidre O'Neil." Then so quietly that Hannah could barely hear him, he said, "She knows."

"What does she know?"

178

"She knows about Judge Walker, about the baby . . . she knows everything."

The room spun and Hannah grabbed for something to steady herself. John took hold of her arm and guided her to a chair.

Hannah's mind was awhirl with questions. "How can she know? Who told her?" Her eyes focused on John. "And what has it to do with you?"

"She threatened to tell the elders. I couldn't allow her to besmirch your name. She's been demanding goods from me . . . otherwise she'll speak to the reverend and the church leaders."

Hannah's shock swelled into fury. "How dare she?" Hannah stood. "Where is she? I'll speak to her!"

"It will do no good. I've tried to reason with her. I even tried to bully her, but nothing made a difference." John gently grasped Hannah's arms. "I didn't want you to know. I'd hoped that she'd let it go, but she continues to demand goods for her silence." He rested a hand on her shoulder. "I'm sorry. I've botched things terribly."

"No. It's not your fault. And I'm sorry I thought you and she . . . were . . . well, you know."

"I can see how someone might think that. But I thought you knew me better."

"I do. I'm sorry." Hannah let out a heavy breath. "How does she know? I told no one except Lydia and Catharine."

"Perhaps she overheard a conversation."

Hannah thought back to the day she'd talked to Lydia in the main dining room. Deidre hadn't even been living here at the time. Catharine would never say a word. "If she asks for anything more, don't give it to her."

"Hannah, you don't know what she's like."

"Oh, there you are," Lydia said. "I was wondering—"

Hannah's anger flared and she turned on Lydia. "Did you speak to Deidre? Did you tell her . . ." She quieted her voice. "Did you tell her about Judge Walker and the baby?"

Lydia's eyes grew large and she pressed a hand to her mouth.

"Did you?"

Lydia looked at the floor. "When she first came, I . . . She acted so nice . . . and when she asked what was troubling you, I told her." Lydia hurried on. "I'm so sorry. I didn't mean to break a confidence, but she seemed to be a thoughtful, kind person. I never—"

"I trusted you." Hannah felt betrayed to her core. Unable to look at Lydia, she said, "John, we're leaving." She kept her eyes straight ahead and walked toward the front of the house. What excuse could she give the Athertons?

"I'm sorry, Hannah. Has something happened? Did Deidre say something?"

Hannah turned on Lydia. "Oh yes! She's said something! She's threatened to tell the elders if we don't keep her larder full! I'll be ruined." The hurt was so deep and powerful, it seemed to choke Hannah. She couldn't speak.

Lydia stepped toward her.

Hannah moved back. "How could you?"

"Please forgive me. I . . . I never intended any harm."

"I don't care what you intended. It's what you've done. Not only have you placed my reputation in jeopardy, but John's as well." She glanced toward the veranda. "Mrs. Goudy believes him to be an adulterer."

"Oh." Lydia's hand went to her mouth. "I'll make sure to set her straight."

"How can you do that without telling her what's happened? I'd say your mouth has caused enough trouble already."

Lydia looked befuddled. "I can't tell ye how deep my regret is. I'm so sorry. Please forgive me."

"I can't forgive you. Not ever." Hannah swept out of the room.

15

As John approached Patrick Roberts's cottage, his stomach felt as if it had been tethered with a leather band. All was quiet and it seemed no one was about. He slowed his horse and studied the small, drab house. It was made of bark planking and had a thatched roof. The family obviously had little means. An extra mouth to feed would be a burden.

Patrick Roberts had been Charles Davies' closest friend, and when Thomas was orphaned, he and his wife had taken in the lad. The word about the district was that they couldn't manage and sadly were forced to find another home for the child.

John sucked in a breath and considered turning about and going home. No one had seen him. They wouldn't know he'd been here.

I've not given this enough thought. I've not even talked to Hannah.

Ever since hearing about the accident, John's thoughts had often traipsed to Thomas, wondering what had become of him. When he heard the Robertses were looking to find a home for the boy, he'd acted on impulse and come here straightaway.

I ought to speak to Hannah. I'm sure it's not necessary, she'll want him. She's been pining for a child. John knew he was simply putting off asking the Robertses, afraid he was too late and someone else had already come for the boy or that the Robertses had changed their minds and decided to keep him.

He stared at the house, hoping someone would open the door while at the same time afraid that they would. John pulled the reins over the horse's neck and turned him back toward the road and moved away. *No one is here, at any rate.*

He wondered if he'd ever seen Thomas. He didn't remember the boy. *I wonder what he looks like.* He imagined a strapping young lad with a quick smile. *It doesn't matter. He's a lad who needs a home. And Hannah and I need a child.*

Hannah had been especially lonely since her falling-out with Lydia. Plus another month had passed with no baby. Perhaps this boy would be the balm she needed. Although John had hoped for a child of his own, he was beginning to believe it would never happen. He feared God truly was holding Hannah under discipline. They had been married nearly a year with no pregnancy. *Perhaps this is our child. This is the one God has chosen.*

He glanced over his shoulder, then turned the horse around and trotted back to the house. When he reached the porch, he stopped, swung out of the saddle, looped the reins over the porch railing, and stepped up to the front door. He listened for any sound from inside. Nothing. He stared at the door and then lifted his hand and knocked. No one answered. He knocked again.

"Who's there?" a woman's voice finally asked from behind the door.

"John Bradshaw. I'm here . . . on personal business." He heard a latch lift and the door creaked open. A bird-thin woman

183

dressed in a faded green gown peered out from the dark interior. "What can I do for ye?"

John managed to smile. "I heard you and your family took in Charles Davies's boy."

"That we did." She opened the door a bit wider. "Why do ye ask?"

John removed his hat. "Would you mind if I came in?"

Uncertain blue eyes studied him. "I guess it would be all right." She moved back and opened the door wider.

John stepped inside. The room was clean, but contained only necessities—two wooden chairs, a small table, a mat on the floor, and a rope bed partially hidden behind a quilt. The only exception to the starkness was a delicate china cup and saucer, which sat on display on a wooden mantel.

"I'm John Bradshaw, ma'am."

"I've seen ye 'bout town. Ye work for Mr. Atherton, don't ye?"

"I used to. I've my own place now, me and my wife." It felt good to be able to say he owned his own property. "We're not far out of Parramatta."

The woman nodded. "I'm Mrs. Roberts. Me husband's not 'ere just now."

Even without Patrick Roberts there, John had to speak his mind; he just didn't know exactly what to say. Mrs. Roberts relieved him of the responsibility.

"Are ye 'ere 'bout the boy?"

"Yes. I heard about what happened and that he's in need of a home."

"He's not to be used for labor. He's a fine lad and deserves better than that."

"No. Of course not. I—"

"Ye best talk to me husband. He's the one to make such decisions. He's in the back pasture." She opened the door and stepped onto the porch. "Just go 'round the house and follow the trail."

"Yes, ma'am." John replaced his hat and moved outside. Mrs. Roberts wasn't exactly the friendly type. He wondered if he'd misunderstood about their wanting to find a home for the boy. He moved to his horse.

"Do ye have other children?" the woman asked.

"No. We don't. We'd like to, though."

Mrs. Roberts nodded. "Ye best speak to me husband. He's out there with our two, and Tommy."

"Thank you." John climbed into the saddle.

"He's a fine lad. I wouldn't want him going to someone who'd be harsh with him. He's had enough hurts in his life."

Her concern warmed John's heart. "I'm looking for a son, not a hired hand. And it would seem he needs a father."

Sorrow touched the woman's eyes. "Good, then." She started to close the door, then stopped and said, "We'd keep him if we could."

"I understand." John tipped his hat. "Good day to you."

He followed the trail leading to the back pasture. The sun was hot and flies swarmed, but John barely noticed. He could feel hope growing inside and imagined how he and Thomas would get along, how they'd work side by side, go fishing together, and build a friendship, and one day, if God were good, Thomas would see him as his father. *Don't be hoping for too much*, John cautioned himself.

The trail followed a broken-down fence where hungry-looking cattle grazed on tufts of grass. There was little natural feed to be had. John wondered why any man would stake out such a poor piece of ground.

He hadn't ridden far when he saw a tall, thin man and three boys unloading posts from a dray. They stopped and watched him. Two of the youngsters were tall and thin, like the man, and the other was short and stocky.

"Good day," the man said.

"Good day," John replied.

Swiping his hat off his head and gazing up at John, he wiped his forehead with his shirtsleeve. "What can I do for ye?"

John dismounted. "I'm John Bradshaw. I have a place north of here."

"Patrick Roberts." The man offered John his hand. He looked scrawny, but his grip was strong.

"I was hoping I could have a word with you . . ." John's eyes went to the boys. "About a personal matter." He tried not to stare at the stocky lad. "Could we speak in private?"

"That we can." Mr. Roberts resettled his hat on his head and turned to the boys. "Allen, ye can drive the dray up a ways by that tree there, and then the three of ye can unload the rest of those posts."

"Right, Dad." The older of the boys clambered onto the seat of the cart, taking the reins in his hands and slapping the hind end of a mule, while the other two youngsters clambered into the back.

John and Patrick watched them move along the fence line. "The work never ends. But they're good 'uns, all three of 'em." Patrick turned pale blue eyes on John. His faced was tanned and lined from years of working in the sun. "So, what is it ye wanted to speak to me 'bout?"

"Thomas. I understand he's in need of a home."

"That he is. He's a fine lad. Wish we could keep him with us, but we've not enough to feed another mouth." Patrick folded his arms over his chest. "Why is it ye want him?"

John felt uncomfortable. He wasn't used to sharing his private life with a stranger. "My wife and I have been married nearly a year and we've had no children. In time they may come, but with Thomas needing a family, I thought we might be of help to each other. I've a farm not far from here. Hannah and I don't have a lot, but we've more than enough to share with a young lad."

John's eyes went to the boy. "Is he the smaller one with the blond hair?"

"That's him." Patrick's voice seemed to catch.

"He looks strong."

"He is and a hard worker too." Patrick scrutinized John. "Ye a God-fearing man?"

"I am, my wife too. We rarely miss Sunday services."

Patrick watched the boys and then turned to John. "Ye wouldn't be lookin' for free labor, would ye?"

"No. That's got nothing to do with wanting to take Thomas into our home."

Roberts was silent for a few moments. "I figure ye and yer wife would make good parents. I've heard yer name spoken well of. If his mother and father knew he ended up in a respectable home, they'd rest easy." His voice diminished to a whisper. He blinked several times, then continued, "Charles and I were mates. We come over on the same ship. His missus and mine were close too."

He watched as the dray continued to move up the path. "I'll tell ye, though, Thomas hasn't been himself since . . . well, since it happened. He's usually bright and cheery, but he's been low

187

and doesn't talk much. He'll come 'round given time, though, I'm sure."

"Of course."

Roberts shoved his hands into his pockets. "I suppose ye ought to meet him."

John's arms and legs felt tight, the palms of his hands were wet, and his mouth was dry. He rolled his shoulders back, trying to relax his muscles. Walking alongside Mr. Roberts, he thought about what he ought to say.

"Hold up there, lads," Patrick called. The one driving the dray yanked on the reins, and the mule stopped.

"I've got someone I'd like ye to meet." The boys climbed off the cart. Patrick turned to John. "This is John Bradshaw. He's got a place near here."

The youngsters gazed at John and said quiet hellos. John smiled and nodded. "Good to meet you." His eyes stopped on Thomas. He was a handsome child with blond hair and blue eyes.

Patrick moved to the boy. "Thomas, Mr. Bradshaw wants ye to live with him and his wife. They've a fine farm. And they're good people."

Thomas's eyes widened and then narrowed, his mouth became a tight line. He glared at John and then turned a bleak expression to Patrick. "I thought I was goin' to stay 'ere with ye."

"We want ye to, lad, but . . . well, we just don't have the means." Patrick knelt in front of the boy. "Mr. Bradshaw's a God-fearing man, and him and his wife are wanting a son. It's the right thing for ye." He gently squeezed the boy's arms, then abruptly he stood. "Go on with ye now. And make sure to stop by the house and pick up yer things."

188

Patrick squared back his shoulders. Thomas stared up at him. Patrick didn't look down, but set his gaze on the distant field. "No time for gawking. Go on now."

Not knowing just what to do, John rested a hand on the youngster's shoulder.

Thomas flinched and pulled away. "I'll go with ye, but yer not me dad." Hands shoved in his pockets, he walked down the trail toward the house.

⁕

With Thomas riding behind him, John tried to think of something else to say. He'd asked the boy questions about what he liked to do, and had told him a little about the property, but Thomas made it clear he wasn't interested in chatting. And somehow, he'd maintained a space between himself and John while keeping his seat.

"Our farm is right on the Parramatta. It's nothing fancy, but one day it'll be grand." No response. John tried again. "There's good fishing on the river. Do you like to fish?"

Thomas didn't answer.

"We've some new lambs that'll need special looking after. You ever work with sheep?"

Thomas remained silent. Finally, John gave up. *Perhaps Hannah will do better. Women have a way with children.*

When they turned onto their drive, John said, "That's our place. The house is new. Your room is upstairs." When Thomas didn't say anything, John continued, "We've a garden. It's coming along nicely. There are carrots and turnips, potatoes too."

Jackson loped toward John and the boy. "Oh, and we've a dog. His name's Jackson."

Thomas made no reply.

189

Jackson beat the air with his tail, ready to greet John and the boy.

John stopped in front of the house. "Hope Hannah's got dinner ready. You hungry? She's a fine cook."

The front door opened and Hannah stepped out. She wiped her hands on her apron. "John. I was beginning to wonder where you'd gotten to." She looked at Thomas. "Who do we have here?"

"This is Thomas Davies." He turned and offered Thomas a hand down, but the boy ignored the assistance and threw one leg over the horse's backside and dropped to the ground. Still wagging his tail, Jackson sniffed the newcomer. Thomas pulled his arms in close and pulled away, ignoring the dog's greeting.

John dismounted. Placing a hand on the lad's back, he guided him closer to the front porch. "Hannah, you remember that Charles Davies . . . died a few weeks ago."

"Yes . . . I do."

"Well, this is his boy, Thomas."

Hannah's eyes widened slightly. She stared at Thomas and then looked hard at John, as if trying to read his thoughts. She pressed a hand to her mouth, then asked in a controlled voice, "John, what have you done?"

"He needed a home." John hesitated. Hannah didn't look at all pleased. "He'll be staying with us."

Hannah dropped her arms to her sides, looked at Thomas and then John. "How long will he be staying?"

"Indefinitely."

Hannah couldn't hide her shock. "You said not a word to me."

Oh, Lord, John thought, realizing he'd made a terrible mistake. Hannah was angry, not pleased.

190

"I know this is unexpected, but if you give it some thought, I'm sure you'll see what a grand idea it is. And I'm certain you and Thomas will get on splendidly." He looked at Thomas. "Would you mind putting the horse in the stock pen? Give him a drink of water and a handful of grain too, eh. There's some just inside the barn door. And an armful of hay would be good as well."

Thomas didn't do as asked immediately. Instead he set cool blue eyes on Hannah. His frown deepened, and finally he turned, grabbed hold of the horse's reins, and plodded toward the pen.

Hannah watched him, then moved close to John and whispered, "How could you?"

"How could I what?"

"Bring home a child without speaking to me about it."

"I thought you'd be happy. We've been wanting a child. And the poor boy needs—"

"You said we weren't to worry, that you were certain we'd have our own, that God wasn't punishing me." She glared at him. "You didn't believe that at all. It was a lie." She whirled about and stomped into the house.

"Hannah." John followed her. "I just thought Thomas needed us and that we needed him."

"That's not true. You thought my sin so grave that God would withhold his blessings of children. I know I'm not deserving of a child, but as long as you believed, I could too." Hannah's eyes brimmed with tears. "I'd hoped. I thought you did too."

Hannah's response startled John. "I haven't lost hope. But sometimes we don't get what we want. I just thought he'd be a child for us to love. He needs us."

Hannah picked up the broom and swept up embers from around the hearth. "I want children of our own, not someone else's child." She stopped, and gripping the broom handle, she stated, "He can stay until you find someone else to take him. I can't be a mother to him."

"Lower your voice. He'll hear you." John pulled off his hat. "If you could mother Lottie, why not this lad?"

"It was different. We were on the ship and survival was our utmost thought. She needed me to survive."

"And he doesn't?"

Hannah's eyes went to the window. "I just can't, John. Not now."

"There is no one else. And think what it will do to him if we send him off. He's suffered enough." Hannah's reaction shocked John. He'd never expected this. He moved to the window and watched Thomas. His arms full of hay, he moved toward the crib. His expression was grim.

"There's something wrong with him, John." Hannah's tone was firm. "He didn't speak a word and his eyes were filled with hate."

"Not hate, sorrow . . . and rejection. He's lost everything. How would you expect him to react, especially when you looked at him as if he had two heads? Where were your open arms? I thought you'd be a mum to him. That's what he needs."

Regret and sorrow replaced John's anticipation and his dreams. He'd made a grave error.

Hannah dropped onto a chair. Silence pervaded the room. Finally she said, "I'm sorry, John. I don't want to hurt him. I'm just shocked. I'm not prepared. You should have told me before bringing him here."

The anger in Hannah's eyes was gone.

"I'm sorry, luv. I heard that the Robertses needed a home for him, and so I went. I was sure you'd be thrilled. We've longed for a child."

"Yes. Our child. John, you should have asked me first." Tears shimmered in Hannah's brown eyes. "I believed what you said—that God wasn't going to punish me. I see now that you were just being kind. God will never give us children."

"But he has—this boy."

"Thomas is not ours."

"He will be if we make him so."

"I'm sorry, but no. Can't you take him back to the family he was with?"

"No. I can't." John squared his jaw. "I won't do that to him. His mum and sister died on a prison ship two years ago. Now his father's gone too, and the people who were looking after him gave him away. They had no means."

"And neither have we."

"If you were carrying a child of our own making, we'd find a way. There'd be no question about if we could care for it."

Hannah stared at John through tears. "You've brought this boy into our house without a word from me and now you're saying I must live with your decision, that I have no choice but to become his mother?" Hannah shook her head. "I don't want to be his mother."

A board popped, resonating from the front of the house. Hannah and John turned to see Thomas standing in the doorway.

His blue eyes were hard, his mouth set, and his hands were balled into fists. "I didn't ask to be 'ere. I don't need ye. I'll not trouble ye further." He turned and trudged down the steps.

16

John stopped the wagon in the churchyard, then looked at Thomas who sat in the back. "Well, this is it. You'll like church. We've good friends here and the reverend's a fine man."

Thomas glowered and didn't respond. He sat with his knees held tight against his chest and stared at nothing in particular.

Hannah glanced at the boy. She felt no love for him and puzzled over why. She'd always thought of herself as a caring person. But Thomas was different from the children she'd known. Since the first day, he'd been trouble. When he'd run off, John had gone after him, and the boy came only when forced; John had to drag him part of the way. It had been a terrible scene and she and John had quarreled. They didn't speak to each other for a full day.

Thomas had threatened to run off again at the first opportunity, but he hadn't. Hannah was certain the only reason he didn't flee was that he had nowhere to go. He felt no affection for either her or John and wanted nothing to do with the farm.

Sadly, she had to admit that it would be best for all if he lived elsewhere. She closed her eyes and sent up a quick prayer. *Lord, I pray for patience. And if it's possible, help us to love each other, all of us. Please put an end to what's going on in my home.* The peace that had once been part of her and John's life was gone; instead, each day was a series of emotional challenges.

"Come on, lad," John said, climbing down from the wagon. "Make the best of it, eh? You can try it. You just might discover there are people here you like. There are several lads your age. I'm sure you'll find a friend among them."

Still looking surly, Thomas climbed out of the back.

Hannah noticed his hair wasn't properly combed and his clothes looked like he'd slept in them. He'd refused any help or instruction, and she'd not pressed her standards of dress and cleanliness for fear of another clash.

Thomas shoved his hands into his pockets and trudged toward the church. He walked around to the side, leaned against the building, and stared at the ground. John watched him for a moment and then gave Hannah a hand down from the wagon.

"John, what are we to do with him? He hates us. He doesn't want to live with us. Perhaps it would be better if you took him back to—"

"They can't keep him, Hannah. You know that."

"Perhaps someone else would take him in."

"Hannah." John's voice was tight. "We can't do that. We've got to stick to this and find a way." He turned toward Thomas. "Look at him. He's already so downtrodden that I don't know if he'll recover. What will happen to him if we pass him off to someone else?"

"I understand, but how can we help when he hates us, especially me? After what I said, I doubt he'll ever forgive me."

"He needs time. If we remain steady in our love, eventually

he'll know he's safe. And he'll come round." John gave Hannah's hand a quick squeeze and then strode toward the boy.

Watching John walk away, Hannah could muster little hope that things would improve. Even if Thomas learned to tolerate them, she didn't know if she could ever fully be a mother to him. She walked slowly toward the church. Catching sight of Deidre, her mind turned to the other trouble in their lives. What would they do about her?

<hr />

"Come on, lad." John rested a hand on the youngster's shoulder and turned him toward the church steps.

"I'll go in, but I'm not singing and I'm not listening to anything the reverend says."

"Just sit then and be quiet." John looked at Hannah, his frustration evident.

"God's got no use for me and I've no use for him," Thomas said.

Hannah felt a pang of regret and grief. She remembered feeling just as Thomas had. Once, she'd believed God had turned away from her. How, then, could she have so little sympathy for the boy? *Lord, I've been despicable. Forgive me. I want to love him fiercely, as I would my own, as you have loved me.*

"Hannah," Gwen called, hurrying toward her. She glanced at John and Thomas, then said quietly, "Perry told me 'bout Thomas. How kind of ye to take him in. Ye must be thrilled to have a child in the house."

Hannah smiled. "Of course we're pleased."

John and Thomas walked toward Perry who slapped John on the back and then bent to shake Thomas's hand.

"He's still unsettled and distraught as you can imagine," Hannah continued. "But at least we can offer him a place to lay his head at night and food to fill his stomach."

Mr. and Mrs. Atherton's carriage rolled into the yard. One of the servants' wagons followed. Hannah caught sight of Lydia but immediately looked away, turning her back on her onetime friend. She couldn't speak to her.

Catharine Atherton stepped out of the carriage and moved toward Hannah. "Good day, dear." She kissed Hannah's cheek. "We missed you last week. I heard you took in the Davies boy. It's splendid that he's living with you. I know you'll make fine parents."

"We'll do our best," was all Hannah could say. She couldn't bear for Catharine to know the truth of the situation. She looked at John and the lad, and then her eyes locked with John's. The two silently heartened one another. Hannah smiled at Thomas, but his expression remained gloomy. Inwardly, she quaked at her own weakness. *I can love him*, she told herself. She hoped that underneath Thomas's angry exterior there lived a child who needed to be cherished and who wanted to love others.

Lydia approached. She slowed slightly and glanced at Hannah as she walked past. Although Hannah knew she was there, she refused to look at her or acknowledge her in any way. Lydia moved on.

Catharine watched Lydia walk up the church steps and disappear through the front door. "What's happened between you two?"

"I can't talk about it."

"You two were so close. There must be something that can be done to repair your friendship."

"People aren't always who you think they are." Hurt welled up as if she'd just learned of Lydia's betrayal.

Catharine let out a sigh. "It's hard to believe, after all you've been through together that—"

"Some things just can't be mended." Hannah caught John's eye, and wanting to avoid any further discussion, she said, "Please excuse me. John's waiting."

John met Hannah at the bottom of the stairway. "Shall we go in together?"

Hannah leaned in close to him and looped her arm through his. She smiled down at Thomas and felt a stirring of affection. "I'm glad you're with us, Thomas. Truly."

He stared back, his blue eyes cool and wary.

Hannah tried to hang on to the warmth she'd felt. "Shall we go in?"

She and John walked up the steps together and into the church. Thomas followed. When they moved indoors, neighbors and friends greeted them warmly, offering congratulations and greeting the new member of the Bradshaw home. Thomas kept his lips shut tight and refused to respond to any of them, not even offering a nod. Hannah was awash with guilt. It seemed everyone saw her and John as the boy's saviors, but she didn't feel in the least like one.

Charlotte Smith, Lottie's adoptive mother, grasped Hannah's hand. "I heard," she said, barely able to contain her joy. "How wonderful for you and John. And for Thomas. I've never regretted adopting Lottie. She was a gift from the Lord. And now you've been blessed in the same way." She kissed Hannah's cheek. "I know you'll make a wonderful mother."

Hannah's emotions tumbled inside. She wasn't sure what she felt. There was guilt over not treating Thomas the way she ought, while at the same time she also felt that his coming to her home might well be a blessing, an opportunity to be a

198

mother—if only she could hang on to that. And the jealousy she sometimes felt over Lottie hung in the back of her mind like a shadow. She loved the little girl. If only things had been different, if only she'd been able to keep Lottie. When Charlotte had offered to adopt her, Hannah knew it had been God's hand that put the two together. Charlotte had longed for a little one, and prison was no place for a child.

Hannah glanced at Thomas. Was he God's gift to her and John? *Lord, I need your heart, not mine.*

She focused on Charlotte. "John and I are doing our best."

"Oh, I know. It's not always easy."

"No, it isn't." Hannah managed to smile. John and Thomas moved on, finding a seat near the back of the church.

"I want you to know that Charles and I are praying for you. In the beginning it can be difficult, but one day you'll love that boy just as if he were your own."

Hannah was startled to hear such advice coming from Charlotte. She'd always assumed that Charlotte and Lottie had instantly bonded. "I'm sure you're right," Hannah said. "And thank you for your prayers." Her eyes found Thomas. Staring straight ahead, he sat beside John. She tried to imagine the boy loving her but couldn't visualize such a thing.

"You know, at first Lottie wasn't happy to be with Charles and me. She wanted to be with you."

Hannah stared at Charlotte, surprised over such an admission. "Really? I had no idea. But that is reassuring. Thank you."

Hannah moved toward the pew. Thomas sat board straight, his arms crossed over his chest. He stared at the back of the pew in front of him. *Oh Lord, he's nothing like Lottie. She was always so open and trusting. This is utterly impossible.* But even

199

as her thoughts pressed her into unbelief, she knew nothing was beyond God's ability to accomplish.

She stepped into the row just as Pamela Hughes moved down the center aisle, snuggling a newborn against her. Hannah couldn't help but look at the infant. *She's beautiful.* She moved closer and peered at the child tucked inside a crocheted blanket. "Is it a girl?"

"Yes. Isabelle Marie."

Hannah drew in a breath of sorrow and her insides ached. "She's lovely. How old?"

"Just two weeks."

That's when Thomas came to us—two weeks ago.

Pamela smiled down at her daughter and rested an index finger against her pink cheek. She looked at Hannah. "Would you like to hold her?"

"May I?" The baby was passed to Hannah. She held the little girl against her breast and caressed the infant's cheek. Her skin was as soft as rose petals. Inside, Hannah wept for the baby she'd never have. Dropping a kiss on the little one's forehead, she handed her back to her mother. "God has truly blessed you. She's beautiful."

"Thank you." Pamela took the infant and moved on to another pew. As Hannah sat beside John, she could still smell the fragrance of the newborn and feel the soft bundle of life. Her throat was tight as she held back tears. She wanted to leave, go someplace where she could weep. Instead, she clasped her hands in her lap and, like Thomas, stared at the pew in front of her.

The music played and Hannah sang, but she didn't hear the words or feel God's presence. When the reverend spoke, she stared at him as if she were paying attention, but she didn't hear a word. Her heart and mind couldn't tear themselves from the little girl and her own longing for a baby.

When the service came to a close, all she could think of was escape. In her mind, she understood that God was in the midst of her circumstances and that he knew what was best for her and her family. But her heart wanted something else. How could she do what he was asking? She glanced at Thomas. She didn't love him, not the way a mother should cherish a child. He was a sullen boy who wanted nothing to do with her.

Lottie galloped up to Hannah, auburn curls bouncing. She threw her arms about Hannah's waist. "Good day." She smiled up at Hannah. "I heard ye got a boy living with ye."

"That we do."

"Is he a good boy?"

"He's very sad right now." Hannah caressed Lottie's hair. "Remember how you felt when your mum died?"

"Yes." She turned and looked at Thomas. "Is that him there with Mr. Bradshaw?"

"It is."

"Would it be all right if I said hello to him?"

"Of course."

Lottie hugged Hannah. "Maybe ye can visit and bring him with ye. He looks to be 'bout my age."

"He is at that. I'll make sure to bring him next time I come."

"Good." Lottie hurried off toward John and Thomas.

Hannah thought back to how she and Lottie had met. The little girl had started chatting with her while on deck of the prison ship. She'd lost her mum and needed a friend. Hannah had loved her right off. *Why do I love her and not Thomas? The circumstances were different,* Hannah reasoned. *We were trying to survive and she was suddenly without a mother.* A quiet voice whispered inside, *Not so different.*

When Lottie reached John, she said her hellos and then in a very grown-up way offered Thomas her hand. He looked at it, then without acknowledging her, he moved past the sociable child and out of the church. Not to be put off, Lottie followed.

A few minutes later, she returned to Hannah. Leaning against her, Lottie said, "He must be real sad, mum. He won't say a word. But I figure in time me and him can be friends. Do ye think?"

"Maybe. We'll see." Hannah rested a hand on Lottie's shoulder.

The little girl spotted her mother. "Time for me to go. Don't forget, please come visit."

"I'll come soon."

She skipped away to her mother.

Hannah walked toward the church door where the reverend stood just outside, greeting parishioners as they passed. When Hannah approached, he said, "Grand to see you. Is everything well with you and John and your new addition?"

"Yes, quite well," Hannah lied.

"I'm pleased to hear that Thomas is living with you. But I can see that he's sorrowing. He's a good boy, though. And he'll be a fine addition to your family. He needs loving people like you and John."

Guilt twisted inside Hannah. "Right now he's quite a sad little boy, but we'll do our best." Even though she stated words of hope, Hannah had trouble believing them.

"Trust in the Lord. He'll see to him and to you." The reverend's eyes twinkled. "God has placed him exactly where he belongs. And we must remember that he sees the beginning and the end. I'm absolutely convinced that he has great plans for you and John and Thomas."

Hannah wondered if the reverend could see right through her to her aching heart. Was he telling her what he truly believed or only saying what he hoped would make her feel better? *May his words be prophetic*, she prayed.

"I'll remember you all in my prayers."

"Thank you, Reverend." Hannah stepped past him and onto the porch. She'd been forgiven so much, and now it was time for her to give away some of what God had bestowed upon her.

The thought vanished when she saw Deidre with John. They stood beneath an ancient gum tree. Until this moment, she'd forgotten that she'd seen Deidre when she arrived at church. Her insides recoiled. *What does she want now?* Hannah took the steps quickly and hurried toward her husband and that woman.

Before she could reach them, Deidre had walked away. She approached John. "I have a mind to tell her what I think of her scheming."

John reached out to Hannah and pulled her close. "It will do little good. Please, say nothing."

Hannah glanced about at the last of the parishioners. "John, people are talking. They think the worst."

"I doubt that. They know us too well for that."

"I hope you're right. What did she want?"

John took in a breath before answering. "Food stuffs and the bull calf."

"But we can't . . . we won't. Not this time."

"Hannah, quiet your voice. People will hear."

"If you go to her house, it will only give them more to talk •

about, especially if you're seen giving her something as grand as a bull calf. John, it must stop."

"People are not going to talk. I'll be careful to make sure no one is about." He took her arm. "Let's go home. We'll discuss it there."

"I'm going to speak to her." Hannah pulled her arm free.

"No. I'll tell her . . . no more."

"What makes this different from the last time?"

The light in John's amber eyes was gone. "I don't know."

"We must put a stop to this." Hannah glared at Deidre's back. "I don't believe she'll say anything. If she does, everyone will know what she's done. She'd not be able to show her face in town."

"And if she doesn't care about that? What then? Your reputation will be ruined."

Hannah stared at John. She knew he was worried about her, but there was more to it than that. "Is it possible that what you're most troubled about is *your* reputation? People will know that you're married to . . . to someone like me. You're ashamed of me." Hannah couldn't keep her voice from trembling.

"I'm not." John started to say something more, then closed his mouth. "It's true that I do care what people will think. I don't want you hurt." He glanced at the church. The reverend closed the door and casually walked down the steps. "But I'll admit to being apprehensive about how it will affect my standing in the community. I've only just started our place. It could ruin us."

Hannah knew she was asking a great deal of her husband, but she needed John to love her so much that the consequences of that love didn't matter. "I need you to not care about that. I need you to care about me."

"I do. But loving you also means taking good care of you, being able to provide for us."

It wasn't what Hannah wanted to hear. Dejected, she walked to the wagon and climbed up onto the front seat. She sat with her spine straight and her hands clasped tightly in her lap. She stared down the road, her vision blurred by unshed tears.

When she'd married John, all she could see was a bright future stretching out before them. Now life had become complicated and overwhelming. What had happened to their plans—to their dreams?

17

Hannah pushed her fingers underneath a weed, loosened the soil, and then pulled. It came free in her hand, and she shook the dirt from it, then tossed it into a wooden box before moving down the row of carrots. Although the garden was doing well, there seemed to be as many weeds as vegetables. She wriggled another weed loose and dropped it into the box.

Sitting back on her knees, she breathed in the rich fragrance of soil and vegetation. She liked working in the garden. It quieted her soul. She glanced at the blistering sun. The day was heating up quickly, and she'd soon be forced to take refuge in the shade.

She stared at the long row of vegetables ahead of her, then looked out over her garden. The potato vines were thick and green, the beets and turnips were nearly ready to harvest, and the cornstalks were sprouting tassels. They'd need attention soon. With her household duties, it was difficult to find time to properly tend the garden. And today it needed watering. She dare not let the plants go thirsty in this heat.

She rubbed at a sore spot behind her right shoulder and wished John were here to help her. He'd left early to attend an auction where he hoped to find good prices on ewes and a ram.

They'd had a successful lambing, and the flock was growing. John had plans for a significant venture, which meant purchasing more animals. A good ram could make the difference between vigorous lambs and substandard stock.

A clattering came from the barn. Hannah shaded her eyes and looked to see what might be making the racket. Thomas didn't appear. Before John left that morning, he'd told Thomas to clean the stalls and pitch in new hay.

Thomas had wanted to go with John. When he'd been told he'd have to stay behind and work, he'd grumbled a bit but had not openly defied John. A bond, of sorts, seemed to be developing between the two, which pleased Hannah. She wished something similar were happening between her and Thomas. He still had little to say to her.

She let out a long breath. *In time. It will happen.*

Life in general had settled into a more comfortable rhythm. John and Thomas usually set out in the morning to share chores, then came in for breakfast. Most days they worked somewhere on the farm while Hannah saw to the needs of home.

While she'd adjusted to having Thomas with them, she still had to bite her tongue and pray through his sullen moods, and there were times when she could barely tolerate him. But that was happening less often. She was still convinced that he loathed her and wondered how long it would take before he could let go of that first day when he'd overheard her say she didn't want him. John continued to encourage her to be patient and seemed certain that Thomas would learn to love them both. *What if he never does?*

Hannah swatted at a fly buzzing about her head. How grand it would be to have a son to love and raise, a child who returned her affection. Was it possible that Thomas would become her son fully just as John had said? There were times she did feel like his mother, but it happened rarely. And he'd still not responded to her in the same way.

The clatter of wagon wheels and harnesses carried up from the road. Hannah stood and looked to see who was traveling the highway. *Most likely someone passing by.*

She kept watching. It had been some time since she'd had a visitor. When the wagon came into view, she couldn't make out the driver right away. As it drew closer, she realized it was Lydia.

"Not today." She pushed her fingers deep into the soil and lifted out a handful. "I'm not ready." She watched, hoping that by chance Lydia was simply traveling past on the way somewhere else. Instead, she turned the horses up Hannah's drive and the wagon rattled toward the house.

Hannah tossed the dirt aside. Jackson, who had been sleeping in the shade, stood and barked, then approached the cart, his tail beating the air.

Lydia stopped the team in front of a stock pen, pulled the brake, then looped the reins around the lever and climbed down. Shading her eyes against the sun, she searched out Hannah and headed toward the garden, ignoring the eager dog.

Hannah's stomach tightened as she watched the sturdy woman stride toward her. Lydia walked like someone with a purpose. Hannah readied herself for an assault. Although she'd missed the friendship she and Lydia had once enjoyed, Hannah was still angry and didn't feel she could trust the woman. Brushing dirt from her hands, she waited.

Lydia stopped a few paces away. Her green eyes looked spirited as she studied Hannah and planted her hands on her hips. "It's time we talked. I've waited and waited, and I can't wait any longer. I miss ye and I've told ye how sorry I am. I'm here to tell ye again. I'm truly sorry. And I hope ye'll forgive me."

A tightness formed around Hannah's heart. She longed for the friendship, but she couldn't think about what Lydia had done without growing angry. Each time, the wound felt raw and exposed. "I know you meant me no harm, but I can't talk about it. Not yet."

"Hannah, please."

"You hurt me. You betrayed me. How can I trust you? I can't." She watched a spider drop from a cornstalk and climb across a broad, green leaf. She turned her attention back to Lydia, meeting the woman's intense gaze. "How can we be friends? I can never again share something from my heart with you. I'll always be afraid you'll tell someone."

Lydia's gaze didn't flinch, but her eyes filled with tears. "I thought ye knew why that happened. It was only meant to help ye."

Hannah knew. But she was afraid.

"What I did was wrong, but we've been through so much together. We've seen the worst and the best. We've kept each other alive, prayed for one another, and held each other up when there was no one else. I can't believe our friendship is beyond healing." When Hannah didn't reply, Lydia continued, "It was a slip of the tongue. And not meant to hurt you."

"What you shared was private and much more than a slip of the tongue. You told Deidre my darkest secret—one that I could barely think of in my own mind." Hannah shook her head. "I still can't believe you said anything."

"I told ye that, when I spoke to her, I didn't know what kind of person she was. I was worried 'bout ye, and she said she wanted to pray and to help. I believed her."

"That may be, but what you did was wrong. You knew it then and you know it now. There's no explanation, no excuse."

Lydia shook her head slightly, defeat in her eyes.

"What you did could quite well ruin my life and John's too. We may have to move. Deidre is still making threats and demanding goods from us. Your indiscretion has cost us dearly." Hannah turned and crouched alongside the row of carrots and went back to pulling weeds.

Lydia stood there for a long while, saying nothing. Then, in a voice of one succumbing to loss, she said, "I shan't ask again." She walked away.

Hannah continued working, pulling weeds and dropping them into the box. She didn't know what else to do. Not until she knew the wagon had reached the road did she look up. Her heart heavy, she stood and watched it rumble away. She knew she was wrong but felt powerless to change her feelings. Her pride wouldn't allow it, and forgiveness seemed out of reach.

When she could no longer see the wagon, the hurt that had lodged inside grew. She'd lost her closest friend, forever. God had pardoned her of so much and yet she was unable to forgive Lydia this.

Why? How must God see me? Please forgive me. Hannah stood in the same spot for a long while, staring at the road. Finally, in resignation, she wiped away the tears and returned to work.

Thomas walked out of the barn and approached Hannah. He kept his hands in his pockets. "Was that yer friend?"

"Yes."

"Why didn't she stay?" he asked as if he really cared.

"It's not something you'd understand."

"I might. I'm nearly a man." His tone was more kindly than usual.

"I'd hardly say being ten makes you a man."

Thomas set his jaw and stared at her.

Oh dear, I've done it again. "Thomas, I didn't mean that you're opinion isn't valued, it's just that you're a bit young still."

Ignoring her statement, he said, "I finished cleaning the stalls, put in new hay, and set the tack to rights. And the stock's been fed. Is there something more ye'd like done?" His tone and expression had returned to the customary sullenness.

Guilt pricked Hannah. He'd tried and she'd been harsh. She stopped working and looked at him. "I'm sorry you couldn't go with John. I know you wanted to. There was just too much that needed to be done here."

"I don't mind working, it's just that . . ." Thomas looked toward the road. "I wanted to go. He's good to me. Sometimes when I'm with him, I forget me troubles."

Hannah felt unexpected tenderness toward the boy. She stood. "Why don't you go off and play for a while and I'll make lunch for the two of us."

"Fine by me." Thomas headed toward the river, his hands swinging freely at his sides. He looked at the ground as he walked. Often, he'd find what he called treasures—unique rocks, bugs, or four-leaf clovers.

"Be careful," Hannah called after him. "The Parramatta might be slow moving, but she still has a hunger for young lives."

Thomas glanced back at her and kept walking.

Hannah pressed a hand over her mouth. *Of course he knows*

that. His father drowned in that river. She wished she could take back the warning.

When he reached the bank, he stood for a while staring at the water and then walked along the bank until he found the right gum tree to climb. He settled on a branch reaching over the river.

Dusting dirt from her hands, Hannah trudged through the field to the house. Perhaps she could make something special for lunch or a dessert for dinner? If the fire in the hearth was still hot enough, she'd have time to make a lemon pound cake. She calculated what she'd need and was certain the larder contained all the necessary ingredients.

A pot of chicken and vegetables was still warming in the hearth. Thomas would like that. She stirred the coals. There was still enough heat to bake a cake. All she needed was to add a bit more wood.

Although adding wood to the fire would make the inside of the house intolerable, Hannah did it anyway. *It's worth it*, she thought, knowing Thomas and John would appreciate the treat.

Taking a bowl down from the shelf, she beat a pound of butter until it was like thick cream, then added twelve egg yolks and a cup of milk and stirred the mixture well. She beat in a pound of flour and added a pound of sugar. She'd been saving the sugar for a special occasion, but what could be more important than making Thomas feel loved? After squeezing in the juice of two lemons, she poured the batter into a cooking pot. Moisture beaded up on her face, and she dabbed at it with the corner of her apron before setting the pot in the coals to cook.

She stirred the meat and potatoes, then went to the door

and called Thomas. She watched as he clambered down from the tree. He seemed to be feeling a bit more like the boy she'd heard he'd been before his father had died.

Hannah went to the cupboard, took down two bowls, and filled each with soup. She set them on the table along with spoons and two mugs for milk. She quickly sliced bread from a loaf and put that on the table as well. It was a fine lunch.

She took a peek at the baking cake. Sweet-smelling steam rose into the air when she lifted the lid. *Thomas will be pleased.* She imagined his delight at the special treat.

After replacing the lid, she went back to the door to look for him. He appeared from behind a batch of bushes along the river and slowly walked up the drive. As he ambled along, he kicked a rock ahead of him.

Hannah waited on the porch until he stood on the bottom step. "Thomas, please take care when you're away from the house. The world is filled with dangers."

"Ye meaning the blacks? I've not seen any."

"Yes. And other things too. There are convicts, and you've got to keep an eye out for snakes."

"I do. I'm not daft." He threw her a derisive look to go along with his disrespectful tone.

Hannah bristled inside, but ignored it. "Of course you're not. Come in, then. I've made a nice lunch for us."

Hannah sat at the table. But Thomas picked up his bowl and spoon and walked outside, leaving the door ajar. He sat on the top step and started eating.

Immediately flies and wasps, enticed by the aroma of cooking, dashed indoors.

Exasperated, Hannah got up to shut them out. *He knows to close the door and should have the decency to sit down to a meal with me.* Standing in the doorway, she said, "Thomas, you've left the door open . . . again. The flies are dreadful. You know better."

He glanced over his shoulder. "Sorry." He returned to eating.

Hannah tried to push aside her irritation. "I set a place for you. It's customary when someone invites you to eat with them that you sit at the table."

He didn't reply but kept eating.

Annoyance flamed into resentment. Hannah shut the door, harder than necessary. *So much for trying. There's no pleasing him.*

Deciding to eat without him, Hannah sat at the table. She picked up her spoon, but instead of eating, she stared at her food, allowing her frustration to build. Finally, she set her spoon in the bowl. "I can't let this pass. What will it be next? It is my responsibility to see that he grows into a courteous, thoughtful adult."

She strode to the door, opened it, and stepped onto the porch. "Thomas, I've told you on more than one occasion to close the door behind you. I expect you to do it."

He stared up at her but didn't say anything.

"Also, I made us a fine meal and expected that we'd dine together. It's extremely bad manners for you to walk out and eat on the porch."

"I wanted to eat outside. It's hot in there."

Hannah stared at him. He could have offered an apology. "It's hot because I've made you a special treat—a lemon cake. And if I can sit inside in the heat, then so can you."

"Ye could 'ave joined me out here."

Hannah didn't know how to reply. She supposed that was true.

He looked up at her through blond strands of hair. "I didn't know ye wanted me to eat with ye. Ye never have before." He turned back to his meal.

His rudeness persists, Hannah fumed. "Thomas, I want you to come in and eat at the table."

"I don't want to."

"You'll do as you're told."

He glared at her over his shoulder. "I don't have to. Yer not me mum."

"Why must you rail against me? I know it hurts to lose one's parents—I lost both of mine. But there's no call to be spiteful or rude."

Thomas set his bowl aside and stood. His expression was hard. "How can ye say it is I who rails against ye? It's the other way 'round. Ye can barely stand the sight of me. Ye made that clear right from the beginning."

"That's not true." Hannah fumbled to find the right response. "I confess to having difficulty managing your sulking and your sour moods. And there's rarely a kind word from you. Not even for dear Lottie who only wants to be your friend."

"How can ye expect me to be friends with her? She's a girl."

"There is such a thing as courtesy no matter one's age." Hannah folded her arms over her chest. Thomas glared up at her and jutted out his chin. Hannah had had enough. "All right, then. You can spend the rest of the day in your room, and you'll not get any cake."

"I don't care about yer cake. And I won't stay in me room. It's hotter than hades up there!"

"Watch your mouth. And do as you're told."

Instead of obeying, Thomas moved down one step. "No. I won't. Yer not me mum. And ye never will be, not that ye wanted to be anyway. Ye never wanted me. It was only John's pity that brought me 'ere. I don't need ye, neither one of ye. I can make it fine on me own."

Hannah was unprepared for his outburst. "Thomas," she said, hoping her tone sounded gentler. "Of course we want you. And we don't wish for you to leave."

"Yer only saying what ye think ye should. But ye don't have to worry. I'll be gone the first chance I get." His blue eyes were red rimmed and it looked like he was trying not to cry. "Why couldn't it have been ye that died instead of me mum and dad?"

He kicked the bowl of stew off the step, leaped down from the porch, and ran as hard as he could. He sprinted across the field, cutting through a mob of sheep.

Her heart aching, Hannah sank to the step and watched until he disappeared over a rise. *What am I to do?*

She closed her eyes and tears trailed from the corners. "I don't know how to be a mother to him. Perhaps I was never meant to be anyone's mother."

Her mind carried her back to her own mum. *I miss you so. Why can't I be more like you?* She felt the comfort of her mother's soft voice, her touch. She was nothing like her. "I need you, Mum. Why did you have to die?"

Opening her eyes, Hannah looked at the last place she'd seen Thomas. How far had he run? Would he return? And if he did, what would she say to him?

She pushed to her feet and slowly walked down the steps. Picking up the bowl and spoon, she gazed out over the field. She felt lonelier than she could ever remember. She'd not meant to hurt him, yet she had. *I'm not the mum for him. Why is he here, Lord?*

216

Hannah moved back inside, set the bowl and spoon in the sink, and then went to the window, hoping to see him at the river's edge or walking across the field toward the house.

He was nowhere in sight, but he was out there, somewhere, most likely sobbing out his anguish. "God, let him know he's not alone. Show him that you love him. And Lord, help me love him the way a real mum should." Even as she prayed, Hannah knew it was too late. Too much damage had already been done. It would take a miracle to repair the relationship.

She'd not realized how much Thomas needed her. She'd only thought about how much she needed a child of her own and not a sullen little boy. The depth of her selfishness revolted her.

Feeling sick, she closed her eyes and rubbed her temples. She could feel a headache coming on. "I've let him down so badly."

Her mind went to John and how much he already loved Thomas. He wanted a son and now he had one. The idea that they could lose him was beyond comprehension.

Show me what to do, Lord.

18

John helped Hannah into the wagon. "You're sure you'll be all right on your own?"

"Of course. It won't be the first time I've made the trip to the Athertons' by myself. I'll be fine. Don't worry."

"I'd go with you, but there's so much to be done here." He glanced at Thomas who was dumping feed into the pig trough. "He's getting to be a great help to me. Maybe the rest will come soon."

"It will," Hannah said, feeling terrible about what had happened the previous day. She'd not told John all that had been said; she didn't want to discourage him. She'd simply told him that she and Thomas had an argument.

Thomas still wasn't speaking to her. And when she'd offered him a piece of cake, he'd refused and gone to bed.

"Try not to worry so."

"I'm fine, really."

John smiled up at her. "You're not good at concealing your emotions, luv. I think your speaking to Catharine is a good idea. She's wise and has an understanding of these kinds of things."

Hannah nodded, wondering if John was referring to her

being barren. "I'm sure she'll be of help. I'm just sorry it's come to this. I wish we'd been able to sort it out ourselves."

"Well, that's part of the reason for friends. We can be of help to one another, eh?"

"Yes. Of course." But as Hannah considered the conversation she'd have with Catharine, her insides churned. It meant revealing truths about herself she'd rather keep secret. "I shan't be late," she said, lifting the reins.

"While you're there, perhaps you and Lydia will have a chance to talk, eh?"

"Perhaps," she said, but Hannah knew she'd do everything she could to avoid such a meeting.

John watched as Thomas headed toward the barn and then looked at Hannah. "I'll be praying you along, luv."

"Thank you." Hannah took the brake off, but instead of turning the team toward the road, she asked, "John, why do you think our life has become so complicated? Sometimes I feel as if I'm trying to make my way through a bramble thicket. I didn't expect it to be like this."

"Like what?"

Hannah moved the reins from one hand to the other. "Things have just not turned out as I'd hoped." She knew talking about it would do no good, yet she felt compelled. "We were supposed to have children, and I was going to spend time with my closest friend over tea, and my secret was going to disappear into the mist somewhere. And instead it's—"

"Hannah, we were never assured of tranquility, only that God would see us through whatever life brings our way. I thought we'd learned that long ago."

"I should have, with all that's befallen me . . . and you. I guess I just hoped it would be easier."

John smiled. "I wish it could be so, but instead we must find the good in the life we've been given." He grasped her hand. "One piece of excellent news—Deidre's not spoken to me recently. Perhaps giving her the bull calf put an end to it all, and she decided enough is enough, eh?"

"I pray so." Hannah lifted the reins. "I'd best be on my way. The day is going quickly."

"Safe travel, luv."

Hannah turned the horses toward the road. The air was already hot and muggy, so much so that even the birds seemed quieter than usual. Along the river the air felt heavy and the flies were thick. Hannah slapped the reins gently over the horses' hindquarters. "Come on. Faster now."

Biting flies tormented her. They crawled on her veil and bit her exposed hands. "I should have worn gloves. My hands will be a sight by the time I get there." She swatted at the flies, but they'd buzz away only to return. "This is ghastly."

When the Athertons' drive appeared, relief, like a cool breeze, swept over Hannah. Gwen and Perry met her as she drove up. "G'day to ye," Perry said, taking the harness.

"Good day. You two not working?"

"We're supposed to be." Gwen smiled lovingly at Perry. "Actually we were sneaking a few moments together."

"We'll be married before long and then we'll have plenty of time together," Perry said.

"You've set a date, then?"

"We have." Perry draped an arm about Gwen's shoulders. "We thought March. Seems a fitting time for a wedding, don't you think?" Before Hannah could reply, he added, "The heat ought to give up a bit by then."

"That's a long wait, four months."

220

"It seems like forever," Gwen said. "But I want my wedding to be perfect. I couldn't bear to be fighting this heat and the awful insects. March is a bit cooler. The world seems lovelier then too."

"Well, congratulations to you. I can hardly wait. I'm sure it will be a beautiful wedding." Hannah looked at the main house and hoped she'd not have an encounter with Deidre or Lydia. "Have you seen Mrs. Atherton? I was hoping to have a word with her."

"She's on the veranda. I'm sure she'll be pleased to see ye." Still holding Perry's hand, Gwen stepped away from him. "I've got to go. I'll see ye later, eh?"

"That ye will." Perry tipped his hat and strolled toward the shop.

Gwen looked up at Hannah. "I'll go along with ye. Mrs. Atherton will be needing some refreshment 'bout now anyway."

Hannah clicked her tongue and drove the wagon toward the house. Gwen walked the short distance alongside the wagon. "Ye've not been 'round for some time. How are ye and John faring out there on yer property?"

"Good. The lambs are growing and healthy. John managed to purchase a fine ram and some additional ewes. He's put up another barn and several more stock pens. He and Quincy even built poor Quincy a new cabin, one that keeps out the flying pests and the snakes. And even with all this heat the garden is flourishing. I'm thankful to have the river so near. It's a wonder what a bit of water can do."

"Sounds like ye've built yerselves a grand place."

"I hadn't thought of it that way, but we have made strides. It's coming along well." Hannah hadn't considered her blessings recently; she needed reminding. "God has been good to us."

221

When Hannah pulled the wagon to a stop in front of the Atherton home, Catharine moved from the shadows of the veranda to the top of the steps. She cooled herself with a small fan. "Hannah. How grand to see you!"

"Catharine." Hannah climbed down from the wagon and walked up the broad steps in the front of the house.

Catharine opened her arms and pulled Hannah against her ample bosom, then held her away and gazed at her. "I can scarcely believe you've come all this way in this unbearable heat." She smiled. "But I'm glad you did. It's been too long. I've missed you terribly."

"You see me every Sunday."

"That's not the same; there's never enough time for a proper visit."

"How true." Hannah's fears quieted. Just being with Catharine made her feel more tranquil.

"Please, dear. Come and sit in the shade. There's a bit of a breeze now and again." Catharine limped to a spindle-backed chair and sat.

Hannah took a seat beside her. The porch seemed buried in greenery and flowers. The fragrance was heady. "One day, I hope to have a veranda as lovely as this one." She breathed deeply. "The lobelia smells heavenly."

"I love lobelia," Catharine said. "But in this heat it's a chore to keep them watered. And poor Dalton has been given the task of keeping them alive. Some days I've seen him watering more than once."

"I've brought tea," Gwen said, setting a pitcher on an occasional table beside Mrs. Atherton's chair. "Mrs. Goudy made raspberry tarts. Would ye like some, mum?"

"That sounds lovely."

Gwen disappeared inside. Hannah sipped the cool mint tea.

Catharine continued to fan herself. "Oh, on days like this I wonder why we ever left England."

"The cool days there were nice."

Catharine stopped fanning herself long enough to take a drink of her tea. "I pray all is well with you and John and Thomas."

Hannah held her glass between her hands. Although she'd come specifically to speak with Catharine about her troubles at home, she wasn't ready to do so just yet. "We're doing splendidly," she said. "John's working hard and he's accomplished so much. Our flocks are growing and we've a bountiful garden."

"And Thomas? How is he?"

Hannah turned the glass counterclockwise and then took a sip. "Actually he's the reason I've come. I need . . . guidance."

Catharine leaned closer to Hannah. "I don't know that I can help, but I can listen."

Gwen returned with a tray of tarts. She set them on the occasional table.

"Thank you," Catharine said.

Hannah picked up one. "They look delicious." She took a bite. "Mmm. Tell Mrs. Goudy thank you for me."

"I'll do that," Gwen said as she walked indoors.

Catharine turned to Hannah. "So, you were saying something about Thomas."

"Yes." Hannah set the tart on the plate. "He's unhappy . . . mostly with me. He and John seem to be getting along well, but things are not good between me and him. And I've been too harsh. I'm having a terrible time being tolerant."

"I find that hard to believe." Catharine sat back in her chair. "And what do you think is causing the strife?"

"I'm not sure. From the first day there's been trouble."

"How so?"

"First off, John brought Thomas home without consulting me at all. He simply showed up with him. I was quite taken aback and ill prepared when they arrived at the house. And I didn't handle it well. I said some things I shouldn't have, and Thomas heard." She set the glass on the table. "He's been angry ever since. He told me he doesn't want to live with us. Never did.

"So, as you can see, we started out quite badly. And I've been struggling since, angry one minute, contrite the next, and hopeful and then hopeless." She brushed damp hair off her face. "Sometimes I feel angry with Thomas without cause."

"And why do you think that is?"

"I don't know. I've not been myself since . . . well, since I told John about the baby, about everything." Hannah clasped her hands tightly together.

"I'm glad you told him."

"Yes, but we had a terrible fight, and he left. That's when the convict broke into the house."

"I thought there was something not quite right when you came to visit."

"Anyway, when John returned, we talked about it all, and I told him I was afraid that we'd never have children. He assured me that he was confident we would. And that God understood how I'd felt and why I'd done what I did and that he wouldn't punish me."

"None of us can know exactly the mind of the Lord, but I tend to agree with John. I don't think God is punishing you, dear."

"I'd like to believe you, but why haven't we had a child?"

Mrs. Atherton turned thoughtful. When she spoke, she chose

her words carefully. "Hannah, do you think God was punishing me? I have no children."

"No. Of course not. You're a wonderful person."

"Thank you." She smiled. "I used to wonder why William and I never had children, and I even questioned whether or not there was some sin I'd committed that would cause God to withhold his blessings. But in time, I came to understand that we each have our own path to walk and that path has a specific purpose. We must trust where God leads."

Hannah nodded, feeling her sadness lift just a bit. "When John told me he thought we'd have children, I believed him. It gave me great comfort to know he believed in me and in us. But when he brought Thomas home, it was as if he were saying he didn't believe. I felt he'd lied to me and thought I deserved God's punishment."

"Oh, Hannah." Catharine reached across and placed a hand on Hannah's arm. "I don't see that at all. John simply wants children and this boy needed a home. There's nothing wrong with that." Catharine poured herself more tea and added some to Hannah's glass. "I see no cause for you to react so negatively."

"You're probably right, but . . ." Hannah stared at her hands. "I can't believe it. Every time I look at Thomas, I see John's doubt."

"That's why you're having so much difficulty with Thomas, dear. You're placing the hurt and frustration you feel toward John on that boy." She cooled herself with the fan. "And is it possible that you're afraid to love him because that means you agree there will be no children?"

The idea slammed into Hannah. Was that what was wrong?

"It's perilous to allow our minds to control us, dear. If we give in to every emotional whim, we can cause great harm. Scripture says we're to take our thoughts captive. We must see things as Christ sees them. Pray and he will reveal his will to you."

Hannah straightened her legs and crossed them at the ankles. "I know you're right, but I'm not sure what to do about Thomas. He's made it clear that he doesn't want to live in my house. I'm wondering if he'd be better off living elsewhere. I think he hates me."

"Of course he doesn't. He's just a boy."

"He does. And . . . I don't love him. Some days I can scarcely tolerate him." Hannah's throat tightened and she could barely speak. "I pray, but it's not getting better. Some days I think that perhaps we're growing closer, and then something will happen and things are worse than ever. Just yesterday, Thomas and I had a row and he told me that he'll leave the moment he can."

If Catharine was shocked, she didn't show it. Calmly she asked, "How about John and Thomas? How are they? You said they were getting along."

"Yes. I think Thomas likes and respects John. And John wants it to work so badly. He loves Thomas but manages to restrain his affection, knowing he must wait until Thomas is ready to be loved."

Catharine sipped her tea and sat back. "Although John made a commitment to the lad without your consent, once he brought him home, you were also committed. You can't send him back, even if there were a place to send him to. Thomas deserves better than that."

She leaned closer to Hannah. "The Holy Spirit lives inside of you, and he will provide the love you need. But you must be willing to allow it to bloom. And as to whether or not there are any babies—that's God's choice."

"I know he can do all things, but sometimes I doubt he will do them for me. I want my own children so badly . . ."

"As did I." Catharine's tone was sharp. "I waited too long, hoping that one day I'd be able to give William a child of his own." She shook her head sadly. "By the time I realized I was waiting on the wrong dream, it was too late to adopt a child. We were too old." She smiled softly, her eyes glistening with tears. "It doesn't have to be like that for you. This child is a gift, if only you would see him as such."

"Even if I do, that doesn't change the fact that he hates me."

"He doesn't hate you. He's hurt and angry. The people he loved the most in the world were taken from him, and he's been shuffled about and hasn't felt wanted. How would you respond?"

Hannah knew how it felt, but it seemed she was still unable to overcome her own problems. "I want it to work, but so much has happened. I doubt he'll ever forgive me."

Catharine grasped Hannah's hand. "I don't think you're giving God enough credit. He can do anything." She squeezed gently. "You pray and listen to his leading. He'll do what he must. That boy needs a mother and you need a son."

Blinking back tears, Catharine cleared her throat and sat back. "Now, tell me why you've been staying away and why you and Lydia aren't speaking to each other."

Hannah was taken off guard. She hadn't intended to share any of that. She didn't want to talk about it.

Catharine waited.

"There is something." Hannah picked up her tea and took a sip. "It has to do with Deidre."

Catharine raised an eyebrow, but said nothing.

"Lydia told Deidre about what happened in London and about the baby."

"It's not like her to carry tales."

"She only meant it to help," Hannah admitted. "Deidre made her think that she cared about me, and Lydia told her. Now Deidre's threatening to expose the truth. She's been demanding we provide her with . . . things. If not, she'll speak up."

"Things, like what?"

"Food and livestock."

"Oh dear. And you've been giving in to her demands?"

"Yes. We didn't know what else to do."

"You mustn't give her another thing. People like her will never be satisfied. I'll see to it she's terminated immediately."

"Oh no. Please don't. If she knows I've said anything, she'll speak to the church elders."

"That may be true, but I doubt she has the courage. You can't allow this to go on." Catharine stood. "I knew there was something not right about her, but I'd hoped . . ." She looked out over the grounds. "I'll tend to it."

"I really wish you wouldn't say anything. She's quite vindictive."

"All the more reason. And remember, if she speaks out, she'll be exposing her own treachery." She moved toward the steps. "I doubt she's got courage enough for that." She took the first step and then stopped. With her hand on the railing, she turned back to Hannah. "I'll consider what you've said, dear. But I don't know that I can keep that woman in my employ."

"Do what you think is right," Hannah conceded.

Catharine took another step, then looked at Hannah again. "You know Lydia's been sorrowing over the loss of your friendship far too long. You were the best of friends. You need each other." She smiled and then moved slowly down the stairway.

John tossed hay from a loft and then climbed down a ladder. Thomas pushed a pitchfork into the feed and carried some to a crib. "Fine job," John said, taking off his gloves. "I could do with some lunch. How 'bout you?"

"I'm hungry." Thomas pushed the pitchfork into the hay pile.

"Hannah set out bread and cheese before she left this morning. I say we take some down to the river and eat, then have a swim."

Thomas smiled. "Sounds fine to me." He followed John to the house.

John gathered up the cheese and bread and placed it in a cloth bag. "Fruit would be good too, eh? We've some plums."

"I'd like that."

John added several plums, grabbed a flask of water, and walked out the door. "On a hot day like this, a swim will be just the thing." He winked at Thomas.

Thomas nodded and grinned. "I know how to swim. Me dad taught me."

"Good." John hurried toward the river, anxious to eat and get cooled off. He stopped beneath a large gum tree, then sat with his back against the tree, legs bent. Reaching into the bag, he took out a slice of bread and a hunk of cheese and handed them to Thomas. He took some for himself. The two sat quietly eating, enjoying a cool breeze.

"Wonder where the flies got to," Thomas said, looking about.

"Speak quietly; they're never far off," John teased, enjoying the time with Thomas. It felt good, as if they were father and son.

Thomas sat with his legs crossed and quickly ate his simple meal. "I could do with a bit more. Is there any?"

"There is." John started to reach inside the bag when he noticed a ripple in the grass behind Thomas. "Be still. Don't move." The boy stiffened.

Then John saw it—a large brown snake, one he knew to be deadly. It slid through the grass and straight for Thomas. He had no time to find a weapon, so John lunged for the viper, grabbing it directly behind the head. He pressed it into the ground and pushed the boy aside.

Thomas jumped to his feet. "Blimey! What is it?"

John grabbed his knife out of its sheath and quickly sliced the head from the body. He tossed both parts into the river. The body writhed on the surface for a moment and then sank. He wiped his knife in the grass and pushed it back into its sheath.

"That was a big one," Thomas said.

"It was at that." John smiled and tried to hide the tremor in his lips.

Thomas looked around. "Do ye think there are more?"

"No. They're solitary creatures."

Thomas sat down, and John handed him another hunk of cheese and bread. Thomas stared at the food, then looked at John. "Why'd ye do that?"

"He might have bitten you. I had to kill him."

"But ye could have been bitten yerself. Ye could have died."

"I guess I could have at that." John took out a plum and bit into it. Juice squirted and he wiped it from his chin.

"Ye risked yer life."

John heard something new in Thomas's voice—wonder. He stopped chewing. "What is it, lad?"

The boy's eyes filled with tears. "No one 'cept me mum or dad would have done that for me."

"Well, we're family, Thomas. I see you as my son. I'd defend you with my life."

"Ye would?"

"Yes."

Thomas took a bite of his bread and then a bite of cheese. "And what 'bout Mrs. Bradshaw? I think she hates me."

"Of course she doesn't."

"But she doesn't want me 'ere. She never will. It's something she can't change."

"That's not true. I'll admit you were a surprise to her. And she's not used to being a mother, not yet, but she'll come 'round."

"How can ye know that?"

"Because she's got a good heart, and her life belongs to the Lord." He leaned over and ruffled Thomas's blond hair. "We're your family now. You've no need to worry, you'll see."

19

Hannah walked down the steps of the Athertons' home and headed to the wagon. Just as she prepared to climb onto the seat, she spotted Lydia. She carried a basket of clean clothes against her hip and walked toward the end of the house.

Hannah rested a hand on the wheel and pondered what to do. The right thing would be to mend the relationship. God's Word was clear about that.

Mrs. Atherton is right. I need to talk to her. Hannah watched as Lydia disappeared around the end of the house. *What can I say?* Although less angry, Hannah still felt the hurt of what Lydia had done, but she also missed her friend. *I need to forgive her and to tell her so.*

Until Deidre had given away her past, Hannah had always liked Lydia's recklessness; she'd found it endearing. She admired her lack of pretense. *She couldn't have known what would happen when she told Deidre.*

Hannah took a deep breath. "All right, then. It's time." Although the words were meant to boost her courage, they had little effect. Even in the heat, she nearly shivered with trepidation. What if she were too late? Lydia wouldn't necessarily forgive her harshness and her bitterness. Even though it was

Lydia who had made a mistake, it was Hannah who had purposely been unforgiving.

When Hannah rounded the corner of the house, Lydia had her back to her. She folded the waist of a pair of underdrawers over the line and secured it with a wooden pin. She reached into the basket, took out an identical pair, and did the same.

She even hangs laundry in a capable way. The last of Hannah's anger faded and suddenly all she could see was her own sin—her unfair judgment of a friend and lack of forgiveness.

Lydia bent and reached for something else in the basket. "Lydia," Hannah said, her voice barely audible.

Lydia didn't respond. Instead she lifted out a crinoline and placed it over the wire.

Hannah cleared her throat and tried again. "Lydia."

Holding the crinoline in her hands, Lydia turned. Her eyes locked with Hannah's. Silence cut the air between them. Finally, Lydia said a stiff "Hello."

Hannah took a step toward her. "I was hoping we might talk."

Lydia turned back to her work, hanging the crinoline alongside the underdrawers, then lifted an underskirt out of the basket. "I thought we had nothing to say to each other, that our friendship was beyond saving." Her tone was indifferent.

"I was wrong. I'm sorry. I want us to be friends. I miss you."

Lydia hesitated, but then secured the underskirt to the line. When it was in place, she kept her hands on the line.

Hannah moved closer. "I forgive you. I know you didn't mean to hurt me. And I've been utterly cruel." She took another step. "Can *you* forgive me?"

Lydia turned and faced Hannah. Her eyes brimmed with

tears. She compressed her lips, then smiled tremulously. "Of course I forgive ye."

The two friends embraced. Hannah could barely contain her sorrow and her joy, which spilled over in tears. She hugged Lydia tightly. "Oh, how I've missed you." She stepped back. "I'm truly sorry."

"I'm the one who's sorry," Lydia said. "All of this is my fault. If I'd just kept my mouth closed. I wish there were some way to take back my words. I never meant any harm."

"I know that. It's just that my hurt got in the way of my intellect. I know you're a true friend, the dearest a person could have."

They hugged again.

Lydia wiped away tears and smiled. "After I finish hanging these clothes, can ye join me for lunch?"

"I'd like that."

Hannah felt comfortable sitting at the table in the small cottage she and Lydia had once shared. "It feels good to be here. I can't tell you how I've missed you. Everyone needs a good friend."

"I've missed ye too. I've been lonely."

"There's been no one to share my thoughts with, except for John, of course. But he's a man and although he tries . . . well, he's a man."

Both of them laughed.

Still chuckling, Hannah said, "He truly doesn't care a bit about my sewing projects or new recipes, although I've tried talking to him about them. And I don't dare speak to him about other female topics."

Lydia chuckled. "I should say not." She set cups on the table. "Would ye like some sugar?"

"Are you sure you've enough to spare?"

"Mrs. Atherton sees to it that we have sugar." She set a bowl of it on the table.

Hannah chose a small chunk and stirred it into her tea. She sipped and looked out the window. "It feels like another life when I last sat in this place." Suddenly overwhelmed at what she'd nearly lost, Hannah gazed at Lydia and said, "I've felt adrift without you. I've been so foolish."

"Guess we both have." Lydia stirred her tea absently. "I know that I tried to tell ye exactly what happened with Deidre, but I'd like to explain it more now that—"

"You don't have to. I know you thought you were helping. Deidre did seem like someone you could trust, at least to most people. Although I must admit, I never liked her."

"Thought I was a decent judge of character, but clearly I'm not. Is she still giving ye trouble?"

"Not recently, but I've no certainty that she won't. Most likely she'll be back with her hand extended. She's successfully robbed us of two ewes, a lamb, a sow, food staples—"

"I'm so sorry."

"No. It's not your fault. You couldn't have known. Deidre was looking for a trusting soul and she found you." Hannah reached across the table and patted Lydia's arm. "You're kind. And she could see that."

Lydia furrowed her forehead. "Is there anything I can do to help?"

"I don't know that anyone can. Catharine's convinced she'll continue with her evil deeds. She wants to discharge her."

"As she should."

"I asked her not to, and she said she'd give it some thought."

"Why, Hannah? After what she's done, she doesn't deserve to work for fine people like the Athertons."

"I agree, but if Catharine dismisses her, she'll only become worse. I don't know that I'm ready for what may come."

"Well, I'll tell her then. She's a no-good."

"Please don't—not a word. John and I will see to her . . . somehow."

"What are ye going to do?"

Hannah picked up her spoon and stirred her tea again, trying to dissolve the last grains of sugar. "I'm very close to telling her she'll not receive anything more. I'm just afraid it will mean the end of things for John and me here in Parramatta."

"But if ye don't, she'll just go on and on, demanding things from ye. It will never end."

"You're probably right. And I know I ought to speak to the elders myself, tell them the truth. Perhaps they'd be merciful."

"Reverend Taylor is a kind man, and so are the others. I can't see them penalizing ye too terribly."

"They may feel they have no choice, especially if Scripture calls for it."

Lydia leaned on her elbows. "I think ye need to stand up to her. And let God see to the rest."

Hannah took a drink of her tea. "When I think about what could happen . . . I absolutely quake inside. What will become of John and me? We could be ruined." She stood and walked to the window. "Still, I know it's time to put an end to her thievery." She looked back at Lydia. "Catharine thinks she'd be too frightened to speak up because she'd ruin her own reputation along with mine."

"That's possible." Lydia sat back in her chair. "How is Thomas? Is he getting on all right?"

Hannah returned to her place across from Lydia. "He and John are doing quite well. But he and I . . . well . . . we've our differences. He doesn't much like me."

"How could he not?"

"I've not been a good mother to him. But I'm going to do better. We've had some difficulties, but I'm the only mum he's got. I'm going to do my best by him. I just hope it's not too late."

"All things work together for good. Have faith."

Hannah sighed. "Pray for us."

<hr />

Hannah knelt beside Thomas's bed while John prayed. She'd sensed something different between the two ever since she'd returned that afternoon. They seemed very much like father and son. If only she felt like a mother.

When John finished, he stood, then bent over the bed and smoothed back the lad's blond hair. "Good night, Son."

"Good night, sir." Thomas snuggled down.

"Good night, Thomas," Hannah said.

He mumbled something unintelligible.

Feeling wounded, Hannah allowed John to steer her toward the stairway leading down from the loft. "Can I get you your pipe?" she asked as John settled into a chair at the table.

"Thank you."

John had only recently taken up smoking. Hannah didn't mind. She liked the aroma. She filled the pipe with tobacco and tapped it down. Handing it to John, she lit a stick in the embers in the hearth and held it to the bowl while John puffed. The tobacco glowed red and smoke rose into the air.

John moved the pipe to the corner of his mouth and said, "Thank you, luv."

Hannah tossed the stick into the hearth, then moved to a rocker and picked up a sewing basket she kept beside it. Taking out a pair of socks she'd been mending, she went to work darning. John continued cleaning his musket.

"I'll be glad when this hot spell passes," Hannah said. "I prefer the weather cooler and a cheery fire burning in the hearth. And the fire helps light the house."

John set the gun on the table. "If it's all right with you, I'll open the door. It might allow a breeze inside." He lifted the latch and swung it open. Even in the darkness the loud buzz of cicadas filled the night.

John returned to the table. "The heat's hard on the sheep. Shearing should help."

"Do you have anyone to assist you?"

"I've a couple of shearers coming in. We'll be fine. I'm a bit worried about the stream, though. It's down some." He removed a bolt from the musket, and the stock fell away from the barrel. He set them both on the table.

"I spoke to Lydia today." Hannah looked up to see John's response.

"You did? And . . . ?"

"It went well." Hannah glanced up at the loft and quieted her voice. "After speaking to Catharine, I saw Lydia and knew it was time to mend our differences. I don't know how I allowed myself to remain so distant. She's such a good friend. Sometimes my stubbornness is a worry."

John smiled at her. "You can be stubborn, that's true."

238

"Catharine had some wise words as well."

"Oh?"

"She helped me see what a hurting lad Thomas is and how I've been overly sensitive to his rebuffs. She also had some insight . . . into me. I may be holding back because I'm afraid that loving him means I believe I won't have any of my own children. It sounds a bit strange, but she may have something." She smiled at John. "I think I'll be a better mum to him after this."

"I'm glad to hear that, Hannah." John's voice was barely more than a whisper, but it held conviction.

Hannah focused on tying off the thread. "Things seem different between you and Thomas. Did something happen today?"

"Not much really. We worked together and had a bit of picnic down at the river. While we were there, a snake came upon us."

"Was it a dangerous type?"

"Yes. But not to worry. I killed it."

"I hate snakes."

"If we're to live here, we'd best get used to them."

"Yes, but that doesn't mean I have to like them." She tied off the thread. "Why didn't you tell me what happened?"

"Didn't want to worry you."

"I don't need to be protected."

"You're right. Sorry. Anyway, I've felt a change coming on with Thomas, and after the incident with the snake, he seemed able to let go of his distrust. We had a fine day." John smiled. "I feel I've a son."

"Truly?"

"Yes. I think we've made it through the worst of things. And we've only good days ahead."

Hannah bent to her work and simply nodded. She wasn't so certain about how things would be for her and Thomas, but perhaps if he and John were getting on well, it would be better for her too. "You're a good father to him."

"I hope to be." Using a rod, John pushed a piece of cloth into the musket barrel. "Did I detect a difference in your feelings for Thomas also?"

"I'd like to think so. Perhaps I understand him better now and can see how lucky I am to have him. I trust that love will come. I'm more determined than ever to be a real mum to him."

"You will be."

Hannah woke the next morning with a sense of anticipation. Today would be a new beginning for her and Thomas. After John and Quincy left to do some doctoring on the sheep, Hannah spooned the remaining porridge into a bowl. "Thomas, your breakfast is ready," she called up the stairs. There was no response, no sound of footsteps. "Thomas?" Still no answer.

Hannah set the bowl of hot cereal on the table and headed up the stairs. At the top of the steps she stopped and gazed about the large room. The bed was empty. "Thomas?" She found him standing at the window. "I called. Why didn't you answer?"

He continued to stare outside and didn't respond.

Hannah felt the old irritation rise and tried to quiet it. "You don't want your cereal to get cold."

"I don't care. I don't want it. I wanted to go with John."

"I thought we decided that I need you here today. I could use a hand in the garden."

He wheeled around and glared at her. "That's women's work. I shouldn't have to do it."

Patience, Hannah. Patience. She moved into the room. Doing her best to remain calm, she said, "It's not women's work at all. It's farmwork. And we all must do our share. I've got to make candles today, we're nearly out. I don't have time for the garden." When Thomas continued to stare outside and ignore her, she continued, "John said he'll take you fishing when he returns this afternoon."

His brows furrowed and his lips formed a pout, Thomas folded his arms over his chest. "I don't need him to take me fishing. I can go on me own."

"No. You'll wait. I need you to eat your breakfast and to help me first."

"You can't tell me what to do. I'm not yer son."

"That's right, you're not, but you are my charge." Hannah could feel herself getting angry. "And you'll do as you're told." Although she steeled herself against it, she couldn't keep her voice from rising.

"I'm going fishing." Thomas charged toward her and tried to push past.

Hannah grasped his arm, squeezing hard. "There'll be no fishing today." Keeping hold of his arm, she headed down the stairs, dragging him with her. She set him in a chair at the table. "Now, I've made you a fine breakfast. I expect you to eat it. And then you'll do the gardening."

Thomas glared at the porridge.

"I said eat."

He propped his elbows on the table and stared at the bowl.

Hannah went to work on the dishes, hoping he'd give in to her wishes.

Thomas pushed the bowl away.

"Thomas, we'll not waste food in this house." She picked up

the spoon on the table, put it in his hand, and pushed the bowl back in front of him. "Now, eat."

"I don't have to." He put the spoon down hard.

Hannah wasn't sure what to do. Now that she'd made an issue about the meal, she felt she had to win the argument. "Eat. Or you'll go without the rest of the day." She took the spoon and dipped it into the cereal. "It's good; I made it just the way you like it."

"I wanted to go with John."

Hannah put the spoon in his hand. "Please, try it."

Thomas flung the utensil across the room.

Stunned, Hannah shouted, "Pick that up!"

"I don't have to do anything you say!" Thomas stood, knocking over the chair. "I hate you!"

Hannah felt a swell of sorrow and failure sweep over her. Her voice resolute and quiet, she said, "If you hate me so much, then perhaps you should live elsewhere."

Dead quiet cut through the room.

Thomas bolted for the door.

"Thomas. I didn't mean that. I'm sorry."

"You're not. You never wanted me 'ere." He yanked open the door and ran outside, leaping from the porch. He ran hard, heading for the fields.

"Thomas! Thomas!" Hannah went after him, but he was too far ahead of her. He kept running until he disappeared among the deep golden grasses.

Gulping air, Hannah stopped. It was useless. She couldn't catch him.

Staring at the place she'd last seen him, she pressed her hand against her stomach. *Oh, Lord, what have I done?*

20

Heavy of heart, Hannah added wood to the hot coals beneath a large iron pot of tallow. Thankfully John had placed it over the fire before leaving that morning, but the task of making candles was hers. She'd misjudged how many candles they'd need to carry them through the summer months, and now she was forced to make more in the midst of the hot season, something she'd never done before.

It was early in the day, but the air was already sultry. Working over a fire would soon make it intolerable. But Hannah had no other choice. It must be done.

Flies buzzed about the pot, and as the day went on, Hannah knew there would be more of the beastly insects. She shuddered. *Despicable creatures.*

She looked toward the garden. It needed tending, but without Thomas she didn't know how she'd manage to look after it and see to the candle making. Planting her hands on her hips, she gazed out over the open fields and down to the road. Where was he? Had she driven him away for good? *Certainly not. He'll be back.*

She considered what had happened and recoiled over what her impatience had caused. Although Thomas had been misbehaving, she should have maintained her composure. Her sharp words had only made things worse. *When he returns, I'll speak to him. If only he'll listen.*

Using a large wooden paddle, she stirred the tallow. It wasn't hot enough, so Hannah set up drying racks, then cut wicks and draped them over a candle rod. When she'd finished, she checked the tallow again, but it still wasn't ready. She decided that while it heated she'd spend some time in the garden. Perhaps Thomas would be back soon and could finish.

She stood at the end of a row of turnips overrun by weeds. She placed a box on the ground beside her and set to work, pulling the unwanted vegetation. Every few minutes, she'd look up, hoping to see Thomas trudging toward the house. He never came.

She hadn't gotten very far down the row when it was time to check the tallow again. She sat back on her legs and brushed hair out of her face. Once more, she looked across the golden fields, crackling beneath the hot sun. Still no sign of Thomas. A pang of alarm pulsed through her. He'd been gone quite a long while. It was hot, too hot. He'd not taken any food or water with him. *He's probably at the river. It's cooler there.*

She still had candles to make, so she pushed to her feet and brushed dirt from her hands and skirt. *He'll be back soon. I'll apologize.* She closed her eyes and turned her face skyward. *Please help Thomas to forgive me.* With one last glance at the river, she moved toward the house where the pot of tallow cooked in the shade of an acacia.

The unpleasant odor of rendered fat tainted the aroma of heated grasses that usually wafted through the yard. Swatting at flies buzzing about the edges of the pot, Hannah picked up the paddle and stirred. The tallow was now melted and hot—ready at last.

After adding more wood to the fire, she wiped her damp face with her sleeve. If only she had help. She needed Thomas.

Frustration stirred inside, but she caught hold of the undeserved irritation and cast it aside. He was just a child, a hurting little boy. She turned and looked down the drive, praying she'd see him walking toward the house. It was empty and so were the fields.

Letting out a discouraged sigh, she used her apron to wipe sweat from her neck and then rolled up her sleeves. She climbed the front steps and dipped out a tin of water from a barrel beside the door. Her mouth was ready for something cool and refreshing, but the water was warm and brackish. Perhaps when John returned, he would bring up fresh from the river.

Feeling overly warm and already dirty and damp, Hannah poured water into a bucket, then went inside for a washcloth. The house was stifling hot. She'd have to open the windows and leave the door ajar, which meant flies would descend upon the room, but there was nothing that could be done about it.

After opening up the house, she returned to the porch, dipped the cloth into the cool water, and washed away the dirt and sweat from her arms and neck. The sensation was momentarily refreshing. Kneeling beside the bucket, she splashed water over her face, then patted it dry with a towel.

She stood and looked at the cooking pot waiting for her. The idea of working over the fire and fighting flies all day was tremendously distasteful. Hannah vowed she'd never again do this during the summer months.

She immersed the first set of wicks into the fat and lifted them out, holding them over the pot so the extra tallow could drip off. Then she draped the newly born candles over a cooling rack. It would take several more layers of tallow before they'd be complete. She cut more wicks and bathed them in the hot fat and hung them to dry.

Hannah checked the first ones she'd dipped. They didn't look quite right, but she dipped them again. She continued working, but the candles were misshapen and not solidly congealed. She held up a candle rod with the droopy candles hanging from it. They were in such poor condition they'd be unusable. "What did I do wrong?" And then it struck her—the heat. It was too hot for the tallow to set up adequately.

She returned the useless candles to the rack and stared at her hard work—all for naught—another lesson of living in New South Wales. Her back and legs ached and her dress was soaked with perspiration. Every place her skin was exposed, there were welts from biting flies, and she'd accomplished nothing.

Disheartened and feeling foolish, she walked to the front porch and dipped out a cup of drinking water, then sat on a wooden chair. She wanted to cry. Instead, she drank the water and then closed her eyes, enjoying a soft breeze that cooled her damp skin. "I should have known. How could I have been so featherbrained?" She looked at the miserable racks draped with the ugly, useless candles. *What shall we do now? They'll need to be done over, but when the weather is cooler.* Hannah hated the thought.

She hung the cup from a bracket above the water barrel and turned to gaze at the land. Heat waves rippled above thirsty fields and multitudes of cicadas whirred. Hannah didn't remember it ever being so hot. Worry tightened in her gut. It was too hot for a little boy to be wandering about. He should be back. *Where is he?*

Hannah considered taking her horse and going to look for him, but knew it would be unwise. She had no idea where to begin. *Perhaps he's with John. He's probably helping him and Quincy.*

It's not safe for any of them to be out in such brutal heat. She'd expected John and Quincy to return earlier in the day. *What will they think when they see my dreadful candles?* She'd already received a lesson in humility but knew there'd be more. The men couldn't bear to pass up an opportunity for a laugh.

❦

The sun sat low in the sky, turning strands of clouds pink. "John, where are you?" Fear spiked through her. There were so many things that could go wrong, and soon it would turn dusk. *At least the night will be a reprieve from the blazing sun.*

Hannah scooped out another cupful of water and unsuccessfully tried to satisfy her thirst. Replacing the cup, she wondered what she ought to do with the pathetic candles. They would have to be rendered down again. In the meantime, she'd have to see about purchasing some. With a glance toward the road, she walked indoors. She'd been so intent on her candle making that she'd given little thought to the evening meal. Eggs would have to do.

She took a basket and gathered eggs from the chicken yard. The multitude of insects and longer days made for more successful laying. The hens produced more eggs than the family could consume. By the time she returned to the house, the sky had deepened into red and the rasping song of the cicadas had quieted, though there were many who still chanted to the coming darkness. Hannah scanned the countryside surrounding her home, hoping to see John, but there was no one.

She remained on the porch for a while, waiting and expecting to see her family at any moment. She finally set the eggs on the

247

chair and walked to the stock pen. The air remained heated, but the breeze was cooling. Hannah rested her arms on the top rail of the pen and studied Patience. She needed milking. Without her calf to feed, she had an abundance of milk. The thought of the bull calf handed over to Deidre sent a rush of anger through Hannah. Deidre had simply turned around and sold him. *At least we haven't heard anything from her recently. We can be thankful for that, I suppose.*

Her eyes found the river and she considered wandering down to its quiet banks. Perhaps Thomas was there. *If he is, he'll not take kindly to my searching him out. Anyway, he's most likely with John. And they'll be back soon.*

Hannah decided to leave the milking to John, went inside, and set to work fixing dinner. She cracked eggs into a pot, whisked them with a fork, and then set them in the dying embers left from the morning's fire. She sliced bread and cheese for a platter, which she put on the table along with butter. She set out plates and flatwear. And there was cake left. It would do nicely for dessert.

The familiar sound of a dog's bark carried in from outside. "Jackson! That must be them." Hannah hurried out to the front porch. She spotted John and Quincy, silhouetted against the red sky, and young Jackson frolicking, his tongue hanging out. He headed straight for the watering trough and lapped up a stomachful of water. Thomas wasn't with them. Like a fire out of control, alarm swept over Hannah. Where was Thomas?

"Sorry we were out so long, luv," John said. "The sheep were cantankerous, and we and Jackson had more trouble than usual." He threw a leg over and dropped out of the saddle. The dog danced about him. John patted his head. "I'll feed you in good time, boy."

"Thomas," Hannah blurted. "He's not with you?"

"No. He was supposed to stay here and help you. He's not here?"

"No."

"Where is he?"

"I . . . I don't know. I'd hoped he was with you."

"What happened?" His tone was accusatory.

"This morning we had another quarrel and he stormed off across the field. He's been gone since. I'd hoped he'd found you and Quincy."

John scanned the darkening landscape and then whirled around to Hannah. "What did you do? I thought you were set on being a mum to him? You promised to try."

"I did." Hannah felt as if she'd been slapped and she deserved it. "He refused to help me. He was angry because he had to stay behind; he wanted to be with you. I made him breakfast, but he refused to eat it. When I tried to force him, things got worse." Hannah put her palms against her cheeks. "It was awful." She was close to tears. "He said he hated me and I . . . I told him that maybe he ought to live somewhere else." She shook her head. "He's out there . . . alone."

Hannah covered a sob with her hand. "It's my fault. All of it. We've got to find him."

"We will." The harshness was gone from John's voice. He took Hannah's hands in his. "It's not your fault. People quarrel. I'm sure he's fine. Most likely he's not far from the house, probably hiding in a tree somewhere. He might even be watching us."

"I don't think so. He was really angry . . . and hurt. I saw no sign of him all day." Hannah remembered how he'd stomped off, acting like he was tough when all the while he felt small and trampled upon. "Please find him, John."

"We will." John climbed back into the saddle.

Hannah gazed up at him, barely able to see through a blur of tears. "If something happens to him—"

"Nothing's going to happen. We'll find him. Which way did he head?"

Hannah pointed toward the west. "He ran through the fields."

"All right, Quincy, you go that way and I'll see if he's on the road somewhere. We'll need lanterns."

"I'll get them." Quincy hurried to the barn.

Hannah gazed into the gathering gloom. "John, there's so much out there—dingoes, snakes, convicts . . . the river. He's just a little boy."

"He's a clever lad. He'll be all right. You'll see." John offered an encouraging smile. "Take heart."

Hannah watched Quincy and John ride away. Their lanterns cast an eerie glow in the darkness. Quincy moved across the field and John headed west on the road. Hannah stood on the porch and watched until they disappeared. She remained there a long while, staring into the darkness. Finally she went indoors. The bread and cheese remained on the table where flies feasted. She shooed them away and covered the food with a cloth, then stirred the eggs. They were burnt and inedible. She lifted the pan out of the coals and set it on the stone lip of the hearth.

A forlorn mooing came from outside. Patience needed milking. Hannah grabbed a washcloth and a lantern and hurried to the stock pen. She hooked a lead on Patience and walked her to the barn and to the stanchion.

Once Patience was secured, Hannah grabbed an armful of hay and set it in the crib. Patience buried her nose in the sweet-smelling feed and was soon grinding it between her teeth. Hannah moved the stool alongside the bovine, her mind outside in the darkness with Thomas. With a pat to Patience's side, she sat and wiped the udder clean with the cloth. Setting the bucket beneath her, she grabbed two teats, and soon milk flowed.

She pressed her forehead against the cow's side, her mind filled with thoughts of Thomas and the stricken look on his face when he'd run off. Sorrow and regret rose up and engulfed her in a large wave. "What have I done? Oh, what have I done?" She sobbed against Patience's rounded belly. "My little boy is lost and it's my fault."

In the midst of heartbreak, the knowledge that she truly loved Thomas swept over Hannah. He was, indeed, her son.

Patience swished her tail and stomped a foot, seemingly irritated with Hannah's delay. The truth swamping her, Hannah straightened, keeping a hand on the cow's side. God had given her a child once and she'd spurned it. And yet God had forgiven her. Then she'd cried out and asked him for another and he'd given her Thomas. Once again, she'd turned her back on the gift. "I deserve nothing from you, Lord, but your wrath. But Thomas deserves more. He needs a family. Please bring him home. I love him."

Through tears and prayer, Hannah continued milking. She pressed in close to Patience, and as the bucket filled, the sound of splashing milk quieted. When she'd finished, she moved the stool and bucket aside and led Patience to her stall. After giving her a handful of grain, she picked up the lantern and stepped into the darkness. The howl of a dingo echoed across the empty countryside. Hannah stopped and listened. How close was it? What if he went after Thomas? *He's a smart lad.*

A dingo's no danger to him. He'll surely climb a tree if need be. She moved on to the house. She stepped inside, and the dingo's mournful cry came again.

Hannah strained the milk and poured it into a container. She placed a cloth over the top and left it so the cream could rise. She'd churn butter tomorrow. Thomas would like that. He liked fresh butter on his bread.

She took her Bible down from a shelf and sat in the dim lantern light, turning to Psalms. The songs of David would comfort her. She turned to Psalm 17:8. *"Keep me as the apple of your eye; hide me under the shadow of your wings."*

Hannah closed her eyes. She could feel the Lord's presence. He loved her in spite of all she'd done. He would not forsake her, nor would he forsake Thomas. She was certain of it. *You know where he is. Keep him safe. Spread your wings of protection over him. And please bring him back to us.*

Hannah read several more Scriptures and prayed until she fell asleep. When she stirred awake, the candle had burned down considerably. She glanced at the clock—1:00 a.m. Was John back? She moved to the window and gazed out—there was nothing but darkness and the sound of buzzing cicadas and the rustle of hot grasses. Hannah returned to her chair and prayed for her son's safe return.

She didn't know how long she'd been praying when she heard the sound of horses. Her heart pounding, she pushed out of the chair and crossed to the door.

Taking a hopeful breath, she opened it. A light illuminated the barn. Someone was there. "John?" Hannah stepped off the porch and hurried toward the barn. *Oh Lord, please let Thomas be with him.* "John? Thomas?"

She moved as quickly as the darkness would allow. It must

be them. It had to be. She stepped inside. Whoever it was, they were in the back. "John," she said and moved inside, walking toward the stalls. "Is that you?"

He stepped out of a stall. "Hannah." He looked tired, the lantern light deepening the shadows on his face.

Hannah's spirits dropped. "You didn't find him?"

He rested a hand on the gate. "No. I did. Thomas."

The lad peered around the stall door.

"Haven't you something to say to Hannah?" John urged.

Thomas stepped out into the open. "I'm sorry, mum. I shouldn't have run off like I did. It was wrong of me to worry ye so."

Love swept through Hannah. "Oh Thomas, it's me who is sorry." She stepped toward him. "I was wrong. I've been wrong from the beginning. I never meant to hurt you. And I'm sorry I did." She knelt in front of him and studied his dirty, beautiful face. "I'm so sorry. Can you forgive me?"

Thomas gazed at Hannah, his blue eyes wide and pooling with tears. "I forgive ye. Can ye forgive me?"

Hannah smiled, her heart brimming with joy. "Of course." She took his face in her hands and couldn't imagine loving him more if he had come from her own flesh. "I love you, Thomas."

A broad smile replaced his look of bewilderment. Hannah scooped him into her arms and held him close. When his arms went around her neck and hugged her back, she was certain she'd never felt such joy, and she hugged her son more tightly.

21

Hannah set two candlesticks with red-tinted candles in them on the mantel and stepped back to admire them. They looked lovely, especially the candlesticks—a wedding gift from the Athertons. They reminded her of a set her mother once had. Caroline would bring them out only at Christmas. Although they had very little in the way of possessions, Christmas had always been a time of rejoicing and thanksgiving. Hannah smiled at the memories.

When her father had been alive, he'd arrive home on Christmas Eve with gifts tucked under his arms—one for Hannah and another for Caroline. He always made the presentation of the gifts a grand affair, teasing and acting as if he'd forgotten Christmas altogether. Afterward, they'd eat a special meal and sometimes sing carols, which was especially fun when friends joined them.

This would be her first Christmas as a mother and their first as a family. It would be a special day, indeed.

Thomas galloped down the stairs from the loft. "Good day, mum." He smiled and ran to Hannah, hugging her about the waist.

"Good day to you." Hannah's arms went around Thomas.

She smoothed back his blond hair, and he looked up at her. It had been two weeks since he'd run off, and the wonder of a mother's love remained with Hannah. Why had she resisted for so long? Her willfulness had nearly cost her a son.

Smiling down at Thomas, she said, "You slept late. Are you hungry? I've made eggs and toast."

"I'm starved." Thomas strode to the table and sat down. "Has John gone off already?"

"Yes, but he said he'd be back for you later this morning. He wants to show you a new fishing spot he found."

Thomas clasped his hands together and rested them on the table in front of him. "Perhaps we'll have mullet for dinner, eh?"

"That would be nice." Hannah looked at the candles. "Do you like the new candles I made?"

"They're nice. Red's a fine color."

"Thank goodness we've had cooler days. Gwen was able to show Lydia and me how to make candles with dye so they'd be special for Christmas, which is only two weeks off."

Thomas studied the candles. "Why did ye make them red?"

"Well, for me, red represents Jesus's shed blood. Do you know about that?"

"I do. Me mum told me." Sadness touched Thomas's eyes, and Hannah knew he was remembering and missing his mother. He continued, "I was only six when I understood 'bout Jesus dyin' for us. Mum told me that because he did I get to go to heaven. That's where she and me sister and me dad are."

"My mother and father are in heaven too. I miss them terribly, but one day we'll be together again."

"I just wish me mum and dad were here now. Why do ye think God took 'em like he did?"

255

"I don't know for sure. But although heaven's a world we can't see, it's a place where there is only rejoicing and no sadness. And our loved ones live there. We should be happy for them."

"I am, but I miss 'em."

"I know. It's something we must trust God with, eh?"

"I guess so." Thomas rested his cheek in his hand. "Will we be having Christmas, mum?"

"Indeed we will."

Thomas smiled broadly. "And will there be presents?"

"Most certainly." Hannah felt a quiver of excitement. John had been working in the evenings to make a new fishing pole for Thomas. He'd also found a copy of *Robinson Crusoe*, which had been one of his boyhood favorites. He couldn't resist and bought it. Hannah had made Thomas a pair of new socks and a warm blanket for the winter months.

She set a plate of eggs and toast in front of him. "It will be a fine Christmas."

"I don't much like it being so warm." He picked up the toast and took a bite. "I used to go skating with me friends."

"It does seem a bit odd, but I don't miss the cold London winters. They could be brutal."

"I wouldn't mind a bit of snow. Sledding would be nice."

"Yes . . . but now you've fishing instead. And that's grand too."

Thomas nodded and took another bite of toast.

The sound of a buggy carried in from outside. Hannah wasn't expecting anyone. She hurried to the door and stepped onto the porch to find Lydia alone and driving the Atherton buggy. Something must be wrong. She hurried down the steps and ran to meet her.

Lydia didn't look at all distraught.

256

"Good day," Hannah said.

"Good day." Lydia seemed to glow from inside. "I couldn't wait to tell ye the news." She tied the reins and climbed down from the seat. "Mrs. Atherton was kind enough to let me borrow her buggy."

Hannah knew that whatever Lydia had to say must be important. "What is your news?"

Lydia didn't answer right away. Instead, she hesitated, as if letting go of her secret might diminish some of its delight. Finally, she held out her left hand. A gold band encircled her ring finger. "David asked me to marry him!"

"Really? How wonderful!" Hannah tried to sound excited, but she had reservations.

"He went to Mr. Atherton and asked permission. And last night right after dinner he asked if we could take a stroll 'round the grounds. And then he asked me." Lydia's eyes shone and her freckled skin looked rosy. "We're to be married the third week in January."

"You've not long to prepare, then. How shall you manage?"

"It will be a simple wedding. And we don't want to wait."

"But you've a gown to make."

"I know. I thought ye might help me with it." Lydia smiled.

"Of course I will. I'd be honored."

"David said I can choose any fabric I like. Will ye come to town with me to pick it out?"

"Today?"

"No. But soon."

"That sounds like fun." Hannah couldn't still a sense of disquiet. Although recently David and Lydia had been getting along splendidly, the difference in class couldn't be ignored.

And it hadn't been that long since David struggled over the disparity.

Hannah hugged Lydia. "I'm so happy for you. Can you come in for tea?"

"Mrs. Atherton told me I could stay as long as I liked."

"Good. I already have tea on."

Hannah and Lydia settled across from each other at the kitchen table, and Thomas excused himself, setting off to take care of outdoor chores. With a cup cradled between her hands, Lydia studied Hannah. "Ye don't seem as happy as I thought ye'd be."

"Of course I'm happy. But I must confess to feeling a bit of hesitation."

"I know what yer going to say . . . 'bout our differences. Yer worried."

"I am, just a little. I know David loves you, but you've had conflicts about the way you talk and dress and—"

"I know our social classes are different, but there's more to us than that. David seems quite happy with who I am. And he says he loves me and doesn't want me to change."

"And his family?"

Lydia shrugged. "They live in London. It's not likely we'll ever meet. And of course they shan't be at the wedding. In fact David and I will be married before they even know of the engagement."

"And what if they do come one day? Has David said how they'll feel about such a match?"

"He said they'd most likely be unhappy, but he doesn't care 'bout that. And he assures me that if his parents knew me, they'd love me just as he does."

Hannah sat back. "Do you believe him?"

"What am I to believe? I can't know the answer without meeting them." Lydia's voice had taken on a sharp tone. "Anyway, it doesn't matter. We're getting married and we can't wait for his parents' approval."

Hannah leaned across the table and took Lydia's hands in hers. "I'm thrilled for you, really. I just don't want you to get hurt."

Weeks of wedding preparations passed quickly, and soon it was Lydia and David's day. Lydia had asked Hannah to stand with her. David had chosen a colleague from Sydney Town.

The morning of the wedding, John, Hannah, and Thomas set off for the church. The air was hot and still, but thankfully the temperatures weren't the suffocating kind.

Hoping to be of help, Hannah and John arrived early. There were only a handful of carriages in front of the church, the Athertons', David's, and another one Hannah didn't recognize.

John held Hannah's hand as she stepped down from the wagon. Thomas clambered out and dashed around toward the back of the church. "Don't stray," John called after him.

"I won't," Thomas reassured him.

"And don't get dirty." Hannah watched the boy. "Some days he acts as if he doesn't have a care in the world. He's so changed."

"That he is. He's happy."

"It's a wonder. I remember thinking he'd never find happiness." Hannah leaned against John. "Although I know God is powerful, he still surprises me."

"He does, indeed." John escorted Hannah toward the church.

Her heart pounded in anticipation, almost as if it were her

own wedding. She stopped at the bottom of the steps and looked at John. "It wasn't that long ago we were exchanging vows."

John kissed the top of her hand. "I remember."

"It's only been a little more than a year."

Hannah's heart warmed at the memory, but the passing of time also reminded her how many months had come and gone and she'd still not conceived. She loved Thomas and the life they had together, but the longing for a baby still remained. Perhaps in time she'd find peace in God's decision.

Shrugging off the melancholy, she hurried up the steps and went to a small room adjacent to the foyer where Lydia should be waiting. Hannah knocked softly.

The door opened and Lydia peeked out. "Oh. Thank goodness. Come in." She nearly yanked Hannah inside and then hugged her. "I've been waiting for ye. I don't know what to do." She paced.

"You look lovely. And I'd say there's nothing for you to do but wait." Hannah gazed at Lydia. "You look absolutely beautiful. David will be overcome."

Lydia stepped in front of a large mirror and studied her reflection. She nudged a lock of auburn hair into place, then held her arms away from her sides. "I must say it doesn't look like me staring back."

"You're stunning. The dress is lovely."

Lydia rested a hand over her abdomen. "Ye don't think it's too tight in the waist, eh?"

"No. It's perfect."

Lydia smiled and did a pirouette. "Ye really think so?"

"I've never seen a lovelier bride."

"Well, I'm sure that's not true, but I'll accept the compliment. It was your good eye for material. Thank you." Lydia smoothed a wide belt made of white satin and peered down at the gown that dropped freely to the floor. "Are ye sure white is proper . . . for me?"

"Lydia," Hannah said in exasperation. "It absolutely is."

"But I'm not . . . untouched."

Hannah remembered the night on board the prison ship when Lydia had been hauled away by one of the sailors. "You are pure. Christ has made you so."

Lydia smiled. "I guess white is just right, then. Thank ye for reminding me."

"Does David know about what happened?"

"Yes. I wasn't 'bout to face the same dilemma ye did with John. I told him straight out. He didn't act shocked or surprised. I suppose being a female prisoner . . . he thought it possible. I think I saw tears in his eyes when he heard what had happened. He reassured me that he loved me no matter what might be in my past."

Lydia moved to a chair and sat down. "Mrs. Atherton is so kind. She tried to get a pardon for me, but the governor refused. He said my crime was too heinous and that he couldn't pardon prisoners at the drop of a hat, that he'd already granted too many."

"Will you stay on at the Athertons', then?"

"No. David's home is too far from there. I've been transferred to the mercantile. They need help. It will be close to David's office, and we'll live in town." She smiled. "It's not perfect, but it's good."

"And it's closer to my home." Hannah smiled.

"That's true." Lydia turned back to face the mirror. "I can't believe I'm about to become Mrs. David Gelson, the wife of a physician and part of an upper-class family." Her eyes teared. "If I were living in London, this wouldn't be possible."

A haunted expression touched her eyes and she hugged herself about the waist. "I remember standing over my mother's husband with a pistol in my hand. He was sprawled out on the floor, dead, lying in his own blood. I knew my future was the gallows. When I was given transportation, it felt like a gift. And it was. Being placed with the Athertons gave me a new life."

"It's so like God to do those kinds of things. He makes treasure out of what we see as rubbish." Hannah felt the sting of tears.

"He does. And I've always believed he could do whatever he chose to do, but there were times . . ." Lydia couldn't continue. She dabbed at her eyes. "I'd best stop or I'll look a mess when I walk down the aisle."

Lydia's green eyes were lit with joy when she handed her simple bouquet to Hannah and turned to David. While the couple vowed to cherish each other and to live out their lives together, Hannah met John's gaze. She knew he was remembering, just as she was, the day they'd promised themselves to one another. It seemed so close, like yesterday. The wealth of God's gift was overwhelming. Her life truly was a miracle. *He's given more than I deserve.*

Making a final pledge, David slipped a ring on Lydia's finger. His eyes were filled with love and devotion, and Hannah's qualms vanished. She was certain he loved her enough to overcome their differences.

The reverend pressed the couple's hands between his own and said a prayer of blessing. He smiled at them and then said, "David, you may kiss your bride."

David tenderly pulled Lydia into his arms and pressed his lips to hers. True to Lydia's forthright way, she responded without hesitation. The couple smiled at each other, their love so powerful that it could be seen, like a great wave, sweeping over them.

The reverend whispered congratulations, then turned to the guests and said, "I'd like to introduce Dr. and Mrs. David Gelson."

David grasped Lydia's hand and led her down the aisle. As they moved through the church, people reached out and wished them well. Feeling especially tender toward John, Hannah grasped his hand and they followed their friends.

Revelry, good food, and music followed. When the sun lay low in the sky, David escorted Lydia down the church steps and helped her into his buggy. Among cheers and blessings, the couple drove off.

Hannah stood on the church steps, John on one side and Thomas on the other. She waved, watching the fading buggy and blinking back tears.

"Shall we go?" John asked.

"Yes. But I need to get my reticule from the dressing room. I shan't be long."

While Thomas and a friend raced through a grove of gum trees, John moved to the wagon to wait for Hannah. He felt quiet inside, grateful and happy. But at the sight of Deidre walking toward him, tranquility fled. She'd not bothered him in some time, and he'd hoped the nightmare was over. He grabbed a handful of grain from a bag and gave some to each horse.

"I'll have a word with ye," Deidre said, striding up to John.

He didn't look at her. "I've nothing to say to you."

"Oh, but ye have. I'm in need of help."

Resting a hand on one horse's broad face, he looked at Deidre, making no attempt to conceal his disdain. "I suppose you would be, since Mrs. Atherton discharged you as she should have."

"She did indeed. But she had no reason. I'm an excellent maid. In fact, I should have been the housekeeper. I'm wondering if someone was spreading tales about me."

"I wouldn't know about that. I'd say you're lucky not to be in prison."

"I've served my time." She glanced at the Atherton carriage driving away. "She'll be sorry for letting me go."

"Is that a threat? I'd be careful if I were you. The Athertons are well loved."

She glanced at the church. "I'm here to speak 'bout my needs. I'm in a bad way and in need of funds. Without work I've no resources."

"Then, I'd say you'd best find employment." He almost grinned, but the sight of her was so distasteful he couldn't manage it. He inspected the horses' harnesses.

Her voice dripping with contempt, Deidre spat, "Turn 'round and face me. Ye don't turn yer back to me."

Slowly, John turned. His eyes bore into hers. They were cold and devoid of emotion. How could he have ever thought her handsome?

"I need cash. Now."

"I've none to give you."

"It's not my concern how ye come by the funds, but ye must pay me."

John despised her. He fought off a desire to strike her. "I'm not giving you another farthing."

She smirked. "Ye think not, eh? Well then, I suppose I'll have to see how the elders feel 'bout yer wife's . . . indulgences."

"Ye won't." John hoped he sounded like he believed what

he was saying. "If you say a word, you'll expose yourself. And you'll be ruined right along with Hannah."

"Ye believe I care what people think of me?" She smirked. "I care nothing for them. And there are other places to live, better than this pathetic settlement." Her blue eyes turned colder. "But ye can be assured I'll not go until I've spoken to the elders."

John knew she meant it. "This will end badly for you."

Deidre laughed. "Maybe so, but all the worse for ye." She rested a hand on her hip. "I suppose ye might hold off and see where it gets ye."

There was no escape. John had nothing to use for leverage. "What happened to the money ye got for the bull calf? I know ye sold him."

"That was gone long ago, as if it were any of yer business."

He stared at her, rage boiling inside. "All right, but this is the last time. Don't ask again."

Deidre smirked. "Certainly."

"I'll get the money for you, but it'll take a few days. I've no funds right now."

"I'll not wait more than a week. And after that, I'll be off to see the reverend." She sauntered away toward a carriage driven by a man John had never seen before.

John's hatred for the woman was deep and powerful, and frightening. He was defenseless. How was it that someone like Deidre could control his life?

He glanced up to see Hannah striding toward him. She was angry.

22

Hannah stepped out of the church just in time to watch Deidre flounce away from John. *What does she want?* Even as the question tramped through her mind, she knew. Furious, she strode toward her husband.

He looked from Deidre to Hannah, then squared his shoulders and faced his angry wife.

"What is it now?" Hannah demanded. When John didn't answer right away, she repeated. "What does she want from us this time?"

"Nothing." John's eyes followed Deidre as she stepped into the carriage.

"So, she was just visiting, eh? I suppose the two of you discussed the weather." Hannah couldn't keep the caustic tone out of her voice.

John clenched his jaw. "No, of course not." His eyes met Hannah's. "She wants money. Mrs. Atherton discharged her and she says she's in a bad way."

"In a bad way? What with all the money she's made selling what we've given her? And her larder is full, no doubt. What more could she have need of?"

John moved toward Hannah, but she stepped away. Just now,

she couldn't bear for him to touch her. She needed him to be strong, to stop this treachery.

"I told her this is the last time."

Hannah glared at Deidre as she settled on the seat beside the stranger. Most certainly she was deceiving him as well. He looked to be someone of means.

Deidre rested an arm on an open window and gazed at Hannah and John. She smiled smugly as the coach moved away.

"It seems she has all the help she needs," Hannah said, her voice prickly as nettles. All of a sudden she couldn't bear the smugness, the ridicule, the treachery. She started after the carriage. "She'll not make sport of us a moment longer."

"Hannah. Stop," John called. "You'll only make things worse." He ran after her.

But before he could catch her, Mr. Atherton's carriage moved toward them. "Hannah . . . John." He smiled, but the friendliness didn't touch the concern in his eyes.

Hannah nodded and smiled and then tried to step around the horses.

Mrs. Atherton leaned out the carriage window. "If you'll just give us a moment. Please, Hannah."

Hannah watched the carriage carrying Deidre drive away. It was too late to catch her. She stopped and let her arms drop to her sides. Still angry, she did her best not to show it as she walked up to Catharine's carriage window. "I didn't realize you were still here."

"I had some tidying up to do in the church. It wasn't much, but I thought it the kindly thing to do." Catharine smiled.

William opened the carriage door, stepped out and approached John. "I've a few projects I was hoping you might do for me." He rested a broad hand on John's shoulder.

"I'd be pleased to. Just what do you need done?"

The men walked away, and Catharine asked, "Will you come and sit with me?"

Hannah didn't want to hear how she ought to be tolerant and forgiving. Deidre deserved neither. She stepped inside and sat across from Catharine. Pressing her back against the seat, she folded her hands in her lap.

"It was a splendid wedding. Lydia was stunning, don't you think?"

"She was." So quickly the joy of her friend's wedding had evaporated. Deidre was good at robbing people of happiness.

"And I'm not sure I've ever seen a more handsome groom." Her eyes sparkled with delight. "Except for John of course."

"A very nice wedding, indeed." Hannah tried to concentrate on what was at hand, but her mind kept carrying her back to Deidre. "I'm happy for Lydia."

"Oh, I'm thrilled for her and for David." Catharine leveled serious eyes on Hannah. "But there is something else I wanted to speak to you about. I know this is a trying time for you and John. And I understand your indignation with Deidre. You're rightfully angry."

Hannah stared at her hands.

"But running after her and confronting her at church is not necessarily a wise way to end her thieving."

"We don't know how to end it. What can we do? There seems to be nothing that will stop her."

"This is something for the Lord to work out. It's beyond human means." Catharine's expression turned mischievous. "Unless, of course, you're willing to allow her to speak out." She rested quiet eyes on Hannah. "I'm not at all convinced she will, but of course she may."

"John and I have talked about what we should do if she tells everyone the truth, her truth. We're prepared to move away from Parramatta."

"Oh, I shouldn't think that would be necessary."

"The farm is only now beginning to do a small amount of business. We've a growing number of sheep, and there should be a profit in the wool. But others must be willing to do business with us. If this were to get out, it could put an end to our dreams. Especially because what she's said to John about what happened isn't altogether accurate; she's colored the story with her own tale." Hannah wanted it all to end, for good or bad. "What shall we do?"

"I'm convinced God overcomes evil with good. I'd say wait and allow him to set his plan in place."

"But when will I know? How can we know what to do?" Hannah shook her head. "I can't allow this to go on any longer. We won't give her another thing."

"And if she goes to the elders?"

"Then she does and there can be nothing done about it."

"And you trust God with that?"

"We must. How can we not? He's been with us through so much. I've no inkling of what is to come, but I do know the Lord walks with us."

Catharine smiled as she reached across and took Hannah's hand. "Good." Passion lit her blue eyes. "We have a God who is powerful and wise, one we trust in all things."

Hannah nodded. "I believe that." She glanced at the road, then closed her eyes and breathed deeply, hoping to find a vestige of peace. "But I'm still frightened."

"Of course. You're only human." Catharine squeezed Hannah's hand. "You have William's and my support, absolutely.

As you've most likely heard, I dismissed Deidre. She's served her previous sentence, but if I were to report her extortion to the authorities, she would most likely be given further gaol time."

"Wouldn't that be cause for her to remain quiet about what she knows?"

"One would think so, but for too many, temptation overrides good sense."

Hannah just wished it would simply go away. "She's insisting on a cash payment this time."

"I've a good rapport with the governor. Would you like me to speak to him?"

Hannah considered the offer. Deidre deserved to pay dearly for what she'd done, but Hannah didn't want prison even for her. "There must be another way."

"I imagine God will see that justice is done. And I daresay, his ways can be the most painful of all."

No longer feeling nearly so flustered, Hannah nodded. "I'm going to speak to her. I won't allow this blackmail to continue."

"I'll be in prayer."

"Thank you." Hannah watched Thomas. He stood beside John, his attention riveted on the men's conversation. She imagined he was enjoying being part of a grown-up discussion. "I'm just not sure about Thomas and what will happen to him if she speaks out."

"I've thought about that. It does add to the dilemma."

"I'd hate for him to become a target of ridicule on my account, but I believe it would be more harmful for him to watch his parents be bullied by someone like her." ·

"I quite agree." Catharine sat back in her seat. "I'm proud of you and John. This isn't an easy thing to face."

Hannah glanced at her husband. "I'm not certain John agrees with me."

"Oh? I thought you were in accord. If not, then it might be best if you waited until you two agree on what should be done."

"I know. And we will." Hannah hugged Catharine. "Thank you for your kindness and your encouragement."

"We need to stand together, eh?" Catharine smiled.

"That we do." Hannah stepped out of the carriage and moved toward John and Mr. Atherton.

William looked at Hannah. "Well, it seems the women have completed their chat." He glanced up at a darkening sky. "And the weather is taking a turn, so I'd best be on my way." He smiled at Hannah. "Good day to you."

"Good day."

John and then Thomas tipped their hats to William Atherton.

Hannah stood a good distance from John while she watched the Atherton carriage move away. Now it was time for her and John to talk and decide their course.

"We should be off," John said as cheerfully as he could manage. He rested a hand on Thomas's shoulder. "In with you."

Thomas clambered into the back of the wagon while John helped Hannah up onto the seat. He took his place beside her and lifted the traces, giving the horses a gentle slap of the reins. They moved toward home.

Wind whipped tree branches and spattered drops of rain. Birds chattered exuberantly in the trees, but in the wagon everyone was silent.

Thomas draped himself over the back of the seat between Hannah and John. "What's wrong with ye, eh? No one's said a word since we left the church. Figured ye'd be talking 'bout what a fine wedding it was. Is something wrong?"

"No. Everything's fine," said John. "We're just a bit tired is all. It's been a long day."

Hannah patted Thomas's hand. If she were going to speak to Deidre, it would be wise to forewarn the boy. "I'm just busy thinking about what a grand wedding it was." She smiled. "Not to worry."

"I know when things aren't right. I've seen enough of it." He pressed his chin into his arm. "Can't help but worry. Once before, I lost everything in me life that mattered. And now I can feel it—something bad is going on."

"It's not like that." Hannah turned and looked at him. "You'll never lose us. I promise."

"Ye can't promise a thing like that. Ye never know what kind of trouble might come. Me mum and sister didn't count on dying on that ship, and me dad and me was just going fishing, that's all . . ." His voice broke.

"I don't know why bad things happen," John said, his voice tender. "But I know we can trust God. I don't think he would have brought you into our lives if he didn't intend for us all to stay together for a good while." He offered an encouraging smile, then his eyes met Hannah's and she could see renewed strength in him.

Hannah and John didn't speak about Deidre the rest of the day, although the woman was never far from Hannah's thoughts. By the time Thomas was ready for bed, she was on edge, needing to discuss what should happen and how.

John and Hannah followed Thomas up the stairs to the loft, and the three knelt beside the bed for evening prayers. Before John could begin, Thomas asked, "Can I pray this time?"

"That's a fine idea," said John. "Your prayers matter to God just as much as mine do."

Hannah was touched by Thomas's desire to pray. *He's a fine boy.* Her mind wandered to Deidre and what she would say to her. She knew her mind needed to be here with her husband and son, but she couldn't keep it from wandering to Deidre and what was coming.

His voice solemn and reverent, Thomas began, "Father in heaven, me life's been a bit of a struggle, but I'm thankful for all ye've done for me. I miss me mum and dad and Catrin real bad, but I love me new home. But there's something bad afoot. I can feel it."

Hannah's heart skipped a beat and she glanced at Thomas. His eyes were squeezed shut.

"I'm feelin' afraid," said Thomas. "I know me new mum and dad don't want nothin' bad to happen, but I think it might. Please do whatever needs done so everything will be all right. Don't let nobody or nothin' hurt us, especially not Mum and Dad. Please, Lord. Amen."

Hannah swiped away a tear, hoping Thomas wouldn't see. When she looked at him, he grabbed hold of her hand. "Try not to worry, Mum."

"I'm fine, Thomas. And I'm certain God will take care of our troubles." Hannah hugged him. She kissed his forehead and then stood. "Now don't you worry about grown-up problems. You go to sleep and have little boy dreams."

"Don't have those kinds of dreams no more. But I figure maybe one day I will." He settled down into bed.

John rested a hand on Thomas's head. "I'd say you're more grown-up than most lads your age. I'm proud of you."

Thomas grinned and then pulled a thin blanket up under his chin. "Good night."

"Night, Son." John followed Hannah out of the room and down the stairs.

"Would you like the last of the coffee?" Hannah asked.

"Sounds fine to me." John sat in his chair and picked up a book he'd been reading. "This author's quite good."

"Who is it?"

"Joseph Andrews. He writes a rousing story."

Hannah poured John his coffee and handed it to him, then sat in her chair and picked up her sewing basket. Setting it in her lap, she went to work repairing socks. Occasionally she'd glance up at John and he'd seem engrossed in his story. *How can he be so unmoved by all that's happened?*

Hannah stitched faster. Now was not the time for an argument. Thomas would hear. She didn't want to frighten him more than he already was. But she couldn't get Deidre off her mind. She'd decided that in the morning she'd go to see her.

The minutes ticked by, and when the clock chimed nine o'clock, John set his book on the table beside him. "I've a lot to do tomorrow. May even have some new lambs. Quincy's keeping an eye on the ewes tonight."

Hannah set her sewing in her lap and looked at John. "I think we need to speak to Deidre. I refuse to give her anything more."

John stared at her for a long moment. "I agree, but I don't want your name sullied. I don't want to risk her speaking out."

"It's my name. And I've decided that keeping the secret is not worth all of this. I'm going to tell her."

"But—"

"Thomas knows something's wrong. And soon he'll know everything. He's a smart lad. I don't want him to see us cowering but rather to know we have faith and that we are strong and courageous."

"He doesn't know about you," John whispered.

"No. But he's heard enough to understand that we're paying someone to keep a secret . . . something bad. And I won't do it any longer."

"Hannah. No. I don't want you talking to her."

"Since I've known you, John, you've never been afraid of anything. Your faith has always been strong. You've been brave and hardworking. I don't understand why someone like Deidre frightens you so much. What can she do to us?"

"She'll ruin your reputation."

Hannah knew the truth, but she couldn't speak it. She needed John to say what was true.

"Everyone has secrets, dark places they don't want others to see," Hannah said. "How many here in Parramatta come from nobility or of good standing? Except for a very few who came in service to the king and their wives, and a handful of businessmen hoping to make their fortunes, most of our neighbors were prisoners. I can assure you there are many secrets being held close."

"Yes. And that's the point. They're private things that no one speaks of. I don't want people talking about you."

"It's more than that." Hannah waited, hoping John would speak up. When he didn't, she continued, "This is about you, John, not me. You don't want people speaking about you and how wretched it must be to be married to a woman of such little integrity—what a fool you were to marry one so sullied."

She stared at him in the flickering lamplight and waited for a response. John remained silent. "Tell me it's not true. Tell me." Hannah quaked inside. *Please let me be wrong.*

John stood and walked to the hearth where he poked at dying embers. "All right. It's true. I don't want to be shamed. If Deidre speaks up, it will go poorly for the both of us, not just you. I've a business at stake. What will happen to it when people know?"

Hannah had known, but hearing it from John made the hurt greater. An ache tightened at the base of her throat. She pressed her lips tightly together and held back tears. "I thought when we married it was for better or for worse. That we were to stand together against anything that might befall us."

"I'll stand with you. I am standing with you. I love you, Hannah. I know what happened was not your fault, and I accept your past."

"Then why are you ashamed of it?"

"I'm not."

"You are." Hannah pushed her sewing into the basket. "I shall speak to Deidre tomorrow. We'll not give her another thing." She set the basket on the floor beside her chair.

"Give me more time. I know I can put an end to it."

"There is no more time." Hannah walked into the bedroom and closed the door. She suddenly felt calm. Removing her day clothes, she pulled on her sleeping gown and climbed into bed. After blowing out the lantern, she pulled a thin blanket up under her chin.

She heard the front door close. Where would John be going this late? Would he leave her?

Hannah closed her eyes. There were no tears, only determination. No matter what, she'd speak to Deidre first thing in the morning.

23

Inside the Bradshaw house, the temperature was warm, but emotions were cool. John set a bucket of milk on the counter. "We've more than we can use."

Hannah poured the milk through a strainer. "Patience is making enough milk for us and the calf. It's too bad we had to give away the bull calf." Hannah knew she wasn't helping matters but hadn't been able to keep quiet. "We've extra milk in the springhouse that can go to the pigs."

"Thomas, can you see to that?" John asked.

"And take the slop bucket too," Hannah said, picking up the broom and setting to work sweeping the floor.

"Right. Will it be all right if I go fishing with Douglas? He said he'd meet me at the river."

Hannah stopped sweeping and looked at him. "Is your room tidy?"

"It is."

John glanced at Hannah. "It's fine by me. A lad needs friends and fun. And Douglas is a fine lad. It's good he has a mate who lives close. And Douglas is from a good family."

Thomas looked to Hannah. She nodded and he pulled on his hat, grabbed the slop bucket, and hurried outdoors.

The door had barely shut when John said, "Hannah, I've decided you're right. We can't give in to Deidre any longer. But I should be the one to go."

"No. It needs to be me. This is about me."

John stared at her. "It's about us."

Hannah took a step toward John. "No. It affects us, but it's about me."

"All right, then. But we need to come up with a way to handle her delicately. Perhaps we can convince her not to say anything."

"Convince her?" Hannah gripped the broom handle, pressing the straw fibers hard against the floor. "How do you propose we do that? She's made it clear there'll be no compromise."

"I doubt she's as set on telling the reverend as she says."

"We can hope that's true, but we can't be certain of it." Hannah rested her hand on the top of the broom handle. "I'm convinced she can't see any capitulation in us—none."

"You're right, of course, but we might come up with something she wants more."

"What can we have that she would want that she hasn't already asked for?"

"What about her own reputation? I know she acts as if it doesn't matter to her, but it's worth a try, don't you think? We can at least remind her of what she has to lose."

"I've hoped she wouldn't speak up for that very reason, but I truly doubt she cares," Hannah said. "What matters most to her is what she can pinch from others. Lydia told me that the day she was let go she was terribly rude to Catharine and even threatened her. She gave no thought to all the Athertons had done for her. She possesses no consideration or gratitude."

Hannah returned to her sweeping. "We simply must stand

up to her and leave the rest to God." She glanced at John. She hated what Deidre had done to him. She'd never seen him feel small, except in this.

She stopped and turned to him. "The Lord tells us to have courage and not be afraid."

"Quite true, but he also cautions against folly."

"By allowing her to coerce us the way she has, we've already committed folly." Hannah caught the look of hurt in John's eyes, but instead of acknowledging it, she swept the dirt toward the door and out onto the porch. "As soon as I've finished here, I'll be on my way." She watched Thomas saunter toward the river, the dog prancing along beside him.

"I should go with you. I don't want you facing Deidre alone."

"John, if you're with me, you'll be tempted to protect me. And Deidre will see that as weakness. I've got to go alone." She walked back inside the house and returned the broom to its place in the corner of the room.

"You're a good man, John—honorable and brave, but you've not yet settled this in your own mind. I'm not afraid." She untied her apron. "I'm ready to stand up to her. And whatever comes will come, for the Father allows only that which is good for us." Hannah took her bonnet from its peg alongside the door, put it on, and tied it beneath her chin.

"Let me come with you. I feel as if I'm sending you alone into a pit of vipers."

"I'm not alone." Hannah kissed him tenderly.

"I'll saddle your horse." His tone was one of defeat and remorse. He led the way to the barn, and after he'd saddled Hannah's mare, he stood beside the animal and held the reins.

"I'll not be bothering with any stirrup stockings," Hannah said, keeping her voice light.

"And you shouldn't. They're a ridiculous nuisance." A grin flashed across his face. Holding the bridle, he offered Hannah a hand up. Once she'd settled in the saddle, John gave her the reins. "I should have stood up to Deidre a long while ago. I'm sorry."

"I understand."

"We're stronger together."

"Not in this." Hannah tightened her hold on the reins. "I'll be back midday."

Although anxious to have this encounter behind her, Hannah kept her horse reined in. The animal must have sensed her anxiety because she was more fidgety than usual and wanted to run. Hannah didn't know exactly what she'd say to Deidre. What could she say other than she and John refused to make further payments to her? *Lord, I need your guidance and your strength. Help me to feel your presence.*

She'd tried to sound brave in front of John, but she wasn't fearless at all. The mare continued to pull against Hannah's tight hold on the reins. Thinking it might do the animal good to canter, Hannah loosened her grip. The horse immediately set off at a sprint down the road. Hannah fought for control and barely managed to rein her in.

The mare's sides heaved and her neck was drenched with sweat. Hannah was overheated as well. She and the horse both needed a drink. She looked for a good place along the river for the animal to satisfy its thirst.

Oppressive heat made the air heavy. And traveling along the river brought no relief; it only seemed to make the overheated world more stifling. Hannah stopped, climbed out of the saddle, and led the horse down the bank and to the river. While the mare slurped up water, Hannah drank from a flask.

After quenching her thirst, she dipped her handkerchief into the river and patted her face and neck with the wet cloth. She felt somewhat refreshed as she sat in the grass and thought about what she would say. Squawking and warbling birds flittered among the trees. Some splashed in the shallows.

The horse nibbled on green grasses, carefully chewing around the bit in her mouth. Leaning back on her hands, Hannah closed her eyes, savoring the breeze and the sweet fragrance of a nearby wattle bush. Deidre's face intruded on her leisure, shocking her back to the present.

She could expect no compassion from her. More likely Deidre would offer a haughty battle. Her insides quivered at the thought of the encounter. Perhaps John had been right and she should approach Deidre with care and hope she chose not to speak out. But even the idea made Hannah feel weak, and she'd had enough of being powerless.

I'll do what I must. I entrust myself to you, Lord.

A rustling across the river startled Hannah. She sat upright and looked to see what had made the sound. Staring back at her were a dozen pairs of black eyes. Among the rushes on the opposite shore, not more than fifty yards away, stood a band of Aborigine men, each with a spear in his hand. They were nearly naked, their bodies looking as if they'd been dusted with dirt. Their wiry hair framed broad faces. And as always there were no smiles or waves of greeting—only stark, penetrating stares.

Hannah's heart hammered. Would they cross the river and attack her? She pushed to her feet. What did they want? She could see hate in their eyes, but she'd done nothing to them.

Why would they hate her? *The reason matters not, they do hate me. I'm white and whites threaten their way of life.* Even though she had no influence over the governmental policies affecting the Aborigines, a flush of remorse coursed through her.

Struggling to control her quaking, she climbed onto her horse. Holding the men's gaze, she eased her way back to the road. The blacks remained still and silent; no one raised a spear or made a threatening gesture. Hannah urged her horse into a gallop and, as quickly as she could, left the band of Aborigines behind her.

When certain she was a safe distance away, she slowed the mare and took in deep breaths, trying to quiet her fear. Her hands shook as she resettled her hat on her head. She could feel the dampness of her scalp beneath the bonnet.

Why did things have to be this way? Would she be forced to spend the rest of her life being afraid? Every time she saw a black man, would she quake? The idea of it was intolerable. Perhaps she and John should consider returning to London. She envisioned the noisy, crowded, filthy city and knew she couldn't live there. This was her home and she'd have to deal with its challenges.

Hannah approached Deidre's cottage. It stood away from the road, nearly hidden among the trees. No one seemed to be about—there was no wagon or horse, nor smoke rising from the chimney. *Perhaps she's not home,* Hannah thought, uncertain whether or not to be thankful or disappointed.

She urged her horse forward and stopped in front of the house. She studied the shack. It was made of acacia with a thatch roof and looked as if it would fall down at any moment. There was one small window in the front, shaded by a dirty piece of broadcloth. A chair made of woven branches sat on a tiny porch that was sorely in need of cleaning. A ragged blanket had been draped across the chair, and a scraggly, mottled-colored cat lay curled on the rag.

This was nothing more than a hovel. Hannah had seen many like it but was surprised to discover that Deidre lived in such squalor. She felt a twinge of compassion, but knowing sympathy would only put her at a disadvantage, she reminded herself, *Poverty doesn't have to mean filth.*

Hannah climbed out of the saddle and tied her horse to a rickety porch railing. The cat opened golden eyes and gazed at Hannah, then bared its claws as it pushed its front legs straight out and then its hind legs in a leisurely stretch. Then with a yawn, it closed its eyes and returned to slumber.

Hannah took in a deep breath, pressed a hand against her abdomen, and then walked to the door. It was rough sawn and filthy, like everything else. She knocked. There was no sound from inside. From the corner of her eye, she saw the curtain flutter. Someone had looked out. She waited, and just as she prepared to knock again, the door flew open.

With one hand on the door and the other on her hip, Deidre stood as if challenging Hannah. She didn't look lovely at all. Her hair needed combing and her clothing was somewhat out of kilter. It appeared she'd been aroused from sleep.

"I daresay, yer the last person I expected to come calling." Deidre closed her lids halfway, nearly concealing her muddy green eyes. "I hope ye've brought the money ye owe me."

"I want to speak to you." Hannah worked hard to control rising anger. "Can you step outside?"

"What? Yer not good enough to come inside?" Deidre

opened the door wide. "Come in. I wasn't expecting visitors, but since it's just ye, I don't suppose the mess matters much, eh?" She smiled, but it wasn't a pleasant expression.

Hannah didn't want to set a foot inside Deidre's house, but if she were to keep this meeting civil, she'd have to. With her arms hugging her waist, she stepped through the door. The room smelled of soot, unclean linens, and spoiled food. Flies were thick. The only furnishings were two chairs, a table, and a straw mattress on the floor.

Deidre meandered to one of the chairs and dropped into it. "I'd offer ye tea, but I've got none and I don't expect ye'd take any from me anyways." She flung an arm over the back of the chair. "Please," she said in an exaggerated tone of graciousness. "Have a seat." She nodded at the only other chair.

Hannah could see that food of some sort was stuck to the seat with flies feasting on it. "I'll stand, thank you."

Deidre gazed at Hannah. "Did ye bring me payment, then?"

"No. I did not. And I shall not."

Deidre's spine straightened and her expression turned ugly. "Then why ye here?"

"To tell you there'll be no more payments."

Deidre sneered. "Oh? Really?" She threw one leg over the other. "I'll tell ye what—ye'll do as I say."

"No. I won't."

Hannah thought she saw a flicker of doubt in Deidre's eyes. "And do ye know what's at stake?"

"I do." Just as she'd prayed, Hannah felt the presence and power of God. She met Deidre's cruel gaze.

"I don't think ye do. I know all 'bout ye. Every detail of yer sordid tale. Yer friend Lydia told me the sad story." She chuckled. "She was quite concerned and hoped I'd be praying for ye."

284

"Yes. I know. She's a good friend who meant well."

"It did turn out well . . . for me."

"Perhaps not." Although still frightened, Hannah managed to smile. "There's a Scripture in Proverbs that says, 'Food gained by fraud tastes sweet to a man, but he ends up with a mouth full of gravel.'" She enjoyed the taste of God's Word on her lips.

Deidre stood and walked to the hearth where she leaned against loose chinking. "I know 'bout yer affair with that judge."

"There was no affair."

"Oh, is that how ye see it, then? Ye were just a poor unfortunate that was taken advantage of, eh?"

"I was." Hannah was shocked that she felt no outrage, only controlled righteous anger.

"When the gentleman was done with ye, he left ye in the family way. Isn't that why he put ye out? Ye sponged off him as long as ye could, offering favors. But alas, when it was clear ye were carrying a child, he was forced to send ye packing."

"That's not at all how it was."

"So ye say. I figured ye decided some recompense was owed ye and helped yerself to some of his property before ye crept away."

So that's how it's going to be, then. Hannah remained calm. "That's not true. None of it."

"Oh, isn't it? What do ye think the elders will believe? Especially when they hear how ye killed the poor innocent babe. Ripped him from yer body the way ye did."

"I didn't." The familiar taste of guilt raised up inside Hannah. She dared not let Deidre see it. "The child died because it was born too early. And I never tempted that man, nor did I steal from him. I only took bread after I'd been on the streets and could find nothing to eat."

"That's not what I heard. I can understand using a man to see to yer needs, but killing a baby, praying for it to die—there's nothing more despicable." She moved to the window.

Again, guilt reached for Hannah. The sin was gone, covered by the blood of Christ. No amount of guilt or shame would change what had happened. She breathed in slowly, nearly choking on the stink in the room. "You can think as you like. It makes no difference to me. John and I will pay you nothing more—nothing."

Deidre narrowed her eyes. "Ye'll be sorry for it. People like to gossip. They'll believe the worst and ye'll be ruined."

"As will you." Hannah knew it would be a wasted effort but felt she must try once more. "When the truth is known, they'll see you for who you really are. You'll have no reputation left."

Deidre smirked. "Ye think I care 'bout that, eh? I've been alone in this world a long while and I've learned to take care of myself. There's always someone wanting a gal to warm their bed. As ye well know."

Hannah understood the implication and had heard enough. Before she realized her intent, she closed the distance between herself and Deidre and slapped the other woman's face.

Stunned, Deidre pressed a hand against her cheek. "Ye'll be sorry for that. Out! Out of my house!"

Hannah stared at her. She felt no remorse for the slap. Deidre deserved worse. "I'll be glad to." She turned and walked out, hurrying down the steps. Her hands trembling, she untied the horse's reins and pushed up into the saddle.

Deidre flew onto the porch and shrieked, "Ye should have

paid me. Things will go badly for ye now. Soon all the district will know 'bout ye. Ye'll not be able to show yer face anywhere."

Hannah sat on her horse and stared at the pathetic caricature of the woman she'd first met months before. Deidre was no longer beautiful but ugly and pathetic. She turned her horse and headed for the road.

Shrewish shrieks and taunts echoed behind her and were finally swallowed up by the forest. There was nothing more to be done now. Hannah's life was in God's hands, as it always had been.

24

The morning sun baked golden fields. "It's impossibly hot," Hannah said, holding her umbrella so that it shaded her and John.

"Nothing is impossible." He leaned on his thighs, holding the reins loosely.

Hannah knew he was talking about more than the weather. Since her visit to Deidre, they'd not heard a word. It had been an agonizing two weeks of mental captivity, but they were beginning to breathe easier. Perhaps she had been bluffing, after all.

"Remember English summers?" John asked, wearing a relaxed smile.

Hannah's mind carried her back to warm days where the heat most often felt comforting. Outside the city it had been green and damp. She smiled at the memory. How lovely the flowers had been. "I remember," she said. "I'd love to be there right now." In truth, Hannah would have liked to be almost anywhere else. Attending church was a difficult challenge. For since they'd not seen anyone during the week, she didn't know if Deidre had spoken up. Those at church would know. And if

Deidre hadn't said anything, she might at any time. It was an ongoing trepidation.

John lifted the reins. "Hurry along, now."

"Why must we hurry?" She leaned against John. "Meandering might be nicer."

"We might miss services."

"And that would be bad, eh?" Hannah tried to make her tone light.

John gave her a hug and continued on.

She dreaded seeing Deidre again. If she'd spoken to the reverend or the elders—Hannah could imagine what she would see in their eyes, especially if they'd believed Deidre's version of her past.

Hannah glanced into the back of the wagon. Thomas sat facing the road, his legs dangling over the back. He seemed perfectly happy to study where they'd already been. He was most likely thinking about the next best place to cast in his fishing line. It had become one of his favorite pastimes. He brought home crayfish, turtles, and mullets. And talked about how he was going to figure out a way to catch a duck. Although Hannah wasn't fond of crayfish, she had found a way to make them edible, but she refused to cook turtles and told him to return the poor creatures to their homes.

"Do you think she'll be there?" Hannah asked.

"We'll know soon. But we've not heard from any of the elders, so she's most likely not said anything."

"Do you think it possible she's moved on?"

"We can hope, but more than likely she's still living in her wretched cottage." He looked at Hannah. "We can only wait and pray."

Hannah thought back to the decision they'd made to move

if Deidre did speak up. She didn't want to leave Parramatta. It was her home; she had friends and the farm was doing well. Changing her grip on the umbrella handle, she quietly asked, "Do you truly think it wise to move away? Our life is here. I'd miss my friends terribly."

John glanced back at Thomas and said in a hushed voice, "I don't want to leave, but I don't see any other way. If we're to stay, people must be willing to do business with me and . . . if things go badly, there may not be enough trade for me in the district." He patted her thigh. "There are other places, fine places to live and to make a fresh start."

"Isn't it possible that we'll still be able to make it? After all, you're an honorable businessman, and that's what matters most to people, don't you think?"

"Of course it matters." He shook his head slightly. "Hannah, I think we've gotten ahead of ourselves. There's no reason to plan on leaving just yet. Deidre's said nothing. And most likely she won't. I'm beginning to think it was all a ruse." He patted her leg. "You did the right thing."

Hannah leaned in closer to John.

"Try not to worry, luv. God has us in his hand."

Hannah closed her eyes and breathed in the peace John offered. *Thank you, Lord, for this good man.*

When John and Hannah's wagon rolled into the churchyard, it was crowded with buggies and wagons, as usual. Children played tag in a field beside the church, and a cluster of men stood at the bottom of the steps. Everything seemed normal.

"All looks well." John pulled the horses to a stop in the shade of a gum tree. He climbed out and gave Hannah a hand down.

Thomas jumped off the back. "Can I play?"

"Yes," Hannah said. "But make sure you're beside us in church by the time services begin." She checked to make sure the food for the church picnic was covered and protected from flies.

"I will," he called and ran to join the children.

Wearing a smile, John watched him. "Seems the youngsters are more interested in socializing than in their faith."

"You consider that unusual?" Hannah teased.

"Not in the least. It was the same for me." He gave her a sideways hug. "And for you too, I imagine."

"As I recall."

John tucked Hannah's arm into his and the two walked toward the church. Hannah was surprised at the peace she felt. *Of course I should feel safe. This is my church family. What better place to feel secure than here among my friends.*

She'd nearly reached the steps when she saw Deidre just inside the door. Peace took flight. Hannah sucked in a breath and pressed a hand against her chest to quiet her thumping heart. "She's here," she whispered.

Deidre remained where she was and met Hannah's gaze. She almost smiled and then disappeared inside the building.

"Pay her no mind," John said as he stepped up to the reverend. "Good day to you."

The reverend smiled and shook John's hand. "It's a fine day, eh. Looks to be a hot one, though."

"That it does."

He doesn't know. Hannah nodded at the reverend and managed a tremulous smile. What would he think of her once he knew? *What has become of your faith? You confronted Deidre with confidence. You felt God's power and presence. What has changed?* Hannah knew God hadn't changed, it was her. She'd allowed her mind to reflect on what might go wrong, rather than staying focused on his promises.

John kept ahold of Hannah's arm and steered her through the door and inside the church. Bright sunlight streamed in through the windows, heating up the room. Needing comfort, her eyes sought out the cross at the front of the sanctuary.

John moved forward, guiding Hannah. She could feel his strength and was thankful for it. He stopped and stood aside to allow her to sit and then moved into the pew beside her. Hannah kept her eyes forward, not sure just what to do. What if Deidre was telling people at this very moment?

Just as Matilda James sat down at the piano, Thomas scooted in beside his parents. He pushed blond hair off his forehead and smiled at Hannah and John, then moved in between them.

Matilda's fingers played over the keys as a familiar hymn resonated throughout the sanctuary. "'All hail the power of Jesus' name! Let angels prostrate fall; bring forth the royal diadem, and crown him Lord of all!'"

Hannah voiced the words, but she barely heard them. "'Ye chosen seed of Israel's race, ye ransomed of the fall, hail him who saves you by his grace, and crown him Lord of all.'"

Voices melded in worship. Hannah tried to feel the power of the words, but she could only think of Deidre. What if today was the day?

Hannah looked about the room and saw worshipful friends. Would they still be her friends if they knew the truth? She had no doubts about the Athertons or Gwen and Perry or Lydia, but she felt no certainty about the others.

The first hymn was followed by another. Hannah kept her hands clasped in her lap. She felt overly hot. Where was Deidre? Hannah glanced behind her. Three rows from the back she sat, looking smug. While she sang, her pale green eyes found Hannah and bored into her. Hannah quickly looked toward the front. *She's going to spread her poisonous lies.*

Matilda stopped playing and the reverend moved to the lectern at the front. "Good day to you all." He smiled. "As a reminder, today is the church picnic. After services we'll gather at the river. I hope you all can join us. There will be games and the food promises to be superb. I understand the women have been cooking all week." He smiled, then cleared his throat and brushed back his graying hair. "Fun and frolic is good for the soul."

He opened his Bible. "Now, shall we look into God's Word together."

"Reverend, I must speak first."

Hannah heard Deidre's voice. She fumbled for John's hand. He squeezed it tightly.

"Reverend, I have a matter that must be addressed."

Hannah kept her eyes forward, staring at the back of the pew in front of her. She heard the rustle of clothing. She glanced back. Deidre stood, looking innocent and wholesome, nothing like the woman she'd seen when she'd confronted her. *Lord, please let there be justice.*

"Miss O'Neil, perhaps you could wait until after services."

"It can't wait. I have a duty to expose a grievous sin."

The reverend's blue eyes were troubled.

"The Word says we're to expose sin and deal with it, am I right?"

He ran a finger under his tight collar. "Of course. But we must keep Scripture in context. Sin is to be dealt with, but perhaps it would best be done after services and not so publicly." He looked down at his Bible.

"I think not. Not this time. I have something to say that

293

everyone should hear." Unable to disguise her ruthlessness, Deidre no longer looked innocent. "God's Word says we are to hold one another to account. Isn't that right?"

"Correct, but not—"

"And doesn't it say we're to go to that person and see to it that they repent?" Deidre's eyes found Hannah. "I'm simply obeying the Word."

The reverend leaned on the lectern. "Yes, Deidre, we are to hold one another accountable, and repentance is necessary to maintain a vigorous relationship with God. But there is a process by which the church must conduct such matters. I'd like to discuss that with you . . . after services."

"No, Reverend. This can't wait." Deidre turned and faced Hannah. "We have a fraud among us!" She pointed at Hannah. "Hannah Bradshaw must be held to account!"

Gasps erupted throughout the sanctuary. The reverend, looking aghast, turned to Hannah.

"She's an adulteress!" Deidre said.

"Deidre, I think—"

Ignoring the reverend's appeal, Deidre continued, "While living in London, she sold her body to a magistrate, and when she found herself with child, she left in the middle of the night, but only after having stolen a costly silver chalice."

Nausea swept through Hannah. She thought she might faint.

Deidre strode to the center aisle and moved closer to John and Hannah.

John stood and faced her. "You are lying."

"Oh and what of you?" Deidre spat at him. "You've accepted her sins and protected her—even though she married you under the false pretense of purity."

"You will be silent," John bellowed. "You do not speak the truth nor do you have an understanding of the truth."

"But I do. As well you know."

Hannah stood. She hung on to John's arm and looked to the reverend. "Please, may I speak?"

His expression grave, Reverend Taylor nodded.

"Deidre is speaking falsely."

"What I've said is true! Ask her about the child."

"I . . . I was with child . . . once. That is true. But the manner in which I came to be in that condition is not as she says." Dizziness swept over Hannah, and she tightened her grip on John's arm. She felt a small hand find its way into her palm and looked down to see Thomas gazing up at her, his blue eyes filled with love and encouragement.

"She was an innocent," John said. "Assaulted by a man of power and wealth. It was he who deserved prison. After he attacked her, Hannah escaped to the streets. It was only when she was at a point of starvation that she took bread from a merchant. That was her only crime."

He turned a gaze of contempt upon Deidre. "If anyone deserves punishment here, it is you." He looked over the congregation. "For months she has threatened to expose Hannah's past, but her version of it, which is a lie. She has remained quiet only because I've paid her to do so. My sin is that I've given in to her coercion and have not stood strongly enough with my wife against this evil."

"And if yer wife didn't commit a grave sin, why would ye pay me then, eh?" Deidre challenged. "It was the child. She destroyed it, killed it with her own hands."

"That's not true!" Lydia flew to her feet. "I was there. The baby was born before it's time. It was too tiny to live. It took not one breath. Hannah had no hand in its death."

Hannah moved to the center aisle. She smiled at Lydia and then looked from John to Deidre and back to the reverend. "Stop. Please stop. I am not innocent. I have committed a grave sin. As my husband has said, my employer, Judge Walker, attacked me and I ran away and I lived on the streets." Hannah felt strength pour into her. "Days later I was arrested for stealing bread. Judge Walker was the magistrate who oversaw my trial. He accused me unjustly of thievery, saying that I had taken a chalice from his home. I was sentenced to transportation to Sydney Town."

Tears slipped down her cheeks. "While on board the prison ship, I discovered I was with child . . ." She glanced about the room, knowing that what she had to say would likely sever her relationship with most of those present. "I prayed that the baby would die."

Gasps and murmurs moved through the congregation. Hannah took a deep breath and continued. "It was a grave sin, one I shall never forgive myself for. The child was born early and it did die." She closed her eyes. "But as someone once pointed out to me, I am not God. It is he who chooses who lives and who dies. Yet, he is merciful and has forgiven me for my shameful request, though I do not deserve it."

Looking at John and the reverend and those she felt closest to, she continued, "And now, I ask for your forgiveness. I've tarnished not only myself but my family and my church family. Please forgive me." She moved back to John and took his hand. "John and I will move away if it is considered a just punishment for what I've done."

Deidre wore a look of satisfaction.

Perry stood. "If she goes, then I guess I'd better go too. I'm a sinner. I grew up on the streets and committed just about every sin a man can." He moved into the aisle.

"And I've committed the gravest of sins," Lydia said. "I murdered a man. I was protecting my mum, but still I took his life." She looked down at David. He stood and offered her his hand. Together they stepped into the center aisle.

Deidre looked unsettled and her bravado dwindled.

Mrs. Atherton was the next to stand. "It was my sin of pride that kept me from adopting a child while I was still young enough to be a mum. Pride is a grave sin. The Lord's forgiven me, but I've still had to live with the devastating consequences. William and I both have." She looked tearfully at William and then at Hannah. "Please stay. I would miss you terribly."

Deidre's bluster had changed to anger. "Can ye hear yer—"

"I believe you've said enough!" The reverend looked out over the congregation. "Please, all of you sit." His gaze was gentle and loving. It rested on John and Hannah. "You also. Please."

Everyone returned to their places. Deidre dropped into her seat with a huff and folded her arms over her chest. "She'll have to go—"

"I said—enough." The reverend turned the pages in his Bible. He stopped and looked out over the congregation. "Romans 3:23 says, 'For all have sinned and fall short of the glory of God.'" He smiled. "I'd say most of us know that verse, eh."

There were words of agreement and nods.

"There is more—we rarely quote the rest of the verse." He glanced down at the Scriptures and then read, slowly and resolutely, "And are justified freely by his grace through the redemption that came by Christ Jesus. God presented him as a sacrifice of atonement, through faith in his blood. He did this to demonstrate his justice, because in his forbearance he had left the sins committed beforehand unpunished—he did it to demonstrate his justice at the present time, so as to be just and the one who justifies those who have faith in Jesus."

He looked out over the congregation. "Everyone in this room has sinned, no one is without fault. But God in his goodness and his kindness offered his Son as a sacrifice." He looked at Hannah with kindness. "He looked down through the ages and he saw you, Hannah Bradshaw. And he sent his Son for you."

He turned his gaze on Perry. "And he knew you, Perry, and you, Lydia and Catharine." His gaze moved from one to the other, touching everyone in the church, including Deidre. "He knew and loved us all even before we were born. And it is his love that saves us. There is nothing we can do but trust in him."

His eyes settled on Deidre. "He treated us with mercy and has asked that we imitate him and offer mercy to one another."

Deidre slumped slightly lower in the pew, but her arms remained tightly clasped across her chest.

The reverend looked out over the church. "We are sinners; that is the sad truth. But we have been created anew and God sees us as holy and blameless because he chooses to."

Again Hannah felt Thomas's hand grasp hers. The ache inside her began to fade, and in its place she felt gratitude and wonder. She'd never experienced God's love more powerfully. Unaware of her tears, she felt John's arm go about her, and she pulled Thomas in close.

"God's greatest commandment is that we love one another," the reverend continued. "And in this church I shall do my best to see that we follow his decree."

He looked at Deidre. "Everyone is welcome in the house of the Lord."

Deidre stood. "I know what yer thinking—that I'm the worst of sinners." She glared at the congregation. "I'm not. I know more 'bout most of ye than ye'd guess, more than ye'd want me to know. And I'll not stay here to be judged by any of ye."

Her hands clenched and her arms swinging at her sides, she strode to the back of the church, then stopped and looked at the congregation. "Yer a weak and pathetic lot." She opened the door and stomped out.

The parishioners gaped at the church entrance and then turned back to Reverend Taylor. He looked bereaved, and then he did something unusual. He knelt beside the lectern and closed his eyes. Soon others were kneeling as well. Hannah and John and Thomas knelt together and prayed. The fragrance of worship filled the sanctuary.

When the reverend stood, Hannah saw tranquility in his eyes. And she recognized the same peace that lived within her own heart, a peace only God gives.

"Let us close with the hymn 'O Love Divine, What Hast Thou Done,'" the reverend said.

He began and the congregation joined in. A sound like angels' voices swelled, and God's divine and holy presence pervaded the room.

Hannah looked at John on one side and Thomas on the other. She'd had so little faith. *How could I have forgotten the goodness of God?*

She closed her eyes and allowed her voice to rise toward heaven—

"'The Son of God for me hath died; my Lord, my Love, is crucified.'"

Acknowledgments

A book is never created alone. There is always a team of people who work together to craft a story.

When I write I rely on others—experts who help me with the details needed to make a story live—editors who insure that what ends up on the page is written in a way that makes sense, writing buddies who hold me accountable and sharpen my work while I create. I'd never have the courage to begin a book without the assurance of a team behind the words.

And so, I owe thanks to many.

To my two editors at Revell, Lonnie Hull DuPont and Barb Barnes: Thank you, ladies. You are true professionals. I'm grateful for your commitment to quality work and for your friendship. Your expertise added luster to this book.

Once again, I had the help of my friends who live in Australia. Mary Hawkins, an Australian author, read the entire manuscript and helped catch errors that I didn't see. And my friend and partner in research, Jayne Collins, shared many hours of her time to lend authenticity to this project. I am exceedingly grateful to you both.

And last but never least, I must say thank you to my critique group, my chums who worked through every page with me. When my deadline loomed, you gave more of yourselves and read chapters thrown at you in a hurry, making important suggestions and crucial corrections. Thanks to Sybilla Cook, Julia Ewert, Diane Gardner, Sarah Schartz, and Ann Shorey. Through the years, we've worked together and you've become more than critique partners; you're dear friends and a gift to me from God.

Bonnie Leon dabbled in writing for many years but never set it in a place of priority until an accident in 1991 left her unable to work. She is now the author of several historical fiction series, including the Queensland Chronicles, the Matanuska series, the Sowers Trilogy, and the Northern Lights series. She also stays busy teaching women's Bible studies, speaking, and teaching at writing seminars and conventions and women's gatherings. Bonnie and her husband, Greg, live in southern Oregon. They have three grown children and four grandchildren.

Visit Bonnie's website at www.bonnieleon.com.